PENANCE

CHARLOTTE BARNES

BLOODHOUND
— BOOKS —

ALSO BY CHARLOTTE BARNES

PROLOGUE

Industrial buildings linger on the outskirts of every city now. Belfast is no different.

From outside the structure looked like a cored office space. She had expected to find contents to match. Instead, the room she occupied looked long abandoned by lodgers and squatters. They'd left behind soiled mattresses and a cracked mirror over an ornate fireplace that had been engulfed by its own flames years ago.

There was a red wall, pink in patches. When she scanned the space, she saw the open window with blades of sun falling through. The heat of it must have slowly taken the wall's colour. The other walls had less character to them. Wallpaper had cracked and flecked, picked off like skin tags around poorly cared for cuticles. The plaster underneath looked damp, and the smell of the room was much the same. Though it was tinged with sweat, too, and when the wind caught her she sniffed a burst of her own perfume.

On the open door there was a body bag and hanger; a change of clothes hidden beneath. She had expected dirt, mud – trace contact. So she'd packed it carefully. There wasn't too

1

much time to waste, though. Her flight was leaving from Belfast International in twelve hours – and from experience she knew this could take as many as eight if she got carried away.

In the corner of the room, she bent down to unzip her bag and take out everything she might need. Otherwise impulse would take over and she'd grab any old thing; that didn't make for a smooth experience. Everything was laid out along a roll of old fabric – one that could easily be burnt up before she left – and each item lay parallel to the next. There was something calming about that.

Nearby, there was a weathered chair that she lowered herself onto with some caution, in case the unloved legs of it were close to giving out. It held her weight, though, and she rested there for a second enjoying the in and out of breath; the quiet of it all, where the city was some miles away in the distance. But from the opposite side of the room there came a rumble of noise; a rat, she thought, trying to scurry free.

She recognised the panic in him. The watering of his eyes, the fidget of bound limbs; he tried repeatedly to move, in short flurries of effort. Not that she was worried; she knew how to bind a man by now.

She flashed a quick smile before she stood and leaned down to collect an old handheld video camera from the equipment on the floor. It was all ready; she only needed to fix it to the stand and press record. It was for show, mostly. She wouldn't keep the film, though she wanted him to believe there would be a record of what was about to happen.

When the camera was ready, she closed the distance between them, pinched her trousers at the knees, and lowered herself to a crouch in front of him. 'You like to film these things, don't you?'

And from somewhere behind three layers of tape, he tried to answer.

CHAPTER ONE

I dragged my case through the front door with a thud that was no rival for the music emanating from the kitchen. I paced through the familiar hallway and found my husband, Simon, rapping along to Eminem.

In those seconds, I felt the familiar rush of home wash over me and I was embarrassingly happy to be back. People at work had told me to make the most of the break – 'It's a free trip away after all!' – and I'd nodded along with a weak smile. But there was nowhere else I'd rather be than leaning against the doorway of a kitchen space that we owned outright, watching my husband pretend to have rhythm while cutting tomatoes into uneven slices. I left him in peace until the end of the track then, when I realised it was on repeat, I trod quietly into the space and hit the pause button on the docking station.

'Dawn, what did I say ab–' He spun around and came to a stop mid-sentence. His smile was expansive; cheek to cheek, complete with dimples I'd fallen in love with just over ten years ago, and they still hadn't lost their appeal. 'You're home!' He closed the gap between us and wrapped himself around me in a hug that felt more like I'd been away for weeks rather than a couple of days. 'She keeps turning my music off because it's uncool. I'm so glad you're back.'

I laughed into his nook; the spot between shoulder and neck. 'We are uncool.'

'She's six. She can't know that yet.' He pulled away and kissed the corner of my mouth; a soft precursor to what would come later. 'Drink?'

I groaned. 'Please!'

He reached for the docking station and glanced up at me; his finger hovered over the play button. 'Once more?' I only laughed and walked around him, to pull out a chair at the kitchen table. 'You're right,' he answered, 'once more is probably overkill. Spotify already thinks I've got a problem.' Instead, he knocked the station off at the wall and went back to his chopping board. 'Balls, drink.'

'I can get–' I moved to stand but he put his hand up to still me. 'Or I can be waited on.'

'You've had a busy day. Well, a busy few days, I imagine.' He was facing away from me, staring into the abyss of a fridge where space was bargained for between the adults – who want food – and their child – who wants an endless supply of Lunchables. I was glad he couldn't see my face. 'I don't know that we've got any white in here, you know...' He bobbed up and down to survey the space fully. I was smiling again by the time he turned. *Christ, it's good to be home.* 'Red?'

'Anything!' I joked.

'It was that bad?'

'Mummy!' Dawn ran from the bottom of the stairs, along the hallway, skidded into the kitchen – in a manoeuvre that only children can really pull off – but overshot the table by a good metre. She landed on the opposite side of the room but made a tornado-ballerina of herself to come back, before landing in front of me and completing a graceful bow. Then she fell over herself with laughter and launched onto my lap. I blew the largest raspberry I could muster into her bare shoulder. Her hair was still damp from bath-time, and she smelled like...

'Is that unicorn I've got a whiff of there?'

Her face was surprised-delight. 'Yes!' Then she turned to Simon. 'See, I told you.'

'Yep, we'll add that to the list of things Daddy got wrong while Mummy was away.' Simon set three inches of wine on the table next to me, then leaned in to kiss the crown of my head. When he moved away Dawn coughed, in a dramatic way, and Simon promptly turned back to kiss her, too.

'Did he get lots of things wrong?' I pretend-whispered to her, to catch Simon's ear. They answered 'Yes' and 'No' in unison.

'Dawnie, what did I get wrong?' he pushed, his attention already on the mince that was simmering on the stove. He probed at it while she listed things off – '*And* he wouldn't let me dance to Little Mix while I got ready for school because he said...' – and I tried to let the normality of it all wash over me. But I still drained my drink too quickly.

'Everything okay?' Simon asked when he saw me reach around him for the bottle.

'It was a nightmare trip back, that's all.' I filled another three fingers. 'I'll tell you about it later.' I kissed the side of his temple to a soundtrack of Dawn making an, 'Eurgh' noise from her post at the kitchen table. 'I know. It's disgusting how much Mummy loves Daddy, isn't it?'

She gave the idea more thought than I expected her to. 'Not *disgusting*, but... Did you bring us anything from your trip?' She was already up and out of the seat, her small feet shuffling towards the doorway.

'Dawn,' Simon cautioned, 'don't be rude. Can't that wait

until after dinner?'

She turned back to throw me a questioning look. 'Go on.'

When she was out of earshot Simon laughed. 'No wonder she prefers you.'

'Oh shush, she does not prefer–'

I'd hardly managed to wrap an arm around his waist when Dawn came through to the kitchen, yanking my bag behind her as though it were loaded with more than its allotted kilograms. 'This weighs a tonne and it's covered in dirt.'

'Dirt?' Simon echoed.

Dawn held up her palms that were muddied with dust, building crust and detritus.

My stomach rolled over. 'You know what it's like when your luggage gets thrown around on a trip. Here, give me those hands.' I reached around for the kitchen towel and took a sheet to her, and then I wiped away any evidence that lingered. 'All clean.'

She shifted from one foot to the other while I unzipped the case, then I reached in to collect something small and secret. When I brought my cupped hands out, I moved them slowly as though a damaged bird might be caught inside. 'Eyes closed.'

She followed orders, pinching her eyes together with an eagerness you only ever find in children.

I opened my hands, then, to reveal a two-inch troll complete with wild red hair, and a small green T-shirt that left its buttocks bare. She'd been obsessed with them since she was about four years old. Simon and I joked that it was a retro addiction, but whenever we found one she didn't have, there was uproar if we didn't take it home. 'Open.'

She gasped as though I were presenting her with a bullion. 'Mum!'

'Oh good,' Simon added flatly, 'another troll in the house.' Though Dawn and I both knew he was joking. 'Dawn, you've got about five minutes to introduce that one to the three hundred others in your room before I start dishing up dinner.'

'Three hundred...' she huffed on her way out of the kitchen. She turned the troll this way and that, inspecting it for identifying marks, I thought, in case some clue to its identity were hidden. 'If only I had three hundred...' she added, before she turned for the stairs. 'You're not going to pull another troll out of that bag for me, are you?'

I stood behind Simon while he flicked at switches, and gave things a final stir. My body was pressed into the curve of his back, and my hands rested in the front pockets of his torn stay-at-home jeans. 'You can have your present later.' I kissed the base of his neck.

'You should go away more often.' I could hear the smile in his voice. But I couldn't muster a murmur of agreement. 'Go and get the troll wrangler, would you? She'll be all day if we're not careful.'

And I obliged, grateful for something to do.

Simon was flicking through television channels in the living room, in search of background noise. He'd carried Dawn up to bed only minutes ago – after she'd passed out, thumb in mouth and troll tucked neatly in palm – on the sofa. I was waiting for the kettle to boil, watching my doting husband through the long stretch of the open-plan space. When we moved in, eight years ago now, we made a mammoth task of tearing down walls and making the place our own. It had been a renovation job for

Simon, but something about the whole process had felt oddly metaphysical for me, too.

'Do you want biscuits?' I shouted into him.

'Oof, now you're talking, woman. Will you have something?'

I thumbed the stem of my wine glass. 'I might finish this bottle.'

There was a long pause, then. 'Okay, babe, whatever you fancy.'

I grabbed the necessary utensils – cup, spoon, sweetener for my heathen husband who refused to drink tea the right way – and then I opened the biscuit cupboard to begin the search. It was another of Simon's weaknesses; anything with buttercream in the middle. I reached up for a packet of crunch creams that hadn't been opened yet – *he mustn't know they're here* – and laid them on the side while I threw tea together. Then I poured another swill of wine, though I told myself I was being restrained this time by measuring out two fingers instead of three. There'd be something for tomorrow, I reasoned. I carried biscuits and brew in to Simon, and then padded back to get my own drink from the side.

'Oh Christ...' Simon muttered.

'An appeal has been launched into the disappearance of...'

'What?' I looked up in time to catch the picture, but the volume on the television was too low for me to hear the narration. Still, it was enough to weaken my reflexes, and before I could grasp at what was unfolding the glass slipped from my hand and shattered across the tiles of the kitchen floor.

'Don't move!' Simon shouted, as he rushed over from across the space. I could hear the tail-end of a news reporter's commentary – 'Police are in the process of speaking with associates of the missing man, one Mitchell Webster...' – but it was soon drowned out by Simon's worrying. 'Babe, stand still, okay, because you don't even have socks on and it's everywhere.'

I watched the television behind him until the picture disappeared; a fade out, like a movie scene transition. And it was only then that I looked down at my husband, collecting up the larger shards of glass from around me; doing his best to avoid what now looked like spilled blood.

CHAPTER TWO

I found that I was both drawn to and repelled from news reports in the days after. Without even noticing a nearby clock, I'd walk into the living room as Simon was putting on the evening news; or as a colleague was turning on the local radio station in time for a bulletin. Somehow, my body clock had become attuned to optimum times that I might catch something I didn't want to hear – only I did want to hear it in many ways, too. I shook the confusion of it all away, then, and tried to be present in the moment; this moment, right here. *Three things I can smell: freshly cut grass; the grease-fry of fairground doughnuts; my husband's aftershave. Two things I can hear: the hum of a car engine; the rabble of children in the park. One thing I can feel: Simon's hand, squeezing my own, once, twice–*

'Celia, are you even listening?'

I swallowed hard. 'You're worried this new client is going to be more trouble than they're worth. But the fact that they're trouble might also mean they're big money. And given how expensive it is to power the house these days, who can afford to turn down big money.' My stare stayed straight ahead but I smiled. 'Did I miss anything?' Simon was a freelance architect –

and a bloody good one, though I realise it's the wife's job to say that.

'It's like a superpower.'

It irked him; I'd always been able to keep one ear on a conversation without being fully present in it. Calling me out on whether I'd been listening at all only meant that I'd parrot everything back – with a good level of accuracy, if his regular huffs and sighs were any indication. I squeezed his hand back and turned to set a light kiss on his cheek. He was watching Dawn, still, showering herself and her friends in the sandbox area of the play zone.

'I think you should take the job,' I said.

He sighed. 'I think I should take the job, too.'

'If it's a pain, it's a pain. How long do you think it'll take, though?'

He answered, but again I switched off to the full frequency of it. It had been hard to concentrate since the news broke. I'd resisted the urge to use any search engines to find out more information about it all. In my head, I imagined all sorts of technological intricacies that a someday detective might track back to me and use as evidence for – something. Something more than nosiness, or idle bystander interest. Though it had crossed my mind that I could use someone else's computer – *hire* a computer even if that's what it took to find out more. But when the option presented itself – Lou had left her laptop unattended in the office for a full ten minutes yesterday – the same compel and repel had happened. I'd fingered the bottom corner of the keypad on my way to get more coffee, and on the way back I'd ignored the opportunity altogether.

'Babe, can we talk?'

He caught my attention with that, and I was no longer in the office with Lou – or in university with...

'Is everything okay?'

I tried to focus. It had been a lovely but long day with Simon and Dawn: a seven-year old's birthday party in the morning; lunch with Simon's parents; now, more playtime at the local splash zone with Dawn's karate cohort. It had been a long time to be involved, normal; my vision felt drunk at the edges.

'Did anything happen while you were away?'

I squeezed his hand like a reflex. 'What?'

'Mum!'

My head snapped up at Dawn's voice; I couldn't tell whether it was panic or excitement. Though I soon searched her out – hanging upside-down from a climbing frame – with her arms hanging long beneath her, and her wild baby-blonde curls falling away from her in a shower of loose corkscrews. *My beautiful girl*, I thought, with a smile and sigh and a wash of calm.

'She'll give herself a headache,' Simon muttered.

I knocked against him softly. 'Please, after today she won't be awake long enough to have a headache.' He huffed a laugh. 'Let her be a wild monkey child for a while, then maybe we can think about some dinner and she can think about bed.' There was a grumbling noise from Simon's throat, and I turned. 'What did you promise her?'

He looked skyward. '*Frozen.*'

'Oh, Simon, for fu–'

'I know, I know.' He laughed. 'She'll grow out of it.'

'She'd better!'

'*Mum!*'

This time, she was on the ground – but still upside-down. She was doing a walking handstand with a friend close by, ready to catch her, and I smiled at the girls' kinship that was already forming. Seven years old and they already knew they'd need to look out for each other. And though the thought formed as a sweet one, it soon turned over in the acid of my stomach to become a reminder of–

'Ce?' Simon squeezed my hand again. 'I know Dawn is doing her absolute best to be a distraction here but...'

'I'm sorry.' I tried to laugh it off. 'You were asking about the trip?'

'I asked whether anything happened on it.'

'Only what you'd expect.' I smiled and felt the pinch of fake dimples; I needed to relax my face, or he'd know I was forcing it. 'We took our panel out for dinner when the conference was over, then I spent the rest of the weekend exploring and eating too much local food.'

I'd been a literary talent representative for nearly four years now, and the trips away were becoming more frequent, every time a highly ranked writer joined my books. Simon didn't say anything, though. He'd only ever been supportive, of everything; although I thought I'd likely made some choices while I was away that he would question... 'And before you say anything, I know there's no such thing as too much when you're on a holiday, yada-yada.' I leaned across and kissed his shoulder. 'How come?' When I looked up at him, I could read all too clearly that he didn't believe a word of it. Credit to him, he was right not to.

'You've been distracted since you got back, that's all.'

I shrugged. 'I mean, it was a lovely trip but it was tiring, too.'

'I don't mean tired distracted.' He shook his head. 'Distracted like... I don't know, you've just seemed somewhere else most of the time.'

'I'm right here.'

'Well, yesterday you were right here, too, but I still stood in the kitchen doorway and watched you stare into the fridge for nearly a full minute before you eventually shook your head and just walked away.'

I belched out a fake laugh. 'I forgot what I was in there for!'

'I'm not sure that helps your case, babe.'

An ugly pause elbowed between us, then. I pulled in a deep breath before I lied to my husband again. 'Nothing happened, honestly. It was just a lot of walking, talking, eating. Such a hard life I lead.' Then I leaned forward to kiss his shoulder again, only this time I turned to rest my head against him afterwards. I didn't want him to read any more accidental expressions. 'What do you want for dinner?' I asked, in a bid to play for a subtle topic change. There came another grumble from the base of his throat. 'What did you promise her?'

'Pizza, I promised her pizza.'

Three things I can remember: overhead lighting that flickered with a dying bulb; the smell of marijuana; the way he pulled pepperoni slices clean away from his pizza like a surgeon performing a skin graft.

'Celia?'

'Pizza, I heard.' I lifted myself upright and searched the playground for Dawn. She was perched on the end of a seesaw with no friend at the other side. 'Now is a good time to grab her before someone else does.' I nodded. 'Do you two want to head home and gear up the film, and I'll do a food run?'

'You don't have to, babe, we can all–'

'Could you?' I interrupted him, then reached across to squeeze his hand. 'Literally nothing is wrong, I promise. I'm just tired and it's been a day and a half, hasn't it? It'll give me some air and then I'll come home all fresh and shiny and...' I laboured over the final point, 'ready to watch *Frozen*.'

He laughed and stood. 'Whatever you need, okay?'

When he went to walk off without a kiss, though, I knew that needing quiet wasn't okay. But it was done now, and I wasn't going to retract this opportunity for a deep breath and a reboot. 'Veggie supreme with a side of spiced wedges and an individual garlic bread?' I shouted after him, and when he spun to amend the order I winked and added, 'Garlic bread times two.'

He hadn't gone far, but what distance there was he closed back to me and leaned over to kiss me square on the mouth. 'I love you.'

'Dad! People are watching!'

'Oh, let 'em watch, Dawnie, let 'em watch.' He turned in time to snatch her into a hug. 'Come on,' he rubbed at the back of her head, 'we're in charge of setting things up at home. Mum's in charge of pizza.'

I stayed in the playground for a moment after they'd left and tried to steady my breathing. I didn't know whether it had been this erratic when Simon had been sitting next to me; *though surely he would have said something?* I scanned the place and picked out everything that started with the letter G. It had been so long since I needed these techniques. But one mention of him on the news; and one slip-up when no one was looking and–

There was a crunch of gravel from somewhere behind me that broke off the thought. Seconds later, a small boy appeared from around the back of my bench; his helmet was on wonky and his stabilisers were squeaking, and there was a worried father, arms spread and waiting, walking close by behind him. He only laughed and gave me an eye roll when he saw that I'd noticed them. It was the universal symbol for parents doing parent things under the pretence of hating it. But we loved it, really. This innocence; this clean slate, born from us, and packed with opportunities we didn't have.

'Be careful,' I shouted after them, 'the next path is a nightmare for skidding.'

'Thank you,' the father answered, still not taking his eyes

from the boy. 'Did you hear that, kiddo? The lady said we need to be extra...' His caution faded from my earshot, then, so I stood and brushed down my creased dress. My own clean slate would be home soon, singing Disney show tunes and demanding food between each chorus. So I set off, and tried to think nothing of how he liked to eat his pizza.

CHAPTER THREE

This was by far my least favourite part of being a parent: this, cramming around a table with crayons and ideas and a talking stick, to join forces with the other mothers.

We liked to pretend that a) there wasn't a chalk line divide down the workers and the housewives among us and b) that anyone truly, honestly, would-attest-to-it-in-a-court-of-law, gave a shit about the fifth fundraiser the school was throwing, to cover the expenses of maintenance work that we *knew* would be covered by our annual fees increase anyway.

But I was still looking for distractions. I'd even agreed to a last-minute couples' night with Simon's friends – hosted at our house, no less – for the sake of having recipes to source, food to buy, preparations to do.

The least I could do to help myself to claw through the afternoon and into the rushed visit to Asda was to sit here and listen to Marie's idea for a bake sale, countered by Olive suggesting a community car wash. In many ways, the two suggestions represented the entirety of the women on the housewives' side of the table. If someone had drawn a perfect line down the core of the long bench we were all perched around, they would have found an exact stripe between those who work and those who don't, with Alberta sitting at the head. Strategically, too, given that Alberta was both heavily pregnant, and still working, and planning to give up work permanently once this second child had been born. She was literally straddling the boundary of us all. Meanwhile, those with jobs outside of the home didn't sub-divide any further than that; the majority of us were too busy checking our iPhones, texting colleagues under the table and refreshing for emails. There were enough people splitting our single selves already without us stoking that particular fire.

'Dolly, did you want the stick next?'

Dolly was sitting opposite me. I knew all eyes would be on her, so I dropped my phone into my lap in good enough time to feign paying attention.

'What if we did some sort of sponsored... thing?' she asked, in a voice that made me wonder what she must sound like during sex. It was a game Simon and I played in every boring situation we'd ever found ourselves in: *But can you imagine them having sex?* Dolly was high-pitched and nervous so no, no I could not, and Simon couldn't either; we'd discussed it. I took a strategic sip of my flat white to shield my amusement while the others quizzed her on what a sponsored something might be.

'What about walking?' Dolly looked around the table for support. 'I see people on social media doing sponsored runs and things all the time. As a group, maybe, we could... I mean... the lot of us must be able to get quite far if we all walked together.' She laughed; another nervous sound. 'Like a relay race, where someone walks one stretch and then meets someone, for them to pick up the baton and walk the next stretch...' And she droned on, for anyone who wasn't yet familiar with the concept of a relay race (which as a group of mothers, of course, *all* of us were).

'Walking doesn't sound very inclusive.' Alberta gestured to her belly. And of course, now she'd played the inclusivity card, walking was most definitely out.

'With the greatest respect, all, if we're looking for inclusive things we can probably knock the car wash on the head, too.' Sasha piped up from next to me. She and I teamed together for these meets since our girls joined the school at the same time. Though we never actually went to the trouble of meeting outside of these gatherings; inside, we were a force. Or rather, Sasha was a force and I always made a point of sitting next to her.

Olive moved to open her mouth – she was clearly going to push back on this – but Sasha leaned across to snatch the talking stick from Dolly, silencing Olive in the process. 'I realise I'm not ordinarily a sentimental sort,' Sash carried on, in the flattest tone she could muster, 'but Alberta is about ready to drop a calf and I'm not having her leaning over bonnets to wash bird shit off for the dads.'

'There's so much wrong with what just came out of your mouth,' Veryan answered; the most motherly and middle class woman of us all.

Sasha waved the talking stick. 'Wait, there's more.'

Veryan rolled her eyes, making no effort to hide the disapproval; which was a terrible move that would only spur Sasha on further. I scanned the café counter for popcorn for the show but there weren't any bags on the stand, which was a true shame.

'Instead of one fundraiser, why don't we host five? We can knock this thing on the head, and avoid any more of these meetings and any more begging emails from the school asking for our bloody money.'

Veryan huffed a laugh. 'And what will these fundraisers be made up of?'

'Quiz night, silent auction, school car boot sale, arts and craft sale, and a playground challenge so there's something to involve the children with at the end. They can design an obstacle course around the school grounds for the adults. We'll hate it, every single second of it, but that'll be the design, I'd guess. The school will at least get some good promotional shots from us all making tits of ourselves. Each fundraiser can have a lead, I'll take one. Celia, I'm sure you will?' She turned to ask though she carried on without me answering. 'Veryan, no doubt you'll throw your hat in the ring to be in a managerial position for an event, I'm sure. Between the lot of us, over the course of a weekend or at most a week, we can clean our bank accounts and get the fucking roof of the old gymnasium finished. Does anyone want another coffee?'

She tacked the final question on the end as though it formed part of her argument, and there were one or two shocked expressions in response to the politeness – or the abruptness that came before it, perhaps.

'Alberta, herbal tea?' Sasha asked as she fought her way free of the bench.

The mother-to-be-again laughed. 'Please.'

'Gotcha. Anyone else? No? Brill. While I'm away,' she waved her hand around those seated at the table, 'throw around your thoughts, let me know.' Then she was away, straight-backed and painfully proud of herself. Sasha had no game face; it was another thing I liked about her.

Flora lowered her voice. 'I can't bloody stand the woman.'

There was a low chorus of agreement like witches chanting around the pot. Though there were also those who started to chatter with some seriousness about Sasha's suggestions, too – 'The playground challenge sounds like great fun...' – so at least the effort hadn't been entirely wasted.

'Do you know,' I said, lifting a leg free, 'I think I will grab that coffee after all.'

When I joined Sasha at the counter she was browsing cakes; her head didn't even lift. 'On a scale of one to ten?'

'Oh, sure as Veryan's tits are fake, they hate your guts.'

She laughed with such an abruptness that she caught the attention of the nearby tables. 'That's a good one, that is.' She righted herself, then, and met the gaze of the man behind the counter. 'Flat white, peppermint tea, a slab of that salted caramel thing and Celia, what'll it be?'

'Flat white again, please.'

'Coming right up.'

'It's terrible, isn't it?' Sasha started and I glanced back at the table we'd left behind. 'No, not them. That.' I followed her gaze to a muted television screen behind the serving station; and there he was, the man I was dying not to think about.

It looked like a mugshot, and the appropriateness of it wasn't lost on me.

'Apparently he was a stand-up bloke...'

There were greying flecks in his hair that felt premature for his age. His jawline was strong, though, and scattered with salt and pepper that was too neat not to be deliberate. I thought there was a scar just visible, above the cupid's bow of his lip, and remembered a piercing that had once been there.

'His wife was on the other day, too...'

Sasha's commentary was the director's cut over a string of images that played on rotation, I guessed, to ensure the maximum chances of someone recognising him.

'Do you think he did a runner?'

'I'm sorry?' I looked back at her.

Again, she nodded behind the counter. 'The bloke that's meant to be making this coffee. Do you think he did– Ah, good man! I worried you'd left us without a caffeine hit and by Christ we need it with the ones over there.' She gestured behind us where the gaggle of women was ongoing.

He laughed. 'It's going well, then?'

'Oh, as well as always, my man, as well as always.' She took the tray that was handed to her and moved away. But I was transfixed by the images, still. There had been one – shown only once – where he can't have been older than nineteen; the lip piercing just about visible and–

'I can unmute it, if you'd like?' the barista offered.

I flashed a tight smile. 'I'll tip you more if you don't. But thank you.' I moved to leave but an idea struck. 'In fact,' I pulled a £10 note from the back pocket of my jeans and wedged it into the tip jar on the counter, 'could you change the channel?'

'Any preference?' He was already reaching up to the buttons underneath the television set.

I shook my head. 'Anything but the news.'

CHAPTER FOUR

There was an earthquake in the living room.

Simon, Wilf, Vita and India were onto their second bottle of chilled white in less than an hour. As a collective, they went all the way back to the days before I even knew Simon existed. They'd gone to secondary school together and, like those mythical groups only ever seen in idealistic film scripts, they had somehow managed to hold together the seams of their friendships through college, university and now, into adulthood. They were a coming-of-age story with an endearing sequel. But when the four of them were in a room together, they were also a nightmare for noise-making, crass humour, and drinking my house dry – which made them exactly the distraction I needed.

Simon had even arranged for Dawn to stay with his mum for the evening, which was the parental equivalent of writing your address on the palm of your hand before you leave for a night out; a sign marked: *Things are about to get wild.*

'Babe!' Simon's voice was already blurred around the edges.

We hadn't eaten, though food wasn't far off being ready, and I thought it would be a wise move to portion out larger servings for the merry drunkards. I hadn't had the stomach for anything for days – apart from red wine, which I looked to be drinking at a steady enough pace to keep myself calm, but not so quick that Simon had noticed the weighty clunk of the recycling bin; the high groan of bottle on bottle as he'd dragged it to the edge of the drive. I made an effort to knock pans together, closed cupboard doors loudly enough to feign ongoing cooking preparations as I shouted back, 'I'll just be a minute.' I took another glug from the glass on the side and the acidity of it hit my dry throat. *It's just any other dinner party*, I lied to myself, *any other normal dinner party with–*

'Babe, seriously!'

'Fuck sake.'

In the living room, Vita and India were lolloped across each other like lovesick teenagers. They were another feel-good movie cliché: the couple who had fallen for each other after years of friendship and had somehow made a stable relationship work, too. They were both in well-paying positions in their respective fields – Vita, a software developer contracted to a major tech development company; India, a physical and well-being therapist at an elite spa retreat that would cost my house and dignity for me to visit – and neither of them wanted for anything.

Meanwhile, Wilf – who was sitting cross-legged in front of the fire that didn't really need to be lit but was for the aesthetics of it – had bounced between being a journalist, editor, English teacher, then a journalist again, but had somehow ended up teaching English as a second language at a local college. It was an in-between job, but for someone without a final destination in mind it suited Wilf for what he needed. In the background, Simon was folded into one of the armchairs with his legs crossed, too, and the posture gave both men something childish, innocent.

The brittle bits of me started to warm through when I saw

them all, then, and even though only seconds ago I'd berated myself for the idea of dinner at all, it made sense why we were doing this – why *I* was doing this. I needed to be tethered.

'Babe,' Simon beckoned me over, 'come and sit with me. Be on our team.'

'She can be on our team if she wants to be a winner,' India answered.

'It's not about winning, Ind, we haven't got a wager on this or anything.' Vita laughed and squeezed her wife's arm. 'Though, if anyone wants to make it interesting...'

Wilf threw his hands in the air. 'I'm not betting on anything.'

'So you *are* unsure whether you're on the right side?' India snapped like an excited terrier.

'Okay, what side and what wager? Someone needs to fill me in.' I tried to use my softest voice and laugh along with them. *Oh, but why didn't I bring my wine?* Simon pulled me closer to the chair until I was perched on the arm of it, his hand resting on my hip, the drunken warmth of him enveloping me. For a second everything was safe until–

'So you know this missing bloke?' Wilf washed the question down with a large mouthful of wine. He snapped his fingers three times over and screwed his face together in thought. 'I want to say Michael?'

'Mitchell,' Vita corrected him.

'That would have been my second guess. So, you know this Mitchell Welcher–'

'Webster,' Vita and Simon said in unison. Though Simon had sounded amused somewhere behind me, while Vita only looked frustrated. 'You're so disrespectful,' she carried on. But India nudged her into quiet.

'I just don't have a head for names, whatever. Celia, you know this Mitchell Webster?' Wilf paused and side-eyed Vita as though proving a point; how well he'd done, to remember a name he heard only seconds ago. I felt my own surge of annoyance at his smugness. 'We're having a friendly debate about where he is. India and Vita think he's...' Wilf petered out, raised a hand and drew a finger across his neck; his meaning was clear, but still he tilted his head to one side and let his tongue loll from his mouth, in case the original gesture hadn't been enough.

Arsehole. I flashed a tight smile while I waited for the rest of the theory. 'Simon and I think that he'll turn up. Maybe him and his wife had a good row, he needed some time, now we're here. It'll be as simple as that. But these bloody-minded cows—'

'The wife claims they didn't have an argument. Where are you even getting that from?' India asked, her tone firm.

'She won't admit to an argument, will she?'

'Why not? If she didn't kill him, if he's *bound* to turn up eventually...'

His wife. I'd managed to keep her at a safe distance. But there she was now, sitting in the empty armchair across the room from me, dabbing away tears and saying something about her husband, how he wasn't the type to take off, how it was so out of character for him to do something so inconsiderate, so hurtful. A shudder ran through me. *She has no idea what her husband is like,* I thought. I could see her so clearly that I almost wanted to offer the woman a drink.

'What do you think, Ce?' Simon gave me a squeeze and pulled me back into the room. I wondered how much of their pondering I'd missed.

'I think this is an odd topic for a dinner with friends.'

'We haven't got to dinner yet.' India laughed. 'Go on, whose team are you on?'

'I...' I looked from one set of eyes to another: India, Vita, Wilf all waiting. Simon must have been wearing a similar expression, too. 'Honestly, why are we even talking about this?' I forced a laugh to try to take the edge off my question.

Wilf shrugged. 'It's popular culture.'

'They haven't made a documentary about it yet,' Simon answered.

'Ah, but they will,' Vita inched forwards, 'if he's never found, they will.'

'Or if he's dead,' India added.

I leapt from the arm of the seat like something had coursed through it and shocked me. 'I need to check the lamb.' It was the only excuse I could think of. Then I hurried from the room and back to the hell-heat of the kitchen where water was simmering and the oven was humming and my glass was empty after two hungry mouthfuls. I gripped onto the edge of the work surface to hold myself steady, eyes closed and– *Three things I can smell: fresh vegetables; Simon's aftershave–*

'Hey.' He stood close behind me and wrapped his arms around my middle. 'Seriously, Ce, what's happening with you?'

I was glad he couldn't see my face. 'Nothing, I just needed to check on things.'

'Like the lamb?'

'Mhmm.'

'Okay.' He pressed a gentle kiss on my shoulder and turned me to face him. 'It's just... we're having chicken.'

Simon told them I wasn't feeling well. He put me to bed with a forehead kiss, a hot water bottle and a strong painkiller. Everyone was operating on the pretence that I was suffering from a sudden migraine; I think I even believed it, too. Though it was less like pain, and more like the hum of white noise that made concentrating on anything else practically impossible.

But you can't tell your husband that, can you? I goaded myself while I lay in our marital bed and stared into the floral swirl of the wallpaper on the ceiling. It was the colour of an americano with flowers in latte shades and it had been a complete fad. At the time Simon had asked whether it was too busy – 'It doesn't seem like something that will help us sleep, Ce.' – but after only a week he'd said how relaxing it was, how it distracted him from thoughts of the day.

While I lay there staring into it, though, it felt like a mirror that bounced back the intricate mess of every day since I'd got back from the work trip. If I'd had the energy, I would have clambered onto the bed and clawed at the paper like a trapped creature. But somewhere between tightening my smile for Simon's friends, and my husband leading me to bed with an arm around me, the energy had seeped out of me. I imagined it running down the stairs like spilt tea; pooling at the bottom, with a steady drip adding to it until there was nothing left.

And strangely, the quiet panic lulled me. The white noise was replaced by the rise of laughter from somewhere downstairs, and I fell asleep thinking how nice it was, that my husband could have a good time, still, while I lay here, counting my misdemeanours as they hopped from one field to another like raucous lambs. And I felt the painkillers start working; or at least, start to numb something. And soon, I slept – right through the news at ten.

CHAPTER FIVE

I t all happened in a single sweep; an arm swiping across a
table full of glasses.

I may have slept through the news, but I couldn't ignore the
sandwich boards at periodic intervals. There were variations on
the tune from one newsstand to the next but the underlying
message from them all was clear: Mitchell Webster's body had
been found. They threw around phrases like 'Warehouse body
find in hunt for missing man' and 'Search for missing man ends
with body in warehouse'; anything that fit neatly into bold print
on an A2 slip of paper. I stopped at one newsstand so long that I
felt compelled to buy something to compensate for my
lingering. I asked for cigarettes – an old and disgusting habit –
and fumbled for my purse inside of my work bag.

'Terrible business, isn't it?' I looked up at the question and
the newspaper seller nodded to the board behind me. 'They
reckon he was in a right state when they found him.'

'Thank you,' I answered, taking the cigarettes. 'Do you take
card?'

He pulled his eyebrows together; a tight frown that implied

I was the strange one for *not* wanting to talk about murder. But at least he accepted Visa.

'You have a nice day now,' I said, and flashed a tight smile. I was five steps away when I realised I didn't have a fucking lighter.

The office had been empty for the majority of the day. When I'd arrived, Rory had been on his way out to a panel discussion in London that I was also meant to be going to. I stole his lighter and asked him to pass on my apologies. Something about a migraine; something about not being fit to travel so far.

'I get it, I get it,' he'd said with a smile, 'I wouldn't be going either if she weren't my client.'

Since then, the day had slipped down the cracks in the laminate flooring. I had managed to stay on top of emails and draft promotional schedules for a string of upcoming events that three of my authors were collaborating on. But whether those plans would be coherent when I looked back over them was anyone's guess. The most productive thing I'd managed to do was burn through thirteen out of twenty cigarettes. The day was already precariously balanced without adding an unlucky number to the mix though, so I resolved to smoke a fourteenth before the hands of the clock hit an acceptable time to leave and panic at home instead of in my open-plan office.

I locked my laptop, closed the lid and grabbed the cigarettes from the drawer. There was a gatekeeper to get by first – Lauren, who operated the front desk at the main entrance to the building, and who had taken to narrating my frequent trips outside over the day already – but it was worth it for the slow in- and out-breath of addiction; the only thing that had managed to steady my heart rate. Though the irony of it clouding my lungs instead wasn't entirely lost.

'That's actually the lady you're looking for, there.' I heard Lauren's voice the second I stepped out of the lift. And when I looked up a glaring spotlight snapped on as to who was looking for me: there were two detectives standing in the lobby. Their occupation was clear from the muted suits, the tired expressions, and the shoes designed for speed and comfort – rather than an overpriced office that specialised in talent management and consultancy work.

'Mrs Nelson, is it?' One of them stepped forward; the woman, with hair scraped off her face and minimal make-up, all of which reminded me of the weekend bliss of being at home with nowhere to be. She didn't extend a hand; only closed the distance slightly, with her male colleague still behind. 'I'm DS Allen, this is my colleague, DC Moss. We were hoping to ask you a few questions in relation to a case we're currently working on.' She looked about us; for a quiet spot, I wondered, or the smoking area, if I was lucky. 'Is there somewhere we can...'

'My office is back upstairs.' I pointed behind me, to the lift. 'I was just about to...' I pointed behind her then, to freedom. 'But that's fine, that can wait. We'll go back up?' I was desperate for one of them to be a smoker – a reformed smoker, even – attached enough to nicotine to understand the importance of an intake of it. But neither of them offered to step aside and let me through, so I only smiled and back-stepped, and waited for the elevator to arrive. The three of us piled in soon after and rode in silence. *Because this isn't at all awkward...*

I smiled at Allen when she caught my eye.

'You must be wondering what this is all about?' Her tone was light, at least.

Still, I thought: *No, I know what this is all about.* The doors opened and I stepped out before I could incriminate myself.

When I was facing away from them both I answered, 'You've certainly got a cloak and dagger about you, I'll give you that much.' And when I heard one of them laugh I could have let out a small strangled cry. *But people with nothing to hide probably don't do things like that*, I reminded myself as I steered them towards the one private spot of the office: a room populated with armchairs, an expensive coffee machine, and space enough for writers to pace and pant and panic. In hindsight, it should have been where I'd spent the day, too.

The detectives dropped into two bucket chairs; DC Moss flashed a surprised expression at the seat, which was obviously lower than he'd expected, judging from the jolt of his body as he sat. I took up space in an easier seat across the room from them, as though a safe distance might shield me from whatever was coming.

'Mrs Nelson,' DS Allen started, but I held up a hand.

'Celia, please? Mrs Nelson makes me feel like I'm at parents' evening, or the bank.'

She laughed. Her smile was a natural one, too, and it made me wonder whether she'd got children at home; it was that shared understanding of the formality, or the responsibility of parenthood. She fidgeted slightly in her seat then started again. 'Celia, we were hoping to have a chat with you about Mitchell Webster. You may well have seen the name mentioned on news reports recently?' she asked, but she didn't seem especially interested in whether there was an answer, and I was glad of that mercy. She turned to Moss, then, who was already clutching what looked to be a photograph; he held it out for his superior to take and I steeled myself for it to reach me. But Allen held on a second longer. 'He was reported missing by his wife some days ago and we pressed on with an investigation into that, which is actually where your name turned up.'

My stomach fell through me. I imagined that if I stood then

it would be left behind me in the seat; a bloodied mess of nerves. '*My* name turned up?'

'Mm,' Moss confirmed. 'You were known to Mr Webster, were you?'

I looked from him to Allen, then to the carpeted floor between us. The main office was laminate but in here it was a soft-touch heap in dark beige; something that absorbed the constant back and forth of worried writers, concerned agents, and office parties. Unfortunately, there weren't handy lies stitched into the fibres, though, so I had to rely on honesty.

'We went to university together,' I admitted. *Remember omission isn't a lie*, I reminded myself, before I added, 'But we haven't really been in touch for a long time now. I don't even think we're connected on anything. Social media, or whatever.'

'Funny you should mention social media, though, Celia. That's where your name turned up to begin with,' Allen took back the reins. I noted her phrasing: *to begin with?* 'Mr Webster, he hadn't reached out to you at all recently?'

They were pushing the line so hard that I wondered whether he had, and in all the panic of the previous days the memory had slipped down the cracks somewhere, too – or into the fibres of the carpet. But no, he hadn't reached out; I was sure of it. I shook my head. 'Like I said, I don't even think we're connected anywhere. I'm not a massive social media user.' I laughed. 'Unless it's for work, obviously.'

'Of course.' Moss made a note of something.

'It looks as though Mr Webster had looked for you across a number of platforms in the last six weeks or so. You mentioned work, incidentally, and that's another thing he seemed to have some knowledge of. He clearly knew what you do for a living, for instance.'

At least I could guarantee that any surprise I was displaying then was authentic; I had no idea he'd go to so much effort to find out anything about me. *Why would he bother now?* I wondered. Then I only shook my head and waited for the officer to continue. 'No reason at all that you can think of, still?'

I didn't like the shift in her tone. 'Honestly, I think the pandemic has made everyone a little nostalgic, hasn't it? Friends who haven't been friends for years are getting in touch. People you hardly know are reaching out...' I tried to keep my tone light, but from her face I knew I'd slipped up somewhere.

'So you *were* friends, you'd say?'

I smiled. 'No, I'd say he falls under people I hardly know.'

'No idea why anyone would kill him, then,' Moss leapt in with blunt force trauma enough to make me wince. He was staring at his notebook when he made the comment – or asked the question, it was impossible to tell – but when no one answered he looked up, first at me, then to Allen. 'Apologies, that didn't come out right at all.' He huffed a laughed and although I couldn't see Allen's face, as she craned round to see him, I wondered whether it was deathly – parental. *She definitely has children*, I decided.

'You'll be aware from the reports made now that the missing person line of enquiry has turned into a murder investigation, as my colleague here has already alluded to.' Allen spoke to me but I imagined the fine-tuned blade of the comment directed at the young man. 'Of course, we have to explore all avenues. Is there anyone else from the university days who we might benefit from talking to; anyone else who might have heard from Mitchell Webster in recent weeks?'

I shrugged. 'I'm sorry, officers. I'm not entirely sure why he was looking to reach out to me, so I can't speak for anyone else.' I took a deep and greedy pull of air – the kind that comes after you've held your nose shut under water – and I tried not to cough when the force of it hit my throat. 'Asthma,' I lied, in case either of them noticed. 'There were a group of them, lads, who

Mitchell hung about with. I dated one of them. I may as well tell you that now. It was fleeting, and it didn't put me in much contact with Mitchell. You know what it's like at that age.' I saw Moss's eyebrows rise. *Are you young enough, still, for that flavour of stupidity*, I wondered. 'I didn't keep in touch with any of them, so I can't speak for whether they kept in touch with each other.'

Allen looked down at the photograph she was still holding, then back at me. *Had I said too much somewhere already?* 'It would be helpful to get those names from you, if you can remember specifics.'

'Of course.' I flashed a tight smile. 'I'll email them? If I can get your...' I petered out as she leaned across to hand me her business card. It was thick and off-white and I was itching to burn it. 'Thank you.'

'Does he look very different?' She held out the photograph, too, and I hesitated in taking it, lest there be something contagious in the print of him. But that would be a hard reaction to explain.

I took it, and only looked for a moment. I wondered how they'd found him. Reports had mentioned an abandoned building, but they'd said nothing about the state of the man; the length of his stay there, before someone had stumbled across him. I swallowed hard and heard the gulp of it bounce about my throat. 'This is the picture I saw on the news.' I forced a smile, then. 'We all grew up, that's all. I hear it happens to everyone eventually. But yes, there's something in his face I remember.' The steel glare of it; the detachment, disinterest; the glass around his pupils. 'It looks like a mugshot,' I commented, echoing the same sentiment that struck me days earlier.

Allen only smiled then stood, and Moss followed her lead. 'Thanks for your time, Celia. If you can drop me those names at your earliest convenience, that would be really helpful to us. We'll be in touch if we need anything?'

I understood she was play-asking permission. 'Please. Anything to help.' They were making for the door when I called Allen back in. 'You forgot this.' I closed the distance between us and held out the image. She took it with a quiet thank you.

When the lift had swallowed them whole I sank back into the armchair behind me and thought more of the image. I wondered how he'd liked it, being captured on camera like that...

CHAPTER SIX

S imon was desperate to go shopping for presents. Since Dawn, birthdays had become even more special to him; though he'd always made more fuss than necessary in the years before as far as I was concerned.

Now, though, there needed to be presents and cakes – plural – and bunting stuck with double-sided tape to the living room walls that looked patchy with colour at the best of times already. I sighed at my own practicalities.

Before Dawn, I'd always imagined *I* might be the fun parent. Fun or un-fun, there were still presents that needed to be bought, and Simon and I always made the effort to join forces for gift-buying. The hope was that one of us would be there to rein the other in. The reality was markedly different but still, it counted as an afternoon together and neither of us had ever been ones to turn that down – we were lovesick like that.

Dawn had been carted off early in the morning by the mother of a school friend; another birthday party, the sacred drop-and-go that brought all parents the luxury of a free couple of hours. *God bless the mothers prepared to host thirty children at a time*, I thought, with flashbacks to the last fundraiser meeting.

Dawn had a playdate immediately afterwards, too, buying us a window of opportunity that Simon was eager to capitalise on. He'd pestered me to leave as soon as the front door was shut behind Dawn – 'Time is of the essence, babe!' – but I'd begged for gym time.

'You seriously want to work out?'

'Is that so hard to believe?' I asked and Simon fell silent. I looked up from packing my bag and laughed at his blank expression. 'Okay, maybe it is hard to believe. I haven't had time all week and I just want a run, that's all. I'll be an hour.' I pulled the zip closed. 'Two hours, max.'

'*Two* hours.' I saw where Dawn got her impatience from; I was waiting for him to stamp his foot, cross his arms and force his bottom lip out. 'You better not be longer than two hours. If all the good toys are gone–'

I'd rushed in to kiss him hard on the mouth to stop the petulance. 'Shut up.'

'Shutting up now.' But he'd caught my arm as I went to leave the room. 'Seriously, though, babe, let's get lunch? Some time together around toy shopping, without Dawnie.'

'We will, I promise. See you later.'

In the gym I set my running pace to 'What's Up Danger' by Blackway and Black Caviar and turned the volume in my earbuds as loud as Apple would allow. Siri generated a message – 'Are you sure you want to burst your ear drums?' – that I dismissed before knocking my phone into airplane mode. If anyone needed me that much they could call Simon; if Simon needed me that much...

I shook the thought away. *This needs to be your time, kid, focus.* I let my feet fall flatter, harder to pound the runway underneath me with the speed rising and falling in time with the music; my heartbeat changing on two-minute cycles according to the lulls in the song. I was desperate to make it louder, to overthrow the white noise of news reports and detectives and—

Three things you can smell: my body spray; cleaning chemicals from the early morning sweep of the gym; sweat. Two things I can hear: vocals, lyrics, rapping; the clock tick percussion of the backing track to the song. One thing I can feel: a knot of anxiety sitting in the bowl of my stomach that could be anything from worries about buying Dawn's birthday presents, nerves about Mitchell Webster, or an unexpected period thrown at me through hormonal disruption.

I forced a stream of air through rounded lips and tried again: *One thing I can feel: the muscle pull in the back of my left leg which must mean the song had been on for ten minutes already.* I swapped tracks to 'Call Me Devil' by Friends in Tokyo and thought of nights on the sofa with Simon, binge-watching episodes of *Lucifer* and eating dinner leftovers straight from the pots they were cooked in and—

I could see the television bounced through the mirror in front of me. It had been muted when I arrived, and I guessed it still was. But the headline was loud: POLICE LAUNCH SEARCH FOR ANOTHER MISSING MAN IN EDINBURGH AREA...

It was too far away to be deserving of panic; a poor coincidence and nothing else. But still I slowed to a stop and took a cautious glance around the room before I dismounted. This was the least popular running studio at the gym, with machines that were outdated in comparison to the other exercise hybrids around the building. It at least meant that I was alone. So I crossed the room, reluctantly turned my music down and hunted out the volume button for the television set. There were three buttons clustered under the set and I pressed them one after the other until a voice boomed from the speakers on the wall.

'...arranging an appeal for witnesses, for anyone who might have seen Uri on the night he disappeared.'

The name meant nothing to me.

The screen was split down its core: one side showed a pristine news anchor in a pristine studio; the other, an offensively handsome man in front of a row of terraced houses. There wasn't any context displayed across the bottom of the screen, though I guessed it must be the missing man's house. *Is it too soon to be calling him the victim?* I scanned the numbers that were hardly visible on each front door and wondered which might be his. *Is this where he was last seen?* I thought and I was suddenly desperate for them to clarify, but they'd moved on to something else, something new – '...spate of disappearances...' – that was even more troubling than the original announcement. I wondered at the word 'spate'; rolled it around my teeth like poorly made pâté that might leave behind grit.

'The police are naturally playing their cards close to their chest on this, and any associated news regarding the other disappearances.'

'But there are early suspicions that there may be a link?'

'It's a hard one to say–'

I hit mute again. *They know nothing.*

I ran until my knees felt like they might buckle under the weight of me. The ground was jelly when I stepped off the treadmill for a second time and I kept a firm grip on the handlebars while I acclimatised to not outrunning anything – even if I had felt more comfortable moving that way.

Still, I'd already been longer than I promised Simon I'd be, and there was only so much patience that man kept in reserve for days when there were a hundred things that needed to be done. I slowly made my way through the gym space and into the changing rooms. They'd been quiet ninety minutes ago but when I pushed back into the space now it was an assault on the senses. There were whole classes of women getting changed from one personality into another, complete with tight-fit exercise gear that was heavily branded to show their social class and their surgeons' skills. I shook the bitchiness away – *You're better than that, Ce* – and powered through them to my locker at the back of the room. There was a hum of a radio in the background, somewhere overhead, fighting to be heard over the chatter – and I was sure I imagined a news report on a missing man.

'Fuck sake,' I berated myself as I slammed the door of my locker closer. I needed to shower off the shit that was clinging to me – before I saw my husband and daughter and perfect life.

The police hadn't been in touch again, and despite my irritability around Mitchell's disappearance – *Murder.* – no one had said anything to warrant the nerves I was carrying around. I hung the towel on a hook just outside the cubicle, turned the water temperature as high as it would go, and stepped in to scald myself – as though I might hit absolution in the washroom of a local gym. Sweat was replaced with the prickle of heat and I stood there until I could breathe at a regular pace. *In and out, just like everyone else.*

'Oof, you've got it like a sauna in here, girl!' a woman shouted over from the cubicle next door and a laugh spluttered out of me. *Thank God for everyone else.* 'Are you okay in there, love?'

I laughed again. 'There was no time in my day for a steam so I thought I'd make my own while I had the chance.' I turned the water off, then, and caught her chuckling.

'There's *always* time for a steam, girl, always time.'

I reached out to grab my towel and secured it around me; flip-flops on, I dodged and darted back to my locker feeling as though flecks of worry had washed away; some of the heaviness in my shoulders certainly had, too. Inside, I dug in my bag for the loose fit dress that would dry easily with me, and I slipped it on and let my towel fall. There was still the sting of sweat in my hair, so I grabbed body spray next and ran a strip of the fresh floral smell along my neckline. I'd keep my hair bun in over the day and wash the last of it away in the bath later. There was something calming about these small steps coming together.

The clock on the wall had been ten minutes fast for as long as I'd been coming here. But even taking that into account, I was still running late. I quickly collected together the scatter of my bag and wedged everything in without any order, bar my phone. I was dodge-darting my way from lockers to door as I turned the handset on, and no sooner had the Apple logo appeared and it hummed alive in my hand to show me three missed calls: one from Simon; two from a number I didn't recognise. Both had left messages.

'Hi, babe. I imagine you're sweating like a... I don't really have an end to that. I imagine you're sweating. Don't overwork yourself. Look, I know I said I'd wait but I'm going to head to town now, I think. Meet me at Joey's bistro? I thought we could grab a drink and make an action plan and I promise not to buy anything until you're there, okay, love you, bye.' He rushed it out all in a single breath and I heard the lie. He'd probably bought three unplanned presents by now – and bunting, so much bloody bunting. But at least the man made me smile.

I deleted that first message and held on while EE introduced the second.

'Hello. I'm hoping this is the right number. I'm looking for a Celia Nelson.' *Potential client on a Saturday?* I pushed through the main entrance door, back into the street. This was the downside of having business cards with a personal-professional mobile number on. I had never learned the error of this– 'It's Debora Webster here.' I froze on the pavement; someone bumped into me, cursed and kept moving. 'I was told that you know... that you knew, sorry, my husband. Mitchell. I realise this call is a little out of the blue but I've got some questions, see, and... it's nothing ghastly... but, I don't know. You may well be the only person who can answer.' Another two people bumped into me in the time it took for her to relay her mobile number. 'Call me, would you, please? If you wouldn't mind. Thank you. Bye now.'

I sped back into the gym to use the customer toilets. The porcelain and my knees cracked in unison as I hit the floor. I brought back the little I'd managed to eat that morning; brown bread and bile and bad feelings.

CHAPTER SEVEN

Debora said she could meet me anytime – 'I'm not at work at the moment... with everything that's... well, happening, still...' – so we arranged to have coffee Monday, late afternoon, after work. I made my excuses to leave slightly earlier than usual on the lie that I was meeting with a potential client; at least if anyone from work were to see us, they'd assume that's who she was.

I told Simon the same story – 'I don't know how long it'll take, hun, I'm sorry.' – though some of my excuse to him had been partly truthful. Debora had suggested the place, Murphy's, a hipster coffee shop just a six-minute walk from my office. But I couldn't marry the sleek outer feel of the place – I'd only ever seen it from outside, until that day – albeit with the limited knowledge I had of her husband. It didn't seem like the type of place where Mitchell Webster might end up with friends, though that left two possibilities: he'd changed a lot, from the man I thought I knew; or his wife was a lot trendier than I'd given her credit for, from the hushed and nervous tones I'd heard over the phone. *But then her husband has just been fucking murdered*, I reminded myself as I pinched my thigh and paced in front of the coffee shop long enough to vape my breathing steady. I'd run out of cigarettes days ago and told myself this was marginally better than buying another packet; not that I'd been sure enough of that to admit either slip to Simon. I exhaled through my nose while pulling in another drag through the mouthpiece. *I can add it to the growing list of indiscretions*, I thought as I capped the machine and slipped it into the side pocket of my handbag. There was a young couple just leaving and I leaned forward in time to grab the door from the woman before it could slam.

Inside, the space was packed with the percussion of coffee machines and idle chatter. I wondered how many people had migrated here following an early finish at the office. But there was only one table in the room that had a solo diner: eyes red, swollen from days of crying, she was nervously fidgeting with the ends of sleeves pulled over her hands. When she looked up to scan the area her eyes settled on me and stretched a fraction in recognition. *Gotcha.*

I flashed a tight smile and made my way through the happy diners to meet my sad one, all the while thinking, *You're asking for trouble, Celia. You're fucking asking for it.*

The abruptness of the thought had me reaching for the back of the chair before I could manage to pull it out and sit. Debora stood and leaned across the table as though to catch me, her hands outstretched, and I instantly spotted the wedding band.

'Are you okay?'

I laughed it off. 'I'm sorry. That's not the greeting you needed.' I pulled the chair out, then, and took a seat, and she soon lowered herself down onto her own chair, too. 'It's been a long day at the office and I haven't eaten enough, that's all.'

'You must work very hard,' she answered, and I couldn't decide whether it was an odd thing to say. Neither could she, I guessed, given the speed at which she added, 'Thank you for making the time for this. I have some questions, is all, which I'm sure you can understand.'

I nodded. 'I do understand. Though I'm not sure how many answers I've got.'

'Better than none.' She opened her mouth to continue but then glanced at the table. She was drinking what looked like herbal tea. There was a tall jug of water with two glasses there as well. I wondered whether she'd hoped for a long conversation – or was only braced for an especially difficult one. 'Coffee?'

I caught a waiter as he moved by us. 'Can I get an espresso, please?'

'And for you?' He looked over at Debora, who only shook her head. 'I'll bring that over.'

'The police said...' She petered out and forced out a long stream of air. 'The police said you knew Mitchell from when you were at university together. That must have been quite a while ago now.'

There wasn't a question, but still I said, 'It was, yes. Fifteen years or so.'

'And now?'

My eyes narrowed. 'I'm sorry, I don't–'

'Espresso.' The young man slid the saucer onto the table.

'Thank you.'

'You're very welcome. Anything else I can get for you ladies today?'

An ejector seat. 'I'm fine, thank you,' I answered, instead, and when he looked to Debora she shook her head again. The woman looked like she was in physical pain; her lips pursed and her eyes full of tears again, as though someone were plucking hairs out with flaming tweezers. I wondered whether anyone else had noticed; whether they wondered what kind of conversation we must be having, to force such a response.

When the waiter was out of earshot, Debora tried to look at

me face-on. I say tried because, more accurately, her glance sat somewhere just above my head. She reminded me of advice I'd been given as a child: 'If you're too nervous to look at them, look just over them.' Either that, or imagine them naked; though I suspected that was a tactic she wasn't altogether keen to employ in this situation. She held her stare just above my forehead as she spoke and asked the question she'd obviously dragged me there for.

'Were you sleeping with my husband?'

I choked on my own spit. A loud cough erupted from me, like someone had smacked my back and blocked my airflow. I reached for the jug of water on the table between us and poured a shaky glass.

'I'll take that as a yes,' she said as I sipped a measured amount, and I felt another wave of something ripple in me. I managed to swallow the second choking fit, though, helped by another swill of water before I set the small glass down.

'I haven't seen– hadn't seen your husband since university.'

She narrowed her stare at my sentence as though inspecting it for holes. She could pull out a magnifying glass for all I cared, shine a light directly behind the statement to see what pattern might shine through on the opposing wall. But it was one of the few truths I'd managed in the last weeks, so it made no difference to me how closely she looked. I sipped my espresso and minded my own business for as long as it took the widow to find her follow-up line of enquiry.

'Then I don't understand why he was looking for you.'

It was my turn to inspect her idea, then. 'You mean the social media searches?'

'I mean everything.' She looked confused; authentically, hurtfully confused. I tried to imagine what it might be like, to find that The Other Woman wasn't that at all; but rather, that my husband had been tracking her down for another reason.

'He was looking for you but...' I thought I saw a light bulb flicker to life over the crown of her head. 'I found you so easily. As soon as I knew your name, I found you.'

'I'm quite public because of work.'

'No, that's my point.' She leaned forward to close the distance between us and rested her forearms on top of the table. Her hushed tone made me feel like a co-conspirator in something. But I didn't like the sound of my name in her mouth; something about it felt like collapsing a boundary. So I leaned back in my seat, to combat the sudden closeness of this woman who I knew *nothing* about – other than she was unfortunate enough to be married to a man who I didn't like. 'If I found you so easily then maybe he wasn't trying to find you at all.'

I sipped my drink again and tried to steady my breathing. I could feel my heart knocking against my ribcage, as though it were about to burst in with an idea or suggestion. 'Where did he look?'

'Social media. You were in his recent searches on Twitter, Facebook, LinkedIn, even! He didn't even *use* LinkedIn. Why would he, with his job?'

I took the question to be rhetorical given that there was no good reason for me to know the answer to it. In recent weeks, I'd gone to great lengths *not* to Google Mitchell Webster, or anything else that might look like I was following the investigation. Simon and I binged through enough true crime documentaries in our early days together for me to know where people slipped up and internet histories were high-ranking on the list. *Look at the problems it's causing for Mitchell*, I thought, a little too smugly given the circumstances. When I didn't answer she continued with her listing. 'He'd looked at your work website, too, more than once. A few times over the weeks before he... over the weeks before.' She hard swallowed and I heard the thud of it. 'Your husband, too.'

At the mention of Simon something greater stirred in me. It wasn't the worry or panic of an old enemy getting back in touch. It was the sting of one part of life encroaching on another. Simon and Dawn both moved the same kind of energy in me: something fierce and primal that was desperate to keep them both bubbled away from anything bad in the world. They were the best things ever to happen to me – and I would keep them that way.

'What about my husband?' My tone was flatter, brittle around the edges, and I wondered whether she would notice. Or – given the recent loss of her own husband – whether she would notice and completely understand. I felt the sudden need to ask if her and Mitchell had children. *But would that only lead her to ask the same of us? And what if she already knows the answer to that, too?*

'Mitchell found his work website.' She looked defensive. 'He visited it once, twice at the most, that was all he knew. Or all he found out through the internet, at least.' She leaned back and ran a hand through her hair; I saw the grease of grief in the underneath layers. 'I don't understand what he wanted with you.'

No, I flashed a tight smile, *I'm struggling to work that one out, too.* I threw the last of my coffee down like I was slamming a shooter in a nightclub. The sharpness of it hit my throat and I was glad to be grounded by it. *Three things I can–*

'That must sound awful.'

I shook my head. 'It doesn't. I don't understand what he wanted with me, either.'

'You'd had *no* contact, at all?'

I shook my head firmly and tried to strangle the beginnings of irritation in my belly. *I'm not a child and asking three times won't change the answer.* 'None.'

'And before, when you were at university?'

'We weren't close,' I snapped my jaws around the words so roughly that I thought she might find teeth marks if she looked too closely at them. The nervous sparrow in my chest kicked and flapped and let out small strangled noises, and I tried hard not to think about Mitchell Webster from Before. 'I'm sorry.'

The smile she mustered made her look more exhausted than she had at the start of the conversation. 'Thank you for agreeing to meet with me.'

'It's okay, really.' I pushed my chair back and reached for my bag. When I looked up at her again I thought I saw a flash of surprise that I was leaving. But what more was there to say? 'I'm sorry to run, but I have a work thing this evening and I need to pop home beforehand, too.' I reached across the table, then, to give her limp hand a squeeze, in what I hoped read as an authentic and not-at-all nervous gesture. 'The police are doing everything they can, and I know it isn't enough. But they'll find something, sooner or later. I'm sure of it.'

'How can you be?'

I don't know, I admitted, *but isn't this what people say?* 'I just am,' I said instead.

'Thank you, Celia.' She let go of my hand and I felt as though I'd been unleashed from prey. 'You take good care of yourself, now.'

I gave her a cool goodbye and pushed through the warm bodies crammed into the coffee shop. The noise of place had me wincing but when I was ejected back into the quiet of the street I found there was nothing to drown out the thrum of heartbeat-panic-flashback-heartbeat that was swamping me. *Three things I can smell: the stain of coffee on my clothes; the perfume from a huddle of women; the man smoking outside.* I fumbled in my bag and dug out my phone as I started to pace away.

I hadn't been able to get through to her mobile in the days before this, so I thumbed my way down to her work number instead. But it only rang twice before it cut through to her voicemail; I knew what that meant – a work trip away – and I wondered when she'd even hear the message, whether it was worth leaving one, still. The recording beep cut in before I could talk myself out of anything, though.

'Hi, it's me. It's Celia. I know you're away, or I guess you're away. But I need to talk to you. Something has happened. Something happened to Mitchell Webster and I... I don't know who else to...'

SHE

The hire car from one part of the country to another had been one that was cleaned to a clinical degree before using. It was good from the perspective of basic cleanliness, but it made it all the more obvious on both legs of the journey – there and back – that she was driving a disguise. Her own car would never be so clean.

Before dropping it at the rental centre she'd taken it to a local valet service; one housed in what was previously a petrol station but was now putting a roof over the heads of four Turkish men making an honest living. Or rather, reasonably honest, given that they knew which customers to do a deep clean for – she was one of them. She always imagined that men and women having extramarital affairs fell into this category, too, if the cars and their owners were anything to go by. Those awaiting a deep clean were always directed towards the back of what was once the petrol store itself; as though there were something seedy and therefore worth shielding about bleach solutions.

There were times when she would lock eyes with a man or woman over the roof of a car – hers or theirs, it didn't matter –

and there was a narrowing of the eyes, as if one were looking for signs of what the other were washing away. Though she wagered hers was always the more interesting of the two, she wouldn't have verbalised the bet.

Once the car was clean enough, she dropped it back at the rental centre and walked the rest of the way to her office. Her travel bag bounced along the pavement for the last six-minute leg of the journey.

From the outside, the building looked like something that was waiting to be ripped down. Inside, it was home. She took the stairs, heaving the bag up clunk by clunk, because the elevator was unreliable at the best of times. On her floor there were two other offices, neither of which were regularly occupied. It made her work even easier, to know there were minimal people around whenever she needed to invite someone to the office.

When she pushed into her open-plan office, it took an additional shove before the door gave way. Either she'd been away longer than she'd realised, or the postman had been especially generous with Pizza Hut delivery offers. It was the latter, she decided, as she kicked her way through the scattered leaflets and torn shreds of paper.

The only thing she could see from an aerial viewpoint was the logo of water and heating bills, which she knew would be minimal, so she left them where they were. Her travel case she discarded in the corner of the room – she'd unpack, burn and/or wash everything later – and she made a beeline for the phone, which was flashing a full memory's worth of new voicemails.

The first two were prospective clients – 'You gave me your card when we met at...' – and she recognised both women as people she'd found during the Dublin trip. The third message caught her attention, though: it was Celia. While she listened, she crossed the room and dug out her mobile phone which had been switched off and stashed in the front pocket of her bag for the majority of the trip.

When the Apple logo kicked into life she walked back and landed in the desk chair; somehow Celia was still talking.

'I'd been trying to call you on and off since my work thing and... I just really need to talk... there's some stuff that I... Christ, just call me, would you?' Celia paused to laugh; a nervous and awkward noise, though. 'I'm a bit of a mess without you.'

She hit delete on the message and lit a cigarette while she waited for the next to start playing.

CHAPTER EIGHT

The living room, kitchen and garden looked as though a unicorn had gargled confetti and bubble mixture, while dancing around the house to Carly Rae Jepson, before violently throwing up over the walls, furniture and floor – and Simon looked elated with himself for it. He'd crept out of bed at 5am and disappeared downstairs like an extra from an episode of *Scooby-Doo*.

Even Dawn was questioning his life decisions when she sleepily crawled into our bed two hours after that and announced it was her birthday – as though I might have forgotten the fourteen-hour labour that brought her to us on this blessed day – before saying, 'Is there something wrong with Daddy?'

Now, staring down the face of a garden full of six- and seven-year-olds all of whom looked to be hooked on crack-sugar, I wanted to rewind time well enough to tell my daughter that yes, there was absolutely something wrong with Daddy. But hours later Daddy was also standing with an arm tucked around me, the curve of his palm cupping the ball of my shoulder, and a look of youthful glee on his face; Daddy, who nodded towards the bottom of the garden and said, 'Doesn't she look ecstatic?'

Dawn was there, surrounded by her friends, while she was having an uneven butterfly painted across her face. And yes, she looked ecstatic. Enough so for me to lean into Simon and, instead of criticising his craziness, to answer, 'You did well, babe.' I turned to kiss his cheek. 'You did really well.'

'Wait until you see the cake.' He sighed, wistfully, like a character from a romance novel – and I was torn between teasing him and joining him. It was the calmest I'd felt in weeks. Though I still hadn't heard back from any of my voicemails and texts, hurriedly left whenever Simon hadn't been looking. I also still hadn't heard from the police – or the widow – again, which I took to be positive signs.

'I guess we'd better hang fire until they've had actual food?'

I laughed. 'You guess right.' I kissed his cheek again as I turned for the house. 'I'll go and get the oven on. Everything has been thawing since this morning, hasn't it? So none of it will take long.' The kitchen island was a mess of half-defrosted party foods: onion rings; chicken nuggets; hash brown bites and more. Simon had bought all of Dawn's favourites to make a feast of them – without a vegetable in sight. Although I was wondering whether I could sneak cauliflower hash browns onto the menu instead. *But it is her birthday...*

I smiled and clicked everything to pre-heat to the right temperature. Once I set the timer I went back outside to find Dawn playing life-size chess with a friend at the bottom of the garden, and another friend – one whose name I didn't but definitely should know – had taken up her turn with the face painter. The lawn looked like a miniature carnival.

'Do I dare ask how much this has cost?' Connie's Mum – Yvonne – appeared at my side. 'Small fortune?'

'It cost so much,' I looked around at each corner of the plot that boasted a different colourful activity, 'that I'm assuming my husband took the freelance job he was on the fence about, and he decided to use his first cheque wisely.'

She snorted a laugh. 'Your Simon, honestly. He's as bad as the kids.'

'Christ, you're not wrong.' I scanned around and spotted that he was talking to Martin – Oliver's dad – with folded arms and a smug expression. 'He loves spoiling her. But I've no idea how he'll top this sort of thing when she gets older.'

Yvonne waved the worry away. 'Bigger job, bigger pay cheques.'

'From your mouth to God's ears,' I joined the joviality. Everything felt normal again. I hadn't checked my phone in nearly an hour, which was a personal best since Mitchell. Simon hadn't triple asked whether I was okay either, which was a personal best for him since my work trip. He always could sense tension a clear mile away. But I was doing my absolute to hide it for the length of the party at least. 'I'm just going to check–'

'Mum?' Connie tugged at the bottom of Yvonne's blouse. 'Can I use the bathroom?'

'Of course you can, honey. Ce?'

'Upstairs, first door on the right.' They were just turning away when I called Connie back. 'Where's Dawn, Connie? I thought...' I scanned the garden as I asked. Connie had been Dawn's chess partner.

'She went to the front door.'

The three of us traipsed through the house, then. Connie and Yvonne tucked into the stairway while I headed for the front door – and there Dawn was. She was perched on the seat of the coat stand, her hands cupping her knees and her face angled towards the glass pane of the front door. Everything about her posture reminded me of a loyal dog, left for an indeterminate period of time and dutifully waiting for their owner to return. But I couldn't marry it with the image of her from moments before, when she'd been pretending to be a queen in search of a pawn to knock over.

I crouched in front of her and caught her attention. 'Baby, did something–'

The latch of the door behind me lifted and cut my sentence down the centre.

'Did somebody say birthday party?'

'Lily!'

I shot up as though scalded. 'Lily, you came.'

She was holding a bouquet of birthday balloons. There was a tote bag slung over her shoulder, too, bursting with what looked like presents. 'Of course I came!' She dropped to her knees with a heaviness that made me wince. 'Get your butt over here, birthday girl.' Dawn fled to her, and I wondered whether this was what she'd been waiting for; the arrival of her godmother, also known as Dawn's favourite person in the whole world. Nothing could beat the excitement of a visit from Lily; not even, it seemed, face painting and party games and all her favourite foods. 'That's a big hug, little bug. Have you been saving them up?'

'We haven't seen you in *ages*, so yes, in a jar, with fireflies.'

'*With* fireflies? Well, no wonder the hug feels so good.' Lily finally unleashed Dawn and held her by the shoulders, at arm's length. 'Look at how grown up you are.' She glanced up at me. 'Tell this kid of yours to stop sprouting, will you? She's making us look old.' Lily kissed Dawn on the forehead and then struggled to her feet; she kissed me on the cheek when she was standing, and the warmness of the gesture moved good feelings through me. 'You doing okay there, gorgeous mama?'

'I've been calling,' I answered, but tried not to sound brutish with it.

'I've been busy.' She winked. 'We'll talk.'

'Lilith!'

'Hey, handsome hubby. How's it hanging?'

Simon opened his mouth to respond but I slapped his arm. 'Little ears.'

'How's what hanging?' Dawn asked and looked between my husband and best friend for an answer. 'How's what hangi–'

'Baby, why don't we go and get that food in the oven?' I pulled her to me for a squeeze. 'Because after dinner, there'll be...'

Dawn's eyes spread as she realised the answer. 'Dad, move, we need to put food in the oven.'

Dawn and Simon swapped places, giving him access to his share of hugs from Lily. 'Comments like that are why Adam had you booted out of the garden,' he said as he pulled her close to him. 'Good to see you, Lilith.' And it was good to see her.

She was immaculate; loose curls that had either taken her hours to master or, more likely, taken a professional only minutes to twist in place. She was wearing dark jeans with a white shirt, a leather biker jacket over the top and studded boots that made a clink-clink-clink on the floor as she followed into the kitchen. I only had limited knowledge of *the* Lilith, but I knew there was something daring and tempting about her; something that had passed through the name's DNA. Lily had always been a force.

She walked into the kitchen with Simon trailing behind her. 'Do you want to put these in some water?' She handed him the balloons which he took with a teenage giggle. 'There's helium in those, FYI, so if the grown-ups get drunk later...'

'Bloody brilliant,' Simon said as he started to tie one balloon at a time to various points around the kitchen: the fridge handle; a dining chair. 'You okay with food, babe?'

I kicked the oven door closed. 'It's all taken care of for thirty minutes.'

'In that case...' Lily dropped the tote bag onto the kitchen counter. 'Presents for the small one.' She looked around as though expecting Dawn to be at her feet, and I thought again of the stray pup image; daughter as loyal dog. It was just like Lily to have people in her thrall. 'These are for you two, though, from my travels.' She leaned across the island to hand me a huge box of biscuits. 'Well-travelled, they are. All the way from...' She waved away the end of the sentence. 'I don't know, wherever it says on the box. Scotland, somewhere.'

'Good trip?' Simon asked as he wrestled the box from me.

Lily shrugged. 'So, so. It was only a work thing.'

'Interesting case?'

'Aren't they all?'

'Anything you can sha–'

'It never is,' she interrupted him and laughed. 'I can't share people's personal trauma. But nice try. How are those biscuits?'

I noted the rapid subject change.

Simon answered from behind his hand, chewing through a full round of shortbread. 'They'd be better with a brew. But they're mighty fine biscuits.'

'You'll ruin your appetite.' I cocked an eyebrow at him. 'And you'll set a bad example to the kids.'

He shrugged. 'If this is the worst of the behaviours I'll pass on...'

'He's got you there, beaut.' Lily shuffled round the kitchen and tucked an arm around me. She looked over the worktop, which was a mess of paper plates, plastic cutlery and unfolded napkins. 'Want me to try to make a swan out of those?'

I laughed. 'I'd settle for squares.'

'Dad!' Dawn's holler came from outside and Simon, who was chewing through his second biscuit, rushed to her aid. I was glad of the chance to corner Lily, though, and I inched to stand closer to her, to shield us from any young eavesdroppers who might be hidden in the room.

'Can we talk?'

She didn't look up from folding. 'About what, doll?'

'My trip away,' I started, and there was already a shiver in my voice. 'And...' I forced out a long stream of air and still she didn't look. 'I think I need to talk to you about Michell Webster, and–'

In a swift motion she dropped the napkin she'd been midway through scoring and snatched at my wrist. Her fingers felt like a cuff. 'If you're about to confess to something, Ce, I wouldn't. Your daughter's birthday party isn't the place for this.'

'Nurse! We've got a bleeder!' Simon came in with Dawn in his arms; her right hand was elevated to show a slim trail of blood rushing down one finger. I rushed to them both, and behind me I heard Lily ferret through the drawers looking for–

'Plasters, plasters,' she chanted as though she might summon one.

Time and a place for this, I reminded myself as I took a slim plaster from the box Lily offered. *Time and a place to confess*. I smiled while Simon kissed our daughter's finger better. *Time and a place for a slight indiscretion*. Dawn stretched her hand across to me, as far as her short arm could reach, and I wrapped the second skin tight around the small cut. *But not here*.

CHAPTER NINE

L ily's apartment building was in a high-end part of the city. It had been a crowning moment in her adulthood when she'd gained the mortgage approval to buy it. We'd celebrated with beer and pizza, straight from the bottle and box, consumed cross-legged on the hardwood floor of her new living room. 'I like to think this particular room, right now, is the one I've managed to buy outright with my deposit,' she'd joked, and we'd cheersed to the idea.

It was a beautiful block of trendy two-bedroom flats, packed into a Victorian structure that had managed to uphold all its original charm from the outside. Though from the occasional complaints Lily made about her neighbours – 'They're having *another* couples' party...' – there was sometimes a lack of charm on the innards.

It had been five years since she moved in, though, after going freelance from the firm she was working with, too, and she'd never expressed a desire to be anywhere else, so I knew she must have nested. That said, I didn't spend much time in her home; not through lack of want, on my part, but mostly because I would inevitably get the world's greatest bottom lip grump from Dawn if I deprived her of too much time with Lily – and I thought Simon felt the same sometimes, too. Besides which, since her work had flourished into a booming business, Lily had taken on the habit of arriving spontaneously; the irony wasn't lost on me that she often disappeared in the same way, too, like a Mary Poppins figure dressed up in a private investigator's costume.

I wasn't in the habit of arriving spontaneously myself. But twelve days after Dawn's birthday party – and thirty-eight missed calls later – I found myself panicked into a corner of my own making. I told Simon I was going out to meet a new client. Instead, I'd taken a taxi straight to Lily's office.

After three unanswered buzzes there I admitted defeat and called for a second taxi; this one to bring me to her home. Two unanswered buzzes had gone by before I managed to catch the door opening by luck. One of Lily's neighbours was leaving the building, and they were kind enough to let me stroll right in. *She'll love that security when I tell her*, I'd thought as I hiked the stairs two at a time. But hammering on her front door hadn't got me any responses. Since then, I'd been sat on the doorstep for such a time that my backside had gone numb, and I knew then that this was another dead-end when it came to finding her.

Fuck sake. A hard and heavy sigh fell out of me; the same style that Dawn makes when she's told she can't have seconds of something with a red sugar content. I dropped my head to rest on my knees and tried to steady my breathing, which was already battering around my chest like a wild thing. *Three things I can smell: exhaust fumes; roses; cigarette smoke. Two things I can hear: traffic on the surrounding streets; an older woman and a younger girl having an argument somewhere. One thing I can feel: the cool of the concrete step underneath me.* I took another big breath and looked up – and there she was.

Lily was standing in front of me with a suitcase by her side;

the type with wheels on the bottom to make it easier to drag behind you. She was wearing brilliant white Converse, ripped jeans and a T-shirt that sported three female Disney villains with script underneath that read: 'We don't care'. I huffed a laugh. She was the only adult I knew who could pull off something quite so–

'It's my favourite T-shirt, and what?' She cocked an eyebrow and lifted a lit cigarette to her mouth.

'I didn't know you were smoking again.'

She exhaled through her nose. 'Stressful work trip. Can I tempt you?' She held the cigarette out to me. 'Our secret.'

'I shouldn't,' I said as I leaned forward and took it from her.

'Yeah, beaut, none of us should. What're you gonna do?' In the time it took for me to pull in a greedy drag, she'd already fished the black box of them out of her back pocket. 'Keep it,' she said, as I reached to hand it back, 'you look like you need it more than I do.' She fumbled a lighter from another pocket, sparked up and said, 'Celia, honey, not that I'm not delighted to see you. But what the hell are you doing on my front doorstep in the middle of the afternoon?'

'I've been calling,' I answered flatly, cigarette smoke tumbling from me as I spoke. *I'll have to tell Simon the client was a smoker,* I thought with another hard inhale. And, *another lie to add to the pile,* I thought on the breath out.

'I've been working.' She sat two steps down from me. 'What's going on?'

I ran my free hand through my hair and looked away from her. 'I need to talk to you about my trip, the work thing, the other week?' I glanced back at her, then, and she nodded. 'Something happened, Lil. Something pretty bad.'

She stood up. 'Well, that's a ridiculous amount of tension building that no woman can stand. Up you get. Let's be having it...'

Lily was sitting on the window ledge of her living room, staring out at some fixed point beyond. There was a bloated pause between us while I was letting her think, and I was keeping myself busy by doing the maths for how many rooms she must own outright by now. I didn't know what Lily's flat fee was for a job but I knew she was always rushed off her feet with work, and often travelling for it, too. I looked around the minimalist space: all glass and sharp edges. There was something cold about it all suddenly, and I wondered how much time she even spent here anymore and–

'Run it by me one more time.'

I pulled in a greedy breath. 'I've already explained–'

'And I'm asking you to explain again.'

The brutishness of her voice felt new to me. I wondered whether she spoke to clients like this; whether I was getting a formal treatment, to make the bitter pill an easier one for her to swallow down.

'I met him in the hotel bar. I was drinking alone, after all the work stuff had properly ended for the day. He said I looked sad and did I want company.'

She sighed; a heavy, weighty judgemental sigh. 'And you did.'

'We didn't sleep together.'

'You told me that part already,' she snapped.

'I've told you all of this already!' I matched her tone.

She dubbed a cigarette out on the outside wall of the building and dropped it into the ashtray next to her. 'And this is what you've been freaking out about, since the trip? This is why you're being weird with Simon?'

The question hit me like a tap to the cheek. 'What?'

'At Dawnie's party. He said– he more asked, actually,

whether I knew if there was something going on with you. He said you'd been... I don't know, I think the word he used was unsettled? Or something like that. Unsettled or nervy, since your trip. I told him you're a hard worker and you're probably tired.' She turned to look at me, then, for the first time in at least a quarter of an hour. 'Stick to that story, okay?'

Another slap. 'What story?'

'You're overworked, you're tired. You'll snap out of it.'

'You don't think I should tell him?'

The tables turned, then, and it was Lily who took the shock of a slap. Her eyes spread so wide that I waited a beat to see whether a dropped jaw would accompany them. 'Why in fucking fuck would you tell him?'

'Simon and I don't have secrets, Lily.'

She laughed. 'Well, now you do.' She reached for the cigarette box but then seemed to think better of it. 'Are you in a rush to get home?' I only shook my head. 'Excellent, in which case, red or white?'

'Lil...'

'I have gin, if that's your poison at the minute, but I have to say it feels a touch early in the day to crack it open. I wouldn't rule it out entirely. Though I suppose that all depends on what you've got to tell me next.' She crossed the room as she spoke and wandered into the kitchen; I followed and stood against the doorframe while she rooted through cupboards. 'How do I not know where a thing is in my own fucking house?'

'Mitchell Webster is dead,' I announced, flatly. It was the first time I'd been able to make such a blatant admission out loud. I couldn't have said it at home; it would mean sharing it all with Simon and... I shuddered at the thought. But Lily didn't even react. 'Lily, I said–'

'I heard what you said, beaut. I'm just in the middle of– Aha!' She spun round with a bottle of red in her hand. 'This will need to breathe, I guess, but there's definitely white in the fridge. Preference?'

'Lily,' I raised my voice and felt every bit the boring parent. But despite her nervous energy, I couldn't muster the energy to pretend I was okay with Webster's death; not after weeks of pretending already, at home, at work, with the police. My stomach turned at the memory of them, then, and I dropped into the nearest kitchen chair for fear of something grim pulling me down to the floor otherwise. 'I told you I needed to talk to you about him–'

'Which him?' She undid the screw top on a bottle of white as she spoke.

'Fair point, but still...'

'You nearly cheated on your husband with a beautiful man you met at a hotel while you were away. Sweet girl, I don't mean to piss on your chips, but you're not the first or the last.' She leaned forward and set a half-empty glass on the table in front of me. 'People like you are literally my bread and butter when it comes to my line of work.' She winked. 'Bottoms up.'

'I told you I needed to talk about Mitchell, too.'

'Don't use his first name like that. We weren't friends with him, Celia, he was shit on our shoes at the best of times, never mind after...' We locked eyes, then, and I was glad I was already sitting. 'Just, after.'

I imagined a naughty child playing cat's cradle with my insides; one organ looped around another. At least that's how it felt in the seconds that passed between us. Lily was the only person who knew about Mitchell Webster – about all of them – and if I couldn't turn to her with this, *Who the hell am I meant to talk to?* There was a rise of tears moving through me and I pinched my eyes closed.

Lily sighed. 'I'm sorry.' I heard her set her glass down, but I couldn't open my eyes, still. She must have walked across silently because the next I knew her palms were over my knees, and when I opened my eyes she was crouching in front of me. 'He's a waste of space, they all were, and are. But if you need to talk, if this has brought stuff up for you, I'm here. I'm here always.' She held a pinky finger up to me and I laughed, then reciprocated the gesture: The Best Friend Code.

'For all you know I could have been coming here to confess.'

She laughed. 'Confess to what?' She walked back to her side of the room and lifted herself up onto the kitchen work surface. She was perched in the corner, her head rested gently on the cupboard door directly behind her. I felt a pull, a flashback to our trips home from university; Lily hardly cared for her own family, so she'd become a shared owner in mine. We would sit, just like this, and wait for Mum to feed us samples of whatever she was cooking. And something about that sudden memory calmed me. I even managed to match her humour.

'He was murdered, you know?' I sipped my wine. 'Maybe I was coming to confess to killing him.'

She snorted booze through her nose. 'Okay, Ce, good one.'

'You don't know!' I joked along and enjoyed the ease of it all, then. 'How do you know I didn't kill him?' It was a crass conversation, but it had lifted my spirits from the moments spent on Lily's front steps earlier. 'How do you know?' I pushed, and tried to raise my eyebrow in a cocksure gesture but I wasn't sure I'd managed it.

'Because.' She shrugged and then smiled. But the smile seemed to belong more to her than it did me. 'Because I know who did...'

CHAPTER TEN

S imon thought it was a migraine.

I called in sick for work and then turned my phone off. He was working from home for the day, which meant he was periodically checking on me. But whenever the bedroom door opened I scrunched my eyes shut like a child feigning sleep and Simon had either believed it, or he'd taken it for the sign that it was: I didn't want to talk. This dance continued until lunchtime, on the day after I'd seen Lily.

When I refused even a mouthful of soup Simon became less sympathetic – 'Babe, if this is the world's worst hangover then...' – but his accusation had died when I filled up with tears and placed a hand flat against my forehead, as though the pain, the pressure, was too much; which it was in many ways, even though it wasn't a physical ailment.

He threw his arms around me, then, and pulled me to him, in the same way I'd seen him do to Dawn when she was hurt with a 'baddy'.

I didn't have the stomach, yet, to tell him the baddy wasn't a headache. The baddy was a short walk away, taking commissions, claiming lives – and I knew their name and home number.

The only time Simon disappeared from the house was to fetch Dawn from school. Everything was too quiet, then. The walls of the bedroom shifted around me and I rolled to angle myself over the side of the bed, in case an upchuck was imminent. Everything was too unsteady to make it to the bathroom, even, and I wondered whether the lie of a migraine had somehow manifested one.

I took deep, lengthy breaths – in through the nose and out through the mouth just like they taught us in how-to-be-a-functioning-human school – and I tried to ground myself in the here; in the safety of the bedroom. *Three things I can smell: the new laundry detergent that I still can't decide whether I like; the sweat from my own pillowcase; the ghost of Simon's aftershave. Two things I can hear: the sound of children having just escaped school, somewhere on the outside of this panic; a clock ticking in the hallway. One thing I can feel: someone watching me. Is that a feeling?*

My eyes snapped open and caught Dawn lingering in the doorway.

'Should I get Daddy?'

Her face was a picture of childlike worry. I scooched further back in the bed and lifted the duvet up. 'I reckon that if I had a little cuddle, I'd be right as rain in no time.'

She smiled, then, though the expression was a nervous one. Still, she crossed the room and jumped into bed and snuggled into me – her head under my chin – like she would have done as a toddler. *One thing I can smell: the sweet-sweat-playground-rush-around in the crown of her hair.*

Unprompted, she told me everything about her day while we lay there and even though half the names brought up only a watercolour memory of who she was talking about, there was still a kind of bliss involved in listening to it all – like a favourite track that you put on for the comfort, or for the known background noise.

'Am I missing out on a cuddle puddle?' Simon stepped into the room and cut Dawn off mid-sentence.

'I was telling Mum about my day.'

'Mum is meant to be resting.' He climbed onto the bed behind me and wrapped an arm around us both. We hadn't lain like this in a long time and I was grateful for it – though there was a stir of sadness at what it had taken for me to make time for this kind of family contact, too.

'Lily called,' he spoke quietly, next to my ear, and my whole body tensed against him.

'Hey.' A closer cuddle, then, 'Hey, babe, what was that?'

I sighed. 'I don't know,' I lied, 'a bit of a spasm, I think.'

He reached to ruffle Dawn's hair. 'Madam, come on, I really do think Mum–'

'Don't,' I cut him off. 'Don't, it's okay. This is helping.'

He kissed the back of my head. 'If you're sure. Do you think you can manage something to eat?' He moved away, then, and I wanted to call him back – pull him to me in a way that might barricade everything outside of the 144 square foot prison that I'd managed to make over the course of just a day.

'I'm not hungry.'

'That isn't what I asked, babe.' He was aiming for the doorway but turned back. 'Dawn, is there anything you fancy for dinner? My night to cook.'

She giggled. 'In that case I vote McDonald's.'

'You sneaky little...' He made for the bed again, then, and reached for another ruffle of her hair. She tucked into me as though I could protect her. *Because that's my job*, I thought with another deep inhale from her crown.

'Why don't we let Mum decide?' Dawn suggested and she pulled away to look up at me. I understood the code.

I made a playful show of thinking about it before I said, 'I vote McDonald's.'

'You two are a bloody nightmare!' Simon's back was to us; his arms thrown up in gentle defeat. 'Fine, whatever, McDonald's. What does everyone want?'

'Fish finger Happy Meal,' Dawn snapped.

I shrugged. 'Same.'

'Babe, that's not...' He shook his head. 'McFlurry?' I don't know what face I made but his response was a saddened one. 'I'm just worried.'

He was right to be. As of nineteen hours ago I was an accessory to murder. 'I could go for a McFlurry.'

'Thank you.' He was halfway out the door but stuck his head back in to add, 'Should I invite Lily over?'

Dawn and I said 'Yes' and 'No' respectively. Simon's surprise was evident.

'Honestly, babe, I just think it'll be too much. I want a bit of family time. Would that be okay?' I looked down at Dawn, directing the question more to her than Simon anyway. And she agreed – begrudgingly. 'Thanks, Dawnie. We'll have Lily over another time.' I pulled her to me again for a cuddle – in the hope that it would stop her from reading any signs of the lie that might have stained my expression.

Simon took care of everything: dinner; homework time with Dawn; bath; bed and to sleep in record time. Dawn had never been a bad kid for getting to sleep. Though she often wanted a kiss from both of us before she'd even entertain it.

When Simon had ordered bedtime, though, she crept into me and kissed my forehead before sneaking back out again. She whispered, 'I love you, Mum,' and a tear rolled out of my clenched eyes and onto the pillow. I couldn't remember whether

I'd taken my mascara off from the night before, or whether the face I'd worn to Lily's had stayed with me all day.

She'd tried calling again during dinner – Simon's phone, not mine – and he'd ignored the ring. But I watched as he tapped out a reply to her afterwards, while we were collapsed in a three-heap together watching Dawn's choice of feel-good cartoon.

He told Lily I was sick – 'Think it's a migraine or bug. She'll call when she's up to it. Nowt to worry for.' – and I glanced again when she replied: 'Tell her I love her.' He had, and I'd only grumbled a tired noise; the safest response.

When Simon came back in from settling Dawn he clambered onto the bed and reached for the remote. There was a jolt of panic that ran through me – I worried that he might want us to talk – and it emerged in a flinch when he turned the television off.

He frowned. 'You seem to getting a few of those... tremors?'

'I think it's just my head. Or not my head, but, you know.' I nuzzled into the pillow to hide my lying face from him. 'I think my body is just putting up a bit of a fight on whatever this head thing is.'

He leaned over to kiss the side of my temple. 'I'm sorry you're suffering with it, babe.' He went to stand, then. 'Is there anything you need from downstairs?'

'Are you leaving?' I tried to settle another jolt; I hoped he hadn't noticed.

'I'm only getting a drink.' He smiled. 'And anything you want.'

'I just want you here.'

'Okay, well, I can manage that.'

In the minutes he was away I braved a look at my phone. It took a second to boot up but as soon as the Apple logo faded and my home screen appeared, the messages started to flood in.

The last of them hit me like a small rock landing in the well of my belly:

Ce, you didn't even let me explain.

She was right, I hadn't. But the world around me didn't feel steady enough for her explanations yet.

Instead, I set the phone down and tried to settle myself in the only way I could think to. *Three things I can smell: fish, burgers and fries we ate for dinner hanging around like the last guests at a party; the same washing detergent, that I'm still unsure of; Dawn, the soft smell of her from where she'd nestled in the duvet. Two things I can hear: the kettle whistling to a stop downstairs; the tap of pipes in the bathroom. One thing I can feel: panic. No, not panic. Try harder. What replaces panic?* I pulled in a greedy breath and forced it out in a stream; then again, and then again. *One thing I can feel: the weight of the bed shifting underneath me as someone else climbs onto it.* I inched open my eyes and there he was again.

'Feeling sick, babe?'

'Unsteady. I might just...' I struggled upright in bed. 'I think it'll help to sit up for a while rather than lying.' As though taking this as a cue, Simon lifted an arm up for me to nestle into the side of him and I obliged. *Three things I can feel: the hard press of his torso; the ball of his shoulder against my cheek as my head drops; the squeeze of his palm around my arm when he drops his hand to me. I am safe,* I repeated to myself, then, to make an affirmation of it, *in this moment, I am safe.* I pulled in another breath. 'Can we play what if?'

I heard his smile crack. 'We haven't played that in years.'

It was a game from the early days of our lying in bed together. We would be strung out on sex and cigarettes and whatever takeaway we'd order in the aftermath of it all. Quite out of nowhere one of us might ask, 'What if the building cracked in half right now, where would you leap?' or 'What if you found out your Mum wasn't your Mum but someone who'd pinched you as a baby?' We never went to a great effort to make them sensible, or even safe, questions. But we'd always had a fun time in trying to answer. I had a very specific question in mind, though, so I was glad when Simon squeezed me to him and said, 'Go on, then, you start.'

'You start.'

He huffed a laugh. 'I thought you'd got something in mind.'

I had. But it was too strong a start, and I needed an idea of where his head was at before I could ask. 'Please?'

'Okay, okay.' He fell quiet for a second; I heard the echo of his heartbeat quicken and I worried where the possibilities might have taken him. *Nowhere as bad as I'm about to, though*, I wagered. 'What if Dawn wasn't Dawn, but Dawn was a changeling?'

A laugh burst out of me. The question had caught me so off guard. But once that first laugh had come there was no stopping the stream of giggles that followed. He would be fine with my question, then, and I wondered whether that was what some of the laughter was about – a kind of nervous eruption – or whether I was really *that* amused by the prospect of our precious girl having been replaced with a naughty Irish myth.

'How do I know she's a changeling?'

'With that girl, that's a very fair question to ask.' He laughed. 'Someone tells you.'

'Do I trust the person who's told me?'

'The person is Lily.' There was an audible turn in my stomach. 'So, yes,' he added when I didn't respond.

'I would start doing my research on changelings, and I would find a way to get her back. I have no idea where to start with that, though.' The giggles moved through me again. 'If I came to you and said, babe, look, this has happened to Dawn, do you sit down and work out a plan to help me get her back or do you—'

'Have you locked up in a heartbeat?' He laughed. 'Is that your question?'

I softly thumped his thigh. 'Absolutely not.'

'Okay, then, your turn.'

I pulled in another greedy breath, though I both felt and heard the shake of it this time. 'What would you do if I'd killed someone?' I wanted to turn to look at him, to inspect him in the silent thought that followed. But I wondered what my own face might give away.

'Why are you killing them?' he asked, but before I could answer he added, 'I mean, why aren't you paying to have them killed? Wouldn't that be the safer option?'

There are no safe options right now.

'Okay, let's say I've paid to have someone killed.'

'That's a separate question.' He kissed the top of my head. 'But I guess...' Another long silence stretched out and there was such a wing-beat of panic in my ribcage that I wanted to retract the question entirely. But then he said, 'What have they done?'

I turned to face him, then. 'To deserve being killed? Can anyone really deserve that?'

He thought about this for longer than he had the other questions and then said, with some certainty, 'Yeah, babe, I think some people can deserve it. So this person, in the question, what have they done?'

BEFORE
2007

CHAPTER ELEVEN

The lads were cramped around a student flat taking it in turns on a poorly rolled joint. Mitchell never had got the hang of rolling them, and the chaps had always complained without making an effort of it themselves.

Raff took a long in-breath and winced as though something in the drug had stung him, then he leaned forward to pass the roll-up to Barnie. This was their second one and they were no closer to working out the logistics for the party, which had been the whole point of this 'meeting'. They were nearing the end of their first year of study, though, and they had to do something to mark the occasion, that much they'd all agreed on.

'Why can we not just fuck off into Bristol town?' Quen asked as he waved away Barnie's offer of a drag. 'It's a damn sight easier than trying to orchestrate a party with piss-all money and no way of agreeing who we want to invite.'

'Well, I'll betcha Celia is going to be there.' Barnie thumped Theo's thigh as he spoke. 'Isn't that right, Romeo?'

'Fuck off,' Theo answered without looking away from the window.

'State of the kid.' Raff landed heavy on the sofa next to him.

'Lemme tell you something, if I knew Shakespeare, I'd be making an arse's job of quoting it in your ear right now, mate. Things still going well with her?'

Theo faced back into the group, then. 'She's pretty special, you know?'

'Has she put out yet?' Quen asked from across the room. He was sitting at the kitchen table; which in student accommodation, was only four metres away from the boxy sofa that took up most of the living room. Everywhere was open plan, which made it easier still for Theo to pick up a pillow and throw it in the general direction of his roommate.

Theo had always thought Quen was a bit of a twat anyway. Still, they'd been assigned the flat together at the start of the year and they'd managed to muddle through.

'I'm not hearing a no,' Quen added as he leaned over to pick the pillow up from the floor. 'Come on, dish the dirt.'

'Lily's the easy one out of the two,' Theo lied. He'd never seen Lily so much as look at a man on a night out. In fact, he'd been quietly convinced since midway through semester two that she might be batting for the other side. But he knew Quen well enough to know he'd take that as a challenge, too. Quen thinking Lily was easy enough to put out at least meant she'd distract him for part of the party – if it went ahead. And maybe even thump him one before the end of the night, too, which was something Theo *had* seen her do on a night out. 'She's your best bet if you want something easy.'

'Celia makes you work for it, then,' Barnie chimed in.

'Can we stop talking about how often Theo dips his wick and concentrate on the actual fucking matter at hand here?' Raff's leg started to shift up and down at a speed. It was the weed hitting, he knew, but he'd had enough waiting around for party plans, too. He stood from the sofa, to try to steady whatever nervous paranoia was rattling around inside him. 'Quen, do you vote town?'

'Aye.'

'What's everyone else feeling?'

Barnie shrugged. 'I think a party would be easier.'

'Than town?' Quen erupted.

'Well, yeah. No bouncers, no kicking out time.'

'He's got a point,' Theo added. 'I'd be happy with a party.'

'Only so you don't have far to drag her at the end of the night,' Barnie joked.

'She might not come.'

'Mate, it's your *job* to make her come,' Quen answered.

'I'm not sure that's what he meant.' Raff ruffled his friend's hair as he scooted around him to reach the fridge for another beer. 'Why wouldn't she come?'

'Parties aren't really her scene, are they?'

'Because she's boring?' Quen snapped.

Theo aimed another pillow at his friend; from sofa to kitchen table, it landed with a soft thud and knocked over an empty beer bottle en route. 'She isn't boring.'

Quen stood, then, and stole the free seat alongside his roomie. 'If you're so sure she isn't a bore, why don't we have the party here after all?'

'I already don't like where this is going,' Mitchell chimed in, then. He was the most passive of the group; everything was decided on his behalf, and he tended to agree with whoever got to him first. It wasn't like him to offer an opinion without being prompted, and the group swapped looks among themselves while they waited for him to add further explanation. 'Come on, the dickhead obviously has something disgusting planned.'

'One man's disgusting is another's sexual stimulus,' Quen answered.

'Fucking hell,' Theo shifted away and turned at an angle to

get a view of his friend's face, 'now *I* don't like where this is going.'

'It's just an idea, and if you hate it then you hate it.'

'Quen...' Raff cautioned from the kitchen. He gestured with his beer bottle as he spoke. 'I know we take the piss but anything that buggers his relationship isn't worth doing.' He focused his attention solely on Theo, then. 'You're allowed to have met a girl and decided you like her, mate. Don't let this fucking Lothario convince you otherwise. Besides, he hasn't had sex in a week, what does he know?'

The group fell about laughing, then, with a chorus of mockery for Quen who protested loudly – 'Oh, get bent, it's been five days if that!' – but joined in the humour, too. The conversation shifted from the party, and any plans Quen might have for it, onto sexual appetites, conquests from the semester and plans for the summer. Someone suggested a tally chart of sexual exploits for while they were away; another suggested proof of sex. Theo avoided eye contact with Quen for the rest of the afternoon, though, and when five o'clock rolled around he quietly slipped away to meet Celia.

CHAPTER TWELVE

L ily slammed the kitchen cupboard and paced to the stove. 'I can't believe I don't have any fucking pesto.'

Celia laughed. 'Middle class problems.'

'Sod off.' She stirred the pasta in quiet then added, 'I'm so *not* middle class.'

The fact that this conversation was taking place in their shared apartment that sat outside university limits – right in the core of Bristol city, otherwise known as 'the posh bit' by students who only ever saw these dizzy heights if they happened to be looking out the top deck of a passing bus – did nothing to help her point.

The place was bought and paid for by Lily's father; the archetypal Daddy's girl, after her mum had passed away there was nothing in the world to put a wedge between Lily and her remaining parent. He'd bought the place as a graduation present – graduating from college, that is – and after two cocktails during Fresher's Week Lily had asked Celia to move in. Celia had been commuting to campus before that – even student accommodation had been out of her financial reach.

When she'd told Lily to ask again when she'd sobered up,

that's exactly what Lily did. It had been the best decision either of them had made during their first year of study – apart from Celia having accepted Theo's offer of dinner, which she also thought of as a mighty fine decision.

'You're thinking about him again.'

Celia's head snapped up. 'I absolutely wasn't.'

Lily snorted a laugh. 'You absolutely were. You get this gooey-absent-minded expression on your face every time he crosses your mind.' She moved around grabbing cutlery, plates, and glasses as she spoke. 'You'd be terrible at poker.'

'So sue me.' Celia dropped back in her seat. 'I'm in love.'

Lily landed in the seat opposite and gave a wide-mouthed stare. 'Are you actually?' When Celia only laughed, Lily reached across the table to grab her hand. 'Celia, this is serious. Do you actually think you're in love with him?'

'Oh, I don't know.' Celia snatched her hand back and ran it through her tangled hair. *Christ, why did I say that?* she thought. 'I don't know that I'm *in* love. I guess– I guess I could love him, at some point. Do you know? I've never felt like anyone the way I feel about Theo, I can tell you that much for certain.'

Lily was up and about in the kitchen again so Celia knew the answer must have settled her. Lily opened the fridge and pulled out a bottle of white that she'd put to chill earlier. *Another middle-class marker*, Celia thought and smiled, but said nothing of it. 'Does he feel the same, do you think?' She poured large measures of wine into two glasses and brought them across.

'How am I meant to know? Men, they're a...'

'There are so many ways to finish that sentence.' Lily laughed. 'Have you thought– Did you want garlic bread with this?' she interrupted herself and Celia raised an eye in answer. 'Stupid fucking question, of course you want garlic bread with it.' She paced back to the fridge and this time pulled out what looked like a garlic and herb flatbread.

Celia couldn't help it, then, the laugh burst out of her like projectile vomit after a bad batch of Snakebite.

'I am *not* middle class,' Lily protested, guessing at Celia's meaning as she ripped into the packaging. 'Have you thought about asking him how he feels about how things are going?'

'Isn't that a bit... direct?'

'And that's a bad thing?' Lily slid the bread into the oven. 'At least you'll know.'

'It's early days still, though, you know? Maybe there's not really anything I need to know. I could just... wait it out, and see what happens and...'

'Go against your natural instincts. I hear you.' She sat down to sip her own wine, then. 'Look, it's just a thought. You don't have to ask him. But wouldn't it be better to know, rather than spend another academic year having mediocre sex with someone who you might not be with by the time you leave?'

The accusation stung Celia, but she couldn't hide a smirk either. 'What the hell makes you think it's mediocre?'

'We share a bedroom wall.'

Celia hesitated. 'It isn't mediocre. That's such an *ugly* word. Besides which, Lil, I might not be looking for the person who I'm going to be with when I leave here. I might just be looking for fun. You don't know.'

'No...' She twirled the wine glass around by its stem. 'But, if you *are* only looking for fun, I'd say that's an even better reason to ditch the mediocre sex and find someone better for the role. Do you see what I mean?'

'I think... I think you mean I should ditch Theo either way?'

She rested a hand on her chest in a theatrical gesture. 'Did I say that?'

'Sod off and check your pesto-less pasta.' Celia kicked her

friend gently under the table. 'What about you, anyway? What's your situation?' Lily never mentioned anyone, and Celia wondered whether that was a deliberate act of privacy or whether there really was no one to mention. Lily was beautiful, though, beautiful and hilarious and clever, and–

'I'm not in the market for anything.'

'Not even mediocre sex?' Celia joked, and Lily let out a curt, 'Ha!'

'*Especially* not mediocre sex.' She served generous helpings of pasta into two ceramic bowls and carried them across to the table. 'If you're thinking of setting me up with someone then don't.'

'Why would you think that I was setting you up?'

'Because I can read you like a bloody book.' She dropped into her seat but then shot up like there'd been a static shock. 'Bollocks.' When she rushed to the oven Celia realised what was missing from the meal. 'See, why would you set me up with someone when I can't even cook garlic bread properly?' She turned to show Celia the charred edging.

'Ten out of ten,' Celia answered, leaning over to snap some crust free, 'would wife you in a heartbeat. I'm basically a kept woman.' She gestured to the room around them, meaning the wider apartment, and she was glad Lily had taken the joke.

'In which case, I definitely don't need setting up with someone. One spouse is more than enough to keep.' She winked as she sat down again, the garlic bread pungent between them. 'And if you're thinking of setting me up with any of Theo's dumb-fuck friends then absolutely don't. I'd evict you in a heartbeat.'

'Not even Quen?'

Her eyes stretched. 'Especially not that fucking numpty.'

CHAPTER THIRTEEN

R aff set a third crate of beer down in the cramped living room. The space looked like a brewery, and he wondered why of all the student accommodations between the lot of them, they'd decided to host the party here. Mitchell's place was much bigger, although it was full of the artsy-twats you tend to find on media and literature courses.

He shook the idea away when he spotted Mitchell in the corner, angling a video recorder just so, and thought: *One artsy-twat at a time is probably enough.* Quen had requested video footage of the evening – said something about saving up memories – and Mitchell had jumped at the chance to play cameraman for the night. Which also meant he was ducking work while the others slogged their guts out lifting booze and industrial-sized boxes of snacks from Barnie's car to the flat.

'How long does it take to set that thing up?' he asked as he passed Mitchell.

'Oh, leave him be.' Quen was in the kitchen making 'party bags', though he was yet to tell any of the chaps what the bags contained. 'I've asked him to do it, don't take the piss.' But Raff was already five steps out of the room and not paying the least attention. 'You all right over there, mate?' Quen asked Mitchell, then.

'Are *you* all right over *there*, mate?' Barnie repeated the question back to Quen, who looked to be all fingers and thumbs with small see-through bags. 'Do I even want to know?'

'Probably best you don't.' He licked his finger and tried to part the lips of another small bag. 'Where's Romeo, anyway? I haven't seen him lift a fucking finger since this lot all started to come together.'

'Where do you think he is?' Barnie cocked an eyebrow. 'He's playing house.'

'He's being a wimp.'

'What, for liking a girl?' Mitchell interrupted.

'No, for letting her call the shots. They've slept together what, a handful of times? And look at him; you'd think he'd never tapped thighs apart before in his life, the gratitude he shows her. Fucking finally,' he shouted the final two words, having just broken the seal on a bag he was struggling with. 'Whatever, this'll loosen her up anyway. Assuming she even agrees to take any. And that's another thing–'

'Mate, leave it with your other things,' Raff snapped when he walked back in the room. 'I can hear you bitching and whining all the way down the corridor. Ever consider the reason Theo is spending less time with you is because you're a demanding little–'

'Chief, I get it, I'm high maintenance. But so is she. That's all I'm saying.'

'Yeah, but,' Barnie paused to lick the inner lining of a roll-up, 'at least she puts out at the end of an evening.'

Theo lingered outside the lecture hall. Celia was in there having a last-minute tutorial for her final assignment of the semester and he'd agreed to meet her for a drink afterwards, maybe dinner, he thought. Though he hadn't checked his bank and he couldn't be sure whether a student loan would stretch for anything better than the on-site café – and he was pretty sure that if he totted up much more on a loyalty card there then it would get embarrassing. Still, he just wanted to be around her.

The party was two nights off happening and he was already sick of the state it had made in the flat. And if Quen said one more thing, one more time about Theo being pussy-whipped, he was pretty sure he'd punch his roommate in the centre of his face – which would be a shitty way to end the year by anyone's standards. Besides which, he wasn't whipped. He was–

Celia pushed through the door and cut off the early annoyance that was rising in him. She was wearing a floral print dress that ended just above the knees, with plain white pumps and a cardigan draped around her shoulders. She was every bit the cute girl on campus, and he loved her a bit for it in these moments. *Not to be confused with loving her full stop, though,* he reminded himself as he stepped forwards to greet her. Somehow, since starting university and falling into his group of mates, falling in love had become the emotional equivalent of picking up chlamydia – only the latter was maybe *less* shameful, and certainly easier to get rid of.

He shook the idea off as Quen talking and slapped on a smile. 'Beautiful.'

'Charmer.' She kissed his cheek.

How does she always smell good?

'Thanks for waiting. My lecturer was going on and on, and on and... you get the idea. Drink?'

'Please. The flat is a bomb site of beer and bad decisions already.'

She laughed. 'Bad decisions?'

'Agreeing to the party is probably the first thing on that list.'

'Oh, no,' she grabbed his hand as they started to walk, 'you're regretting it already?'

'I'm just a grouch from spending so much time around the boys, that's all.'

'Quen?'

He smiled. *She always knows what I mean.* 'Yes, Quen. He...' Theo lingered over how honest he should be. This was a problem he'd started to see, with having a girlfriend who also felt like a best mate; where was the line between being open and telling her shit she just didn't need to know? He shook away the horrible honesty. 'He's just taking the piss a bit more than usual and it's winding me up. He's probably got a lot to get out of his system before the summer hits.' They rounded the corner and the Student Union bar was in sight, then.

'I'll set Lily on him if you like?' Celia joked, but something turned over in Theo's stomach.

'At the party, do you mean?'

'I can't see when else I'd be able to get that pair in a room.' She laughed and gave his hand a soft squeeze. 'As long as you don't mind us coming along? I sort of... God, I invited myself there, didn't I? I just thought...' Her second laugh was much more forced. 'I'm such a tag-along.'

'Hey,' he stopped and span her around to face him, 'you are not a tag-along, at all. Lily might be, sometimes,' he said, though his tone was playful. 'Seriously, though, I want you there, the guys love you too. There's no reason why you wouldn't come. I'm sorry, I didn't mean to be weird about it.'

'You're not planning something stupid?'

He frowned. 'Like what?'

'I don't know, anything stupid that boys do in their final weeks of first year? It feels like something has got you nervous, that's all.' She leaned forward and kissed his forehead. 'But I want to be there, so if you want me, too, then we're all good.' She turned to start walking again. 'And we can light a fire under Lily and aim her at Quen, and at least that'll keep them both busy for five minutes.'

Theo laughed and turned to start walking again. He changed the subject – 'Go on, anyway, tell me more about this tutorial...' – and he tried to stifle whatever bubbles of discomfort were still popping and knocking in his stomach. *It's just a fucking party*, he reminded himself, *how wild could it really be?*

CHAPTER FOURTEEN

'It's just a fucking party,' Lily shouted in from the living room, 'how important can this night possibly be?'

Celia was trying on her third outfit in the space of twenty minutes and she still didn't have an answer to Lily's question – which she'd asked for the third time now, too, with increasing levels of annoyance on each recital.

Celia had been disingenuous when she asked Lily for five minutes of her time to run an outfit by her. But Celia also knew that 'Can I try on thirty-eight outfits and then decide to wear the first, which you already told me you don't like?' wouldn't have convinced Lily to hold still for this long.

Celia decided against the third outfit on her own, though, and instead moved on to a fourth: a plain black dress that came just below the knee. Its thin straps were made up of daisy chains. It was one of her favourites, and she was pretty sure that Theo hadn't seen it yet – which couldn't be said about much else in her wardrobe. She took a deep breath and walked into the living room, where Lily was thumbing through a copy of *Vogue* that she definitely wasn't interested in.

'Will I do?'

Lily's head snapped up and her expression softened. 'Adorable,' she said, and she sounded like she meant it.

'Adorable in a way too cute way, or adorable in a–'

'Would take you for dinner, treat you like a lady, and show you a good time sort of way.' She cocked an eyebrow. 'Which I assume is what you're going for. Though I think it's a bit too good for a frat-boy type party where most of the men involved will be in a pissing contest with each other and most of the women will be wasted.'

'Wasted?'

'Not drunk. But wasted... you know, on the men.'

'Oh. Oh! I get it. Lil, come on, do you have to be so cynical about it all?' Celia trod back into the bedroom but shouted over her shoulder, 'You don't even have to come, you do know that?'

'Of course I do!'

'Why?'

'Because who else will unhinge their jaws, swallow Quen whole and then spit him into the carpet fibres if I don't?'

A snort of laugher erupted out of Celia. The straps on the dress were slipping down her arms already, but mid-undress she rushed back out to her friend anyway. 'You're coming specifically to smack Quen down?'

'Mhmm.' Lily was staring at the magazine again. 'I would never miss the opportunity.'

'I bet it's sexual tension.'

Lily's head jerked up and she narrowed her eyes at Celia, who added, 'Between the two of you, I bet that's why you're always arguing or sniping or trying to smack each other down. I bet it's ripe and juicy sexual–'

'Shut your tart mouth.' Lily was playful in her tone, but there was a hard edge that let Celia know she was serious with it, too. 'I would rather go it alone than go it with Quen Parsons any day, of any week. Now will you get changed so we can go for our run, or am I circling campus on my own tonight?'

'You absolutely aren't. Give me a minute.'

Lily and Celia had taken to running together. Despite Lily's dad's financial situation, she didn't want to fork out for the on-campus gym – and Celia certainly wasn't in a position to. So they'd vowed to keep (relatively) healthy with the occasional run, but they'd also vowed never to go it alone. Celia slipped the dress off and hung it on the back of the wardrobe to keep it safe from the cluster of creases that would be waiting for it if she wedged it back in among the rest of the clothes. Then she searched through the floor-drobe to find what would pass for suitable running gear.

'If you're looking for joggers they're in the tumble dryer,' Lily shouted in.

Celia sighed and trod back out in her underwear. 'Now you tell me.'

'Well if I hadn't I would have missed these delights.' She gestured up and down at Celia's body. 'There's a hoodie in there, too, I think. Get 'em on, let's go.'

Still standing, Celia struggled to get one leg in then the other before ferreting through the dryer for the hoodie. When Celia pulled it out, she spotted that it was actually one of Theo's; four sizes too big, if not more. There was a logo for a sports team she didn't recognise the name of emblazoned across the front, and when she tugged it over her head she caught a whiff of his aftershave. The detergent never quite managed to get rid of it. When she walked back to Lily, she still had her nose buried in the collar of the fabric, pulling in the scent of him like a Wall Street guy might pull in a line of–

'Stop it.' Lily stood up and righted her running gear, which had bunched up around her legs in the time she'd spent waiting. 'You're being sentimental and I'm worried I'll catch it.'

'You'll fall in love one day,' Celia teased, then turned to make for the door.

Lily caught up with her and grabbed her by the elbow. 'So you *are* in love?'

Celia hesitated. *Yes. A thousand times, a hundred per cent, yes.* 'I...' She let out a heavy sigh. 'Why do you think the party matters so much?' she asked, and it felt good to let out pressure that she didn't even know had been building. 'Theo goes home literally the day after and we've got plans to see each other over the summer but who knows whether that'll work out? And I don't want to start the holiday without... I guess without telling him.'

Lily cocked an eyebrow at her friend and smirked.

'Don't look at me in that tone of voice. Like I said, it'll get you one day, too.'

'So that's the big plan for the party; load him with booze and confess your love?' Lily reached for her jumper from the hook on the front door. 'Or do you have something more nuanced planned?'

'I haven't planned a thing, actually.' *Apart from drinking Dutch courage at the start of the night; waiting until the first joint has been passed around; asking for a word with Theo in private.* Celia swallowed the details of the plan. 'All I know is that I love him, and I'm going to tell him just that when I see him next.'

CHAPTER FIFTEEN

Quen dug a bag out of his pocket and passed it to Barnie; it was a practised gesture, the smooth-guy handshake where something was swapped between them without anyone noticing. 'Treat yourself, have a blast,' Quen nudged his friend, 'but stick to the plan, okay?' Barnie hesitated a second before he gave in with a nod and disappeared into the mess of the room.

There were at least five of Quen's party bags doing the rounds by now, so it wouldn't be long before things got louder – and messier, if he had his way. He pulled a joint from his front pocket, sparked up and went to join Raff who was smoking by the window.

'You don't smoke,' Quen said through an exhale of smog.

'It's party-smoking, it doesn't count.' Raff laughed. 'Besides, I needed some air.'

'Having a good time?'

'I would be if Mitchell would get that thing outta my fucking face for a minute.' He nodded to their friend on the other side of the room. Mitchell was ducking and diving with his camera in hand, but no one else seemed to mind. 'Why do you want a camcorder here, anyway? Worried you're going to lose the night?'

Quen flicked ash out of the window. 'Something like that. Hey, Mitch,' he called for his friend's attention and Mitchell's head snapped round. His eyes were wide with weed already and Quen worried at the photo-quality of what was being documented. 'Why don't you set that aside for a second? Dump it in Theo's room. He won't mind.'

Mitchell frowned for a second before letting out an, 'Oh, oh, yeah sure,' that was hardly audible over the music, but the shape of his lips had been clear.

'See, there you go, he's out of the way. You can start enjoying yourself now.' Quen nudged Raff.

'Barnie looks to be enjoying himself enough for the lot of us.'

When Quen turned he clocked his friend upending a party bag into the mouth of a woman he didn't recognise. He laughed. 'She'll be passed out within half an hour, taking it all in one go.'

'Whatever. As long as there's someone to drag her ho– Hey, Theo!'

Theo was forcing his way through the room; his arm was wrapped around Celia like a protective barrier. When he turned to spot his friends, he yanked her along with him. 'Hey, everyone having a good time?'

'Hi, Raff. Quen.' Celia smiled; a hazy smile, though, that made her words watercolour. 'Great party.'

'It'll get there,' Quen answered, 'when it's warmed up.'

'You two having fun?' Raff asked, and Theo nodded.

'We're just going for five minutes' quiet. We'll be back.' He pointed in the general direction of his bedroom. 'Don't break out the good stuff without us.'

'Five minutes' quiet my ass, you dog.' Quen's voice was hard, bitter. 'Don't worry, if we break out the good stuff we'll be sure to bring you a share. We'll knock first, though, for modesty.' This last part he said directly to Celia, and she recoiled at the sentiment. *Still sober enough to sense a tone*, Quen thought, and he flashed a smile, then, though it did nothing to soften him. 'See you later, lovebirds. If you decide you need a third wheel, you'll find me over there,' he pointed somewhere beyond them, to where Lily was leaned against a wall and deep in conversation with three other girls, 'tormenting Celia's minder.'

Celia moved to speak, then, but Theo beat her to it. 'Ignore him, you know she can handle herself.'

'Hey,' Raff pulled their attention back, 'get going. Don't go doing anything we wouldn't in there.' Raff softly punched Theo's arm and sent the couple back into the room; through people dancing, and shots being thrown back, and too much of whatever Quen had cooked up, floating around between sweaty hands.

'She seem drunk to you?' Quen nodded after them.

'High, maybe. She's hardly out of it, though.'

'Quen!' A young woman threw her arms around his neck and landed hard against his torso. 'Babe, I've been looking for you *everywhere*.' She gestured to the full room behind her as she spoke. Quen answered only with a hesitant, 'Hey, you...' which seemed to lull her into talking more. He was grateful for the sudden distraction, though; *this*, he thought, *is at least going to kill some time*.

Celia was staring up at the ceiling while Theo searched through his bedside table for a condom. 'I know I have one...' he said, more to himself than her as he moved through pens – that no doubt didn't work – and flyers for takeaway restaurants in the local area. Then there, wedged at the back of the space, he hit upon the foiled wrapper of a Durex. 'Bingo!' He turned around to face her, brandishing the packet like a winning ticket.

'Hey, before we... you know.' Celia nodded at the wrapper. 'Can we talk?'

'Sure, what about?' He was already fumbling with the foil, though, looking for the right angle to tear through to avoid the latex underneath.

'Us?'

Theo's head shot up, then. 'In a good way or a bad way?'

'Well,' she hesitated. Her pupils were penny wide and her smile so slow to form that for the first few seconds it looked more like a muscle spasm than it did a deliberate action. '*I think that it's–*'

The door burst open and cut her sentence straight down the centre. Quen burst in as though he'd been expected – but behind him there trailed Barnie, Mitchell and a reluctant Raff, too.

'Didn't interrupt anything, did we?' Quen asked, landing hard on the bed.

'Actually...' Celia looked from him to the huddle behind him. Someone had closed the door.

'Mate, now isn't the time,' Theo said, and he twirled the condom between finger and thumb like his was spinning a lucky coin. 'Why don't you give us half an hour?'

Barnie stepped towards them, then. 'Why don't you give *us* half an hour?'

'What?' Theo looked from one friend to another. Mitchell was in the corner of the room, fiddling with his camcorder again, while Barnie had managed to inch so close to the bed that he was very nearly on Quen's lap. Raff lingered by the door like a poor-man's imitation of a bouncer. He looked pissed off.

'What is this, some sort of group outing?' Theo laughed.

Barnie shrugged. 'One way of looking at it.'

Celia had remained quiet up to that point, but her discomfort was clear. She pushed herself up towards the top of the bed and pulled her clothing back into place. Her legs were folded up against her chest with her arms wrapped tight around them, as though to form a barrier between her and the rest of the room. 'Theo...'

'Don't worry, they're just dicking around.'

'You reckon she doesn't matter to you?' Quen said and nodded behind Theo to where Celia was. 'Prove it.'

Like a finger snap, Theo caught his meaning. 'Oh, fuck off, mate, what is this? You're all in this muck-about, are you?' He looked around at the others. The last person he turned to was Mitchell, who was still stood behind the recorder. 'And what about you, Spielberg? You're planning a director's debut?'

'Theo...' Celia said again, reaching to touch him. He shrugged her off, though, as though somehow his annoyance at the situation had bled onto her as well. 'I don't understand what... Quen, what are you...'

'The thing is, Ce,' Barnie moved towards the top of the bed to be closer to her, 'our Theo, he reckons he isn't all that bothered about you, not really.'

Celia looked from Barnie to Theo, then, with the expression of a freshly slapped face; her cheeks were blushed pink, to complete the appearance.

'Now, we call bullshit on that. But we figured the only way to find out if he *really* doesn't care, is for him to treat you like any other girl.' He reached forward to touch her hair. 'Like any of the other party favours in there,' he pointed beyond the room, 'only we get a private audience with you whereas the rest of them get groped against a wall.'

Raff's flat expression broke with a laugh. 'Eloquently put.'

Quen pushed himself up off the bed and stood so his crotch was nearly level with Theo's face. 'What'll it be, then, kid? Are you ready to admit how you really feel?' Quen lowered himself into Theo's eyeline. 'Either to us, or to her.'

Theo's face matched Celia's; a blank, blush shock with a streak of misunderstanding scored as a frown across his forehead. Again, he looked from one friend to another, but no one broke the silence. He shook his head abruptly, like this might be a bad trip he could push away with a deep breath and a hard rub of his eyes. But when he looked up again they were all still there – including Celia, bunched into herself between the two pillows now, and he wondered whether she might fold herself into the space at the back of the bed before this got further out of hand. Quen had pulled stupid stunts before, but nothing ever quite so drastic. And just as Theo opened his mouth to dispute the suggestion entirely, a different idea occurred to him instead.

'Go on, then, if you think you're fucking hard enough for it.' *He'll back down*, Theo thought, *when it comes to calling his bluff, he'll back off.*

'What?' The small sound came from Celia. There were train tracks of tears appearing. 'Theo... what the fuck...' Her voice became louder, though the thump of the bassline from beyond the room was competing for space, and it was clear that no one had heard – or, even if they had, no one was going to intervene. She looked at the door with an expectancy, hoping, no doubt, that someone might burst through. But no one did; no one did anything at all.

NOW
2022

CHAPTER SIXTEEN

I'd been nervous of calling but, when she answered the phone she sounded somehow excited to hear from me – though I thought excitement might have been the wrong reaction.

I booked a day's holiday from the office and told Simon I was seeing a friend – 'Clearing my head after, you know, the migraine and all.' – and he encouraged me up and out of the house, as though desperate for the break, too. It had been two days and by the end of the second I was only too aware of what a difficult patient I was becoming.

But the idea for a conversation – a face-to-face conversation – struck me at last as a sensible option. After her friendly greeting and her rushing to ask how I was, I suggested a proper catch-up: 'There are some things I need for us to talk through, please.' And she'd readily agreed.

I suggested a public setting, somewhere neutral and easy where neither party would feel an advantage. But she suggested her home. And though I was reluctant to make the journey there, I understood, too, that this perhaps wasn't a conversation to be had with prying ears around – lest either one of us collapse in tears, burst open with panic, or worse.

I told her I could be with her by late morning and she said, 'Fine, I can clear my schedule.' Though she said it in an ironic tone that made me wonder whether her schedule had been clear for days already. *Have you just been waiting for a phone call, for company?* I thought as I rounded the corner into her road.

I sucked in a deep breath and pressed the doorbell like it might detonate something. Seconds later, she answered.

'Celia, I'm really glad you called.' Debora's hair was scraped back into a tight ponytail at the back of her head. It looked wet still, and she had that fresh-scent smell that comes with a recent shower. I was touched that she'd made the effort. Particularly when I looked like someone recovering from a three-day bender – which was, incidentally, also how I felt. She flashed me that same tired smile from before and stepped aside to make space for me to move into the hallway. 'Come in, the kettle's just boiled. You must have sensed it.'

I forced a laugh. 'Always have a sense for when there's a brew on the go.'

'Tea?'

'Actually, do you have coffee?'

'Of course, of course. Go straight through.' She pointed to the room at the end of the hall and I trod along ahead of her. 'Do you take sugar?'

'Please, two. Black.'

The kitchen was like having time-travelled. The cupboards were cream, with light wood around the edges; the floor was a linoleum mess of browns and beiges. Even the free-standing furniture looked aged; a table with rough wood that was in need of replacing, and two chairs just waiting to collapse under unexpected weight.

I hovered in the centre of the room while she found cups

and spoons. She opened each cupboard slowly, as though this were her first time in the room as well, and I wondered how tired the poor woman must be to have lost the layout of her own kitchen.

'You're welcome to take a seat.'

I eyed the kitchen table set with some suspicion again. 'Thank you.'

'I really am so glad you called.' She turned with two full mugs, then, and walked across to take the other seat at the table. 'It's important to me, now more than ever, to reach out to Mitchell's friends.'

I swallowed so hard that I wondered whether my larynx might drop into my stomach. 'I know it had been some time since you last saw each other, but still...' She struggled to finish. 'But he must have been thinking of you lately, to have gone searching for you how he did.' She shook her head, then, and a puzzled expression took over. 'Though I still can't work out why he went to the trouble and then didn't contact you.'

Guilty conscience, I thought and I swallowed a mouthful of too-hot coffee to keep the bitterness from tumbling out of me. 'The police haven't had any leads on that, then?' I tried to keep my tone balanced.

She shook her head. 'They said they'd be in touch but...' She dropped her head and a strangled sob fell out. 'It's only too bloody obvious they haven't got a clue what happened.' Her shoulders shook with the admission.

But all I felt was a bloated swell of relief. I might not be certain of what Lily had done – but I was certain I didn't want the police to know yet either.

There was an open box of tissues on the table and she reached for one. 'I'm sorry. You didn't come here so I could weep all over you. You wanted to talk about the good times, I'll bet.' Her sobs gave way to a gentle laugh, then. 'There must have been plenty of those, knowing Mitchell.'

I frowned. 'I don't remember him being a party animal, as such.' *I remember him being a coward; spineless; a ride-along.* I swallowed another two glugs of coffee then pressed my tongue to the roof of my mouth to settle the sting.

'Gosh, he certainly was by the time I met him. Actually...' She stood and disappeared from the room, then, and I tried to use the seconds wisely. My lips formed an O and I forced out a steady breath before pulling another one in.

When she came back, she was holding two binders that I thought must be photo albums; places where they'd pressed memories. And it dawned on me, then, what a fucking dreadful idea this had been. 'I thought these might be of some use to you, if you were looking into the time you spent at university together. There's this one, which I really like.' The binder fell open on the table like a book with a broken spine; scored from this memory having been viewed so often. 'I think this was from his first year at university?'

A noise escaped out of me; something that an animal might make.

'I know,' she reached across the table and took my hand, 'it's funny seeing him that young, isn't it?'

There Mitchell Webster was, brandishing a handheld video camera. His smile was wide and his hair was boyhood messy, and he was wearing a bright purple jumper that I remembered was a favourite from the time when I knew him. Though out of them all, he'd hardly been a flicker on my radar. Still, I could remember him from the night–

'Oh, there was one with everyone's names scribbled...'

I could remember how he did nothing.

'Names?' I shook away the beginnings of a memory that I'd worked hard to stifle.

'Here we go.' She pulled a picture free from a page and placed it in front of me on the table. I leaned back in my chair as though there was something to be gained from a physical distance between me and the men. *Three things I can smell: the orange citrus of Debora's shower gel; the ghost of the perfume I sprayed before I left the house; leftover cooking, food that I don't recognise. Two things I can hear: wind lapping at the outside walls of the building; the hum of the fridge that feels like the loudest spasm of electricity I've ever known. One thing I can feel: Debora's hand, patting the back of my own.*

I forced out another breath.

'I'm sorry, God, I'm just throwing this stuff at you.' She moved the photograph, but I snatched it back.

'It's been a long time since I saw... I saw them all.' I looked at the line-up from left to right. I didn't need the back of the image to tell me who they were: suspects stood side to side, smug faces and schoolboy arrogance that had carried through from their college days to this, their first year of university. There was bunting in the background; two crates of beer just about in the frame; and a few other faces that I didn't recognise. I wondered which party this was. 'You say that Mitchell was quite the partier?'

She laughed. 'He really was. Or from what I heard he was. Though he said it wasn't until much later in university.' She tapped the image. 'I'm not sure he was the drinker among this lot, but they certainly told me some stories in their time, so he definitely loosen–'

'You know these men?'

It was a small fist to the stomach. In my mind, they'd disbanded; the weight of their collective crime too much for their friendships to bear. I'd wanted solitary and lonely lives for them – I didn't want them to have fucking bonded.

'This one,' I tapped Theo's face, 'you know him?'

'Oh, Theo.' She looked sad again, the earlier flicker of excitement at Mitchell's party lifestyle memory having died down. 'It was terrible what happened to him. Even to this day I still puzzle myself over it. Do you know,' she leaned forward as though telling me a trade secret, 'Mitchell told me there was a period when they were at university when Theo went through something...' She struggled for the right word. 'I don't know, something dark is all Mitch would ever say about it. And he thought Theo had put it behind him after their second year, which was the worst of it by all accounts. But then out of nowhere, it must be...' Again, she searched. 'It was probably about six months ago now, out of nowhere it happened. There was no note, nothing. It broke his sister. She and I are in touch, of course, now more so.'

I heard everything she said without being able to piece together the obvious meaning, though, and I stammered out a plea for more information.

'Celia, oh, Celia, I am sorry. I should have... God, there's a more tactful way to have...' She shifted awkwardly in her seat; her role suddenly switching from bereaved to– 'I just thought you'd know that Theo had killed himself.'

A swarm of bees flew in one ear and out the other.

'Six months ago, like I said.' She nudged the tissue box towards me. 'Help yourself.'

I'm not crying. But I took a tissue anyway and pressed it first to one tear duct then the other before balling up the paper. 'How?'

She shook her head. 'Are you sure you...' She petered out when saw my insistent nod; the same enthusiasm that Dawn might use when she was offered more ice cream. 'He was holidaying somewhere on the coast. Or that's what he told everyone he was doing, at least. He was... God, Celia, there's no subtle way of saying this even. He threw himself from a clifftop.

He... I don't know that anyone knows what he was thinking in doing it. But the body, his body, it washed up some days later. He was in a poor way by all accounts, though I suppose he would have been, after...'

Debora spoke like a woman uncorked and I wished I knew how to stop her.

But more than that, I wished I could remember when Lily had last visited the beach.

CHAPTER SEVENTEEN

S imon was a strong believer in the ethos of a tidy house
equalling a tidy mind. By the time he got home from his
Friday afternoon meeting with a new client, I had upturned
every box I could find in the office. Paperwork rested in disarray;
folders were torn open and their contents ripped apart like a
bloody-minded creature had torn through the place in search of
something – which was exactly how I felt.

The room had always been scored down the centre in terms
of ownership, though he worked at home much more frequently
than I had a need to. After blitzing my own corner of the space,
though, I'd moved on to his.

I was on the cusp of emptying his desk drawers when he
walked in and caught me. He coughed from the open doorway,
and waited until he had my attention. 'What in the name of
everything sacred are you doing to my system?'

It was only then that I really paused and took in the state of
place. I ran a hand through my hair – also tangled and
disarrayed by that point – and tried to force a laugh. 'I'm looking
for my diary.'

'The diary that's on your desk?' He pointed to where my

work diary lay, sitting pretty on top of my laptop. His tone made me sound like a raging idiot and while I didn't care for it, it hardly seemed like the right time to argue with it either; given the hot mess of a house he'd walked into. There were drawers torn apart downstairs, too, and I wondered whether he'd spotted them on his way in.

'No, my personal diary. And not my current one either.'

'Okay.' He dropped his bag and took a hesitant step closer. *What must he be thinking?* Between the migraine and the mood swings and the fact that I'd been screening calls from Lily all week, with only a string of piss-poor excuses to explain it away. 'How far back are we talking? Because that'll make a difference to the box.'

I started to keep a diary when I was fifteen, and I was yet to throw one away. The only time period missing from the string of scruffy notebooks was the summer between college ending and university starting – and the fact that those entries were lost felt like evidence in itself that a good time was had by all. Beyond that, though, I had been meticulous in keeping a record of things. It wasn't daily, but it was often enough that if I looked closely I might find – something.

'I'm only talking like, six months ago?' I threw the timeline out like it was nothing. But I was desperate to reel it back in with something on the end. 'Do you... I mean, is there any way of knowing where that might have been... Packed, or whatever.' My hesitations did nothing to make my frantic efforts at finding the diary seem more casual, and I was sure the hand on the hip hadn't helped me either. I was seconds away from trying a strategic hair-flick, too, to cement the Cool Girl demeanour that I was desperate for – despite the Seething Woman that sat under the surface.

He smiled. 'You're a nutter, you are. Follow me.' He turned and walked back into the hallway, up the stairs, and towards the attic latch, all while I hurried behind him. 'If it's a diary that you've finished, like, you've run out of space?' He faced me, then, and waited for a nod to the question. 'Then it'll be up here with the rest of them.' Simon reached up to pull at the string to the attic; the hatch opened, and a set of stairs slowly followed out into our narrow hall. 'Head on up, make a left turn.'

'Aren't there a hundred boxes up here?' I pushed by him to the foot of the ladder.

'Yes, but you'll be looking for the ones marked "Celia's Diaries". I would guess that if it's only six months back, it's your most recent, or close to it. Go for the box on top.' He leaned forward and planted a hard kiss on my forehead. 'Whatever is going on, tell me when you've found what you're looking for.'

There was a family of bubbles in my belly; opalescent and Disney-like. I had a husband I loved; a daughter I adored; and a life that I'd made beyond what had happened. *If Lily is doing this*, I thought, *does it matter?* Guilt took a sharp needle pinpoint to every bubble of love in my stomach, then, and I was awash with bad feeling again: bad feeling for not caring what happened to another human's life; worse feeling, still, for believing this of Lily. But she'd known what happened to Mitchell before I'd told her; she'd *said* she knew who killed him. She'd said– Hardly anything more, before I'd fled the room like a startled bird.

'I love you, Si.'

'I know.' He paced back down the corridor. 'I love you, babe.'

I should be asking her, I thought as I climbed the rickety stairs, *I should be trusting her to tell me the truth of it all.* But somehow, I didn't feel I could.

When I was in the attic I reached for the overhead light and threw the space under a dusty glow.

'I'm not sure you want to know how I know,' she'd said. And she'd smiled as she said it. And–

'I didn't even give her the chance to explain, either,' I said aloud to the hollow space and I heard the soft echo of my disappointment as the words hit the walls. 'I chickened out and left and screened her calls and now I'm here,' I spoke again to no one as I followed Simon's directions to the boxes I needed. I lifted the lid off the top one. 'There could be so many explanations that don't involve...' *Don't involve what?* I didn't know how to end the sentence. Don't involve Lily killing people? I felt a near laugh move up through my gut into my throat at the thought alone. *But she knows something, doesn't she?* Of that much I was certain.

In the search for my most recent diary – the front cover clear in my mind, still – I'd forgotten the circumstances under which someone had bought it for me. Lily, of course. She and I had been having a girls' day out when we'd strolled by a pop-up stationery shop; it was one of many that had taken over the high street as part of a local market. The front cover had caught me from a clear ten paces away, though, and I swooned as we got closer still. It was an abandoned building overgrown with moss and mildew; wildflowers that had forced up from the cracked concrete of the structure.

'She'll take it,' Lily had said, already ferreting her purse out.

'No,' I said to the stallholder, then repeated it to Lily. 'I have a hundred notebooks.'

'I know, you're a fiend. But you like this one.' She handed over her card. 'She'll take it.'

'I'll use it for something special,' I promised her. The memory of it all uncomfortably clear. She'd laughed and told me I wouldn't, and I'd promised again. Now, I ran my hand over the smooth of the photograph on the front cover and wondered what I was doing. *What am I thinking? What am I looking for proof of?* And then, quickly, *Proof for or against?* The questions piled up one atop the other and I was already leafing through the pages. I licked a finger and flicked through weeks at time, noticing from the dates in the top right of each page where the shortfalls in my written memory must be. *What if Theo died in an in-between space? What if I didn't write about Lily at all?* Another stream of questions appeared and accelerated, one worry knocking another out of the way until–

Something fell free from the book. It must have been wedged into a later page. I backed up and reached to collect it from the floor. And there it was, a coastal view of a hillside with a happy looking sky behind it: 'Wish you were here, beaut. xx' scribbled on the back – with the date of Theo's death written in the corner.

———

'And, sorry,' I called back to the attendant for the second time, 'how much time have I got for this?'

'You've got internet access for the next thirty minutes.' He flashed a tight smile. 'Though it's probably more like twenty-seven minutes now, with the questions and all.'

He didn't give me the opportunity for a comeback. Instead, he turned and trod back to his standpoint behind the counter. He couldn't have been older than twenty, and I wondered whether this was a university job for him; something to keep him in beers and bong hits in between the paydays of student loans arriving. *It's arseholes like you that have got me here*, I thought with disproportionate spite. I could recognise the self-importance from every young man who'd been on my course – and every young man who I'd dated, too, though there hadn't been many. There were fewer still after...

I shook away the end of the sentence and turned to the

screen. Prior to this, I hadn't set foot in the coffee shop before. But on my panicked tread through the city – from my front door to the office, which had been my planned end-point – I'd spotted through the window the advertisement for internet, bought by the hour. There probably weren't many internet cafes kicking with life still, and this hardly counted; it was more of a coffee-internet-clothing-doughnut store. But it brought me the anonymity of browsing online without the worry that I was repeating Mitchell Webster's mistakes. I wasn't going to have my history printed and presented to me in a slim plastic folder in front of a jury of my peers any time soon.

It was hard to know where to start. Theo felt like a waste of a search term but still, there were things I needed to know. Debora hadn't mentioned a wife – only a sister – and I wondered whether there'd been some loneliness in his life after all. *Which is exactly what the fucker deserved.*

I rushed past the urge to check on him and instead typed: 'Raff Hall.' It took two pages of search results to find him but there he was, with a wide-open social media presence and posts listed that were only two days old. *So no one has got to you,* I thought as I scrolled down the information shared there. Raff was the archetypal surfer boy: every picture of him showed long hair and a board, apart from one that showed a young girl alongside him. She was looking up to him with a beaming smile that I recognised as one my own young thing wore: this was Raff's daughter. The caption read: 'my world' and it was coupled with an Earth emoji.

I swallowed a rise of bile and back-clicked to the search engine: 'Barnaby Colt'.

I didn't need to know they were well. I only needed to know they were alive. And it was easy enough with Barnie who looked to be whoring himself out on every social media platform available. I was two pages into his online presence when I stumbled across what looked to be a dating profile, too, and I resisted the urge to look. I didn't want to know what false advertising he'd written. There was no standards agency to report him to.

And then there was one: Quentin Parsons.

I hadn't heard or thought of that name in fifteen years. And as the slow wheels of the internet turned and the results appeared one bright white pixel at a time, I realised, then, that I was desperately hoping there would no signs of life for Google to find...

SHE

The place was a dive but at least she knew she wouldn't be recognised. Her contact was at the back of the room – hidden partially by a laptop screen – with a cloud of vapour hanging around him. It made him look mystical. She crossed the space and ignored leering looks from the men around her; it was that sort of place. But at least she knew she could handle herself against any one of them, too.

When she arrived at the discreet table, she pulled out a chair and sat opposite the one she was there to meet. He was typing away furiously with headphones cupped over his ears; he reminded her of a worker-bee. She knew better than to interrupt someone who was doing her a favour, so she held her tongue while he finished tapping and clicking and hacking. She surveyed the space instead, and took in the healthy blend of strong coffee, different flavoured vapour liquids, and men's aftershaves that bled together into something masculine and unfamiliar. She did what she could to avoid being around so many men at once.

A movement from the corner of her eye caught her attention

and pulled her back. The man opposite her removed his headphones and smiled. 'Thanks.'

She held up a hand. 'I know better than to cut you off.'

He laughed, then, and leaned over to reach for something in the bag on the floor alongside him. It was a thick, padded envelope that he pulled out and handed to her under the table. Not that she imagined anyone cared what they were doing, but she still appreciated the discretion of it. That was another part of the back-alley coffee bar's appeal. 'Everything you asked for.' He smiled. 'He isn't married, doesn't have children; no family to speak of either by the looks of it.'

She lifted the lip of the envelope and peered inside. 'And the diary?'

'Also in there. You'll know his whereabouts for the next few months, subject to change. But I went one extra. You'll find a USB in there, too; connect it to the laptop I got you, touch nothing, and you'll get live updates as the diary changes.' He was observably pleased with himself and rightly so; it was a better result than she could have hoped for. 'Is that...'

'More than enough and you well know it. What extra do I owe you?'

He raised his hand to dismiss the question. 'On the house. I had fun cracking it.'

'Thank you.' She laughed, and stashed the envelope inside her own bag. 'And the other tail?'

'I have to say,' he pulled in a sigh and it sounded like there was an undercurrent of a wheeze to it, 'it was a surprise when you asked for this one. But I give the people what they want.'

'Why was it a surprise?'

He shrugged. 'You've never tailed a woman before.'

She didn't like the observation. 'I'm not tailing one now.'

'No, but... you know what I mean.' He turned the screen so

she could see the fruits of his searching. 'You're sure you don't want this stuff printed?'

'I don't want a paper trail. Where's she been?'

With a two-tap manoeuvre the man pulled up a list of coordinates with their corresponding addresses alongside them. She scanned the list quickly then nodded as a signal: *Next*. Another click revealed another page of information.

'I went straight in after her and these were the only things I could pull. The place isn't especially clean, digitally speaking, so it's a little tricky to work out what's hers from this list and what could be other people's. I did what I could to clean it all up for you.'

She scanned the list of entries. 'It's okay. I know what she was looking for...'

CHAPTER EIGHTEEN

I'm going to accuse my best friend of murder. The thought had rolled around my head like a marble lost in a pinball machine for days.

Lily kept calling – though she'd given up on calling Simon, at least, which I was thankful for – and I knew I was well into the territory of panicking on borrowed time. 'You'll have to talk to me eventually, Celia, you'll have to hear me out,' she'd said in one late-night voicemail – and of course, she was right. There was no version of this story that involved me not talking to Lily again – even if it did mean talking to her through the medium of a monitored phone and a sheet of reinforced glass.

I'm going to turn my best friend in for murder was another thought I'd spent too much time with as well. The moral mess of it all had morphed and grown into an ugly creature and it followed me, from room to room, heaving and hacking and gagging on its own worry – and I could feel it like a physical weight that sat in my stomach and bled down into my legs, now lined with lead, almost too heavy to lift. The whole situation felt observable. I worried that if I were to walk past a police officer on the High Street, he or she might stop me and demand to know what it was I knew: 'What's the creature you're carrying around with you?' they'd say, eyeing the animal in the shadow. *I think my best friend is a murderer.*

A laugh erupted out of me like a burp I hadn't felt coming and I was glad the office was empty. I couldn't decide what was worse: being the sad and downtrodden woman or the wild and cackling one. Though I felt myself batted between the two states and neither of them were safe long term. Never mind the police; it would only be a matter of time before those closer to home-made comments – more comments. And I couldn't lie to Simon about this until I knew what I was really lying to him about.

It had been weeks since Lily and I had spoken; the longest stretch in the entire time we'd known each other. I left a note on a colleague's desk – 'Meeting. Totally forgot. Back tomorrow.' – for them to find when they returned from their own call-out, and I slipped away quietly while I could. With Lily's line of work there was no way of knowing where she would be at any time, on any day, and the thought was suddenly a deeply unsettling one. But I decided that I'd start with her home and if that didn't yield results then I'd cross the city to her office. *And if that doesn't yield results...* I didn't have a fail-safe. Wherever she was, I needed to find her, before the bravery for it slipped away from me again.

Lily's neighbour – an older woman, who could have easily been a version of Lily's future self, chain-smoking on the front steps of the building – told me she'd seen Lily leave earlier in the day, which at least saved me the anxiety of banging down her front door and waiting for a reply.

On my pace away from the building I pulled my phone out and thought of just calling her – *what a novel concept* – and asking whether we could talk this all through. But I would lose the element of surprise in doing that, I reasoned, and there was already enough in this that I'd lost the upper hand on. I didn't want her to know I was coming. I wanted her caught out, surprised; taken back enough to be honest, or even make a mistake.

So I stashed my phone away and felt, instead, for the postcard that I'd sealed inside a plastic wallet and hidden in my bag days ago. It was pressed between pages of my daily diary; something I could justify keeping close, and carrying everywhere I went. Even though the postcard had been safe in the attic for months in its quiet hiding place, now it had been unleashed from the confines, I felt as though it were precious cargo – something that needed to be protected from the outside world. Though I'd watched enough crime dramas to know that alone, out of context, it was worthless. There'd be no trace evidence; there was hardly even a real paper trail.

Theo had killed himself in Devon; the postcard had come from Devon: Capstone Hill. 'So what?' the police officer would say – the same one who might have apprehended me and my guilt demon in an earlier scenario. 'So what does it prove, Nancy Drew?' And maybe it proved nothing. I fingered at the edge of the plastic for half a street longer before letting it go again. Whether it proved anything or not, I wanted the satisfaction of slamming it on the table in front of her and seeing her reaction – and a call would only ready her for a confrontation.

It took me nearly thirty minutes to walk to her office block and by the time I arrived I was huffed out and panting. I stopped to get a bottle of water from a convenience store and eyed the full pink bottles of wine on my travels to the counter, too. I imagined the satisfaction of buying one, taking it in with me, and laughing all of this away. 'For a minute, I really thought you might have killed people,' I'd say and Lily would howl; the raucous wail that burst out of her when something tickled her.

Like drunken teenagers, we'd settle down from the hilarity only to glance at each other and start giggling again.

'I really thought it, Lil, I *really* did for a second.'

She'd call me a silly cow – and it would all be over with.

But instead I only got the water, and resisted the urge to buy cigarettes. I hurried from the shop and bundled myself into the open mouth of Lily's building; the front door felt like the gaping smile of a villain. This building had never had a huge appeal that I could see. But even when Lily started to make money enough to afford somewhere better, she'd never expressed a desire to move. I had always thought she secretly relished the seedy feel of the place; the way in which it fit perfectly with everything that everyone thought of private investigators. The grime of the walls and the stale smell of smoke; the fact that the satellite offices around Lily's looked to be made up of businesses and practitioners that were never open – at least, they'd never been open on the handful of occasions I'd visited.

Lily never mentioned neighbours, either, which might have been another part of its appeal: the privacy it afforded her. *Especially if she's killing people...* I drove the thought away with a headshake and a series of tuts as I climbed the stairs. On my first visit here, only a month after Lily had moved her things in, I'd got trapped in the steel drum of the lift – never again, I'd vowed, even if the fourth flight of stairs started to wind me.

I pushed through the door onto Lily's landing and bumped straight into another visitor.

'Shit, I'm so sorry,' I rushed, and tried to catch the door before it could hit her. I was sure it hadn't made contact, but I was sure that I saw her flinch all the same. 'Sorry,' I said, this time in a slightly lower tone – I begrudged apologising twice. But when she lifted her face to meet my gaze, I thought I should apologise again, and again.

Through the bruising, I could still guess that she must be my age. Her hair was a tangled mess of tentacles; grease thickened into strands that you could knot and climb from a building with. It looked like she was trying to smile but the split of her lip made it more like a grimace and I bit back on telling her to stop. Her hand reached for her face then and when she pulled it away she checked her fingers; I wondered how many times the wounds must have cracked open with fresh blood for that to be a knee-jerk response. She ducked her head and went to move around me but I sensed an opportunity slipping by.

'I'm sorry,' I caught her attention. 'Were you visiting...' I gestured the stretch of corridor behind us. I hoped that if I left grey space in the question she might fill it.

She looked over the banister of the stairs, as though checking whether anyone were in earshot of her answer, before she said, 'Lily?'

Bingo. I nodded. 'You were here to see her?'

'Someone recommended her to me. I wasn't sure I'd get in without a card the first time, but...' She pointed to her face. 'I guess this is basically the same thing now.'

I made an encouraging noise; a quiet lie that I understood her meaning even though I wasn't sure of it, still.

'The first time she saw me it wasn't quite this bad. This time... Well, things are different...' She shook the half-explanation away. 'Do you have a card?'

'I do,' I reached for my bag to cement the bluff, 'here, it's in here, safe.'

She tried to smile again. 'I guess it's your first visit here?'

'Is there usually more than one visit?'

She tilted her head from one side to the other. 'I've heard mixed things. Some of the girls at the centre, they told me she dealt with it right away. Some of them, I don't know, they waited longer, I guess... I think. When I came... I told her I wasn't sure what I needed, that I just wanted to talk, to start with, and she said that was okay, too. I'm not really sure how it works for others. I guess it's a bit of an unspoken thing, like something from a film.' She forced a laugh and then caught an immediate cough in her hands. 'Sorry, damaged...' She gestured to her throat. 'I'm healing from...'

'I see,' I answered and I tried to sound as gentle as I could, lest I scare the fragile bird. I thought something as everyday as a sudden movement might send her scuttering down the stairs and out of reach. 'Sorry, you mentioned a centre?'

She gave me a quizzical look, then, and I wondered whether my cover was blown. 'You didn't hear about her there?'

'No,' I shook my head, 'I heard about her from a friend.'

'If it's someone that Lily knows then I'm sure it will be fine,' she answered, though it didn't sound like she fully believed what she'd said. I wondered whether I was walking into some kind of coven. Worse still, *is Lily the leader of a cult?* I housed that sudden thought in the same box as Lily being a murderer and a hit-woman; neither things were options that I'd managed to rule out in the endless days of trying to, so the cult leader idea didn't seem too far-fetched to be true either. *Nothing else makes sense in this situation...*

I forced a smile. 'I really appreciate you being so helpful.'

'We have to stick together all of us, don't we?' She flashed a thin smile, then, too, and it looked easier than her earlier attempt at one. I caught a movement in her hand, and a hesitation that followed it. But she reached forward then, and set her fingers around my wrist in a gentle squeeze. 'Look, I can't speak on a case by case because... I just can't, who can? But I can tell you this much.' She nodded back along the corridor towards Lily's door. 'Whatever the problem is, she'll help you. There's a lot of us that wouldn't have got by without her. That woman, she's an angel.'

I managed to hold myself upright through our hurried

goodbye. The woman disappeared down one flight of stairs and out of view. And when she was far enough away for me not to hear her footsteps, I sank onto the top step with a hard enough thump to bruise my coccyx on the concrete of the floor. I ran a hand through my hair, then rested my forearms against my legs and dropped my head between my knees.

Breaths were coming out like torn strips of fabric; ragged and unpredictable. *Three things I can smell: whatever floor cleaner had been used; the last of the stranger's perfume; the apple vapour that still clung to my clothing from smoking. Two things I can hear: an alarm going off somewhere inside– No, outside the building; the woman's voice, ringing in my ears like siren song: An angel, that woman, an angel that– One thing I can feel: her hand around my wrist, the conviction of that grab, the heavy-press weight of her words.*

CHAPTER NINETEEN

During a late-night confession of, 'I don't know what's been going on with me lately...' I lay with my head against Simon's chest, listening to the soft thrum of his heart beating. It grounded me.

I told him that work had been driving me crazy and there were new clients and a constant stream of information that needed to be ordered and checked to make sure things were being arranged properly for these very same new clients and—

The lies poured out in a torrent and Simon stroked my hair, ran his fingers through the damp curls that were forming post-shower, and listened to every excuse I had to share.

When I finally gave up talking, he leaned forward and kissed the crown of my head. 'Do you have any leave to take or is now a terrible time?'

Now is a terrible time, I thought. Not for work, but to lose the excuse of having work to keep me busy. I still hadn't decided what I was going to do about Lily. After the near panic attack at her office the other day I'd temporarily parked the idea of a direct confrontation. But the thought of turning up at our local police station and dribbling out incoherent strings of half-evidence didn't seem like a viable option in this mess either. *Are you going to turn her in, then? Are you* that *convinced of this?* I shook away the thought before it could get carried away with an extended family of others, and Simon took the gesture to be an answer to his question.

'Well, if you can't take leave, maybe we can at least take some steps to make work easier?' He spoke in a gentle voice, a conscious effort to keep me calm, and I thought again of the woman: *That woman, she's an angel...*

'What kind of steps?' I pressed the words into the space between his pecs and his bellybutton.

'What time can you finish tomorrow?'

'I... I don't know without checking my...' I started to clamber up to reach for my phone on the bedside table. My work calendar was synced to it. But Simon pulled me back to him and squeezed me tight instead.

'"On time" is the answer you're looking for,' he said around the beginnings of a laugh, and I smiled, too. 'I'm working from home all day. Dawn has an early finish at school because of some... I don't know, whatever training it is that they force teachers to periodically hoop-jump through. Finish on time and I'll make an early dinner, and we can have food and phones off and–'

'*Frozen?*' I interrupted him.

He let out a curt, 'Ha.' I loved that sound from him; that surprise laugh he only did when something truly tickled him. It was like a well-kept secret for these moments when we were intimate and silly and safe.

'Yes, most likely *Frozen.*'

'It sounds perfect.' I cuddled into the warmth of him. 'And necessary...'

Simon was a man of his word. By the time I walked in from work the following day the house was alive with smells. I didn't know what he was cooking, but the early works of it were bloody impressive from the minute I pushed through the door – and I realised, then, that with everything going on around me, I couldn't remember the last time I'd eaten a meal and truly enjoyed it. The kitchen was alive with colour, too, the work surfaces covered with different vegetables; like a breadcrumb trail leading to Simon at the end of it all, merrily chopping and so intent on listening to the radio he hadn't even noticed I was there. For a while I watched him – not quite a minute, I didn't think, though perhaps close to it – and even then it wasn't him who noticed, it was Dawn.

'Dad,' she whispered, though she was looking at me when she said it. 'Aren't you meant to be putting the kettle on?'

'Aren't I–' He spun around to face her, but cut himself off when he saw me. 'Ah balls, you were meant to let me know when you were leaving so I could get the kettle on. Dawn, hop to it.' He waved around hands covered in what looked like pulp from something. 'Get your mother a brew.'

'There's really no need.' I walked over to the island and sat on a tall chair. 'I'm okay, Dawnie.'

She hopped down from her own perch. 'No, Mum, we're looking after you.' She was just about tall enough to lift the kettle from its stand but when it came to filling it she needed a little help. 'Ahem,' she caught Simon's attention. The pair of them collaborated on the task. While Dawn waited for the kettle to boil, she plated up a handful of biscuits, too, and carried those over with the air of a professional waitress. 'Madam,' she curtsied.

'Why thank you.' I bowed gently, too, and took the plate. The hunger hit me, then – *Have I even eaten today?* – and I found that I was chewing through a second round of shortbread by the time Simon was putting a full mug of tea in front of me.

'Have you heard this?' He nodded behind him, though he didn't wait for an answer. Instead, he turned back and hit volume up on Alexa, and a newsreader's voice came booming through the speakers.

'After going missing in Edinburgh earlier this month...'

Something in me churned. *Do I remember this?*

'The body of a man thought to be...'

'Mum, you're spilling crumbs.'

Why does this matter? I craned to listen.

'Mum!' Dawn pushed the shortbread box beneath me to catch the spill.

'Okay,' I snapped and made a point of leaning over the box. Of shortbread. Made in–

'Investigations are now well underway to confirm whether this is indeed...'

'Dad, you haven't even told Mum the best bit.'

'Is this the shortbread Lily brought us?' I looked between them though neither seemed to be listening. *Why aren't they listening?* 'Simon?'

'What? Oh, I guess so. Dawnie, why don't you tell Mum the best bit?'

She jumped around in front of me in an excited dance. 'Lily is coming!'

'Here?' I sprayed crumbs across Dawn, the floor, part of the island. 'Lily is coming here?' This time I threw the question at Simon, who looked genuinely delighted with himself for having orchestrated such a thing. 'Why?'

'Because we haven't seen her in weeks?' He collected up whatever he'd been dicing and threw it into the stew pot. 'I know you've been missing her, babe, I can always tell. And when I called to ask if she was free she seemed, you know, excited to be asked. You're both useless without each other, we all know that.' He made a joke of it and found something else to chop. Meanwhile, my insides moved through a meat-blender motion of my soft feelings for Lily being chewed over by the hard-edged suspicion of whether she was a–

'When is she getting here?'

He looked at the wall-clock. 'Any time, I guess. Why?'

Because I have an idea. 'I have something for her, but I left it at the office.'

He sighed. 'If you're going, be quick. And don't you dare bring work into this house.' He made it sound like I was going to smuggle drugs in – and there he was, potentially inviting a murderer to dinner.

'I'll be quick.' I crossed the kitchen and pecked his cheek, then kissed Dawn's soft hair on the way out, too. 'I won't be long. She and I might even cross paths.'

Though it'll fuck everything up if we do...

For the first five minutes of the pace back to the main part of town I followed the same route I would have done for any visit to the office. But two roads diverged – and I took the one that led to Lily's office. At this time of the late afternoon the area felt even dirtier than it did during lunchtime hours. Now, the few office workers were trickling out and something more sinister was rolling in to replace them, as though this stretch of street had a deviant energy all of its own.

Though I couldn't put my finger on what I meant by that – and by the time I was hiking up the stairs to Lily's office, I wondered whether it was less about the area at all, and more about what I was doing there. I paused at every sound from higher up the stairwell, like a rat startled midway across an alleyway. I would wait out the sound until the person scooted past me on the stairs, or the untrustworthy elevator clicked and whirred and groaned into life, and then my scuttle continued. It took twice the time it should have done to land outside Lily's office. But at least there were no signs of life there, or anywhere else along the corridor, when I came to a stop.

For someone who was planning to break and enter into a very private space, I had nothing chill about me. I was only too aware of the tremor in my right hand when I reached up to take the bobby pin out from one side of my messy bun, sending a cascade of curls free – though they would at least cover my face, I thought, and stop me from being recognised. *Because I've seen enough true crime documentaries to know...* I tutted. *Who do I think I am?*

I poked and prodded and shoved at the lock until I felt something give way. Lily had taught me how to do this. I don't think she ever thought it was a skill I'd need – I certainly hadn't banked on rolling it out any time soon, and certainly not for this purpose – but I was grateful, now, for that bored evening at home some years ago when she'd said, 'Have you ever broken in anywhere?' and the whole night spiralled into a skill-swap. Though my skill – being able to tip my head back and make a water fountain of myself with any liquid – had been not only less impressive but also notably less useful than what Lily had brought to the table.

Once the lock was freed I pocketed the pin, pressed down on the handle and– Nothing. The door didn't even blink at my weight, so I tried again with another hard shove and– Nothing. I reached for the pin in the same second that my phone started to ring and I guessed it would be Simon, calling to tell me my grace period was up; I needed to go home and play nice with my best friend the...

Any thought of lock-picking died out when I saw the name on the screen: Lily. I answered – the first time in weeks that I had which I guessed would be suspicious in itself – but she beat me to the greeting before I had a chance to force one.

'There's another lock, at the bottom of the door. You won't be able to pick it.'

Let the earth crack open and swallow me. 'I'm sorry?' My voice was a high-pitched sound of something in discomfort – which I was. 'I don't know what you–'

'Turn around, Ce.' I followed the instruction, expecting her to be there. But instead she added, 'Now look up.'

In a snap my eyes moved from one corner to another and there I spotted it: the brilliant black bulb with a blinking red core, reporting back everything I'd done – to my best friend, the might-be-a-murderer.

CHAPTER TWENTY

Lily asked me in front of Simon – 'Are you free on Thursday night, Ce?' – knowing that I would have to give an honest answer – 'I think so. Oh, I don't know, actually...' – or rather, knowing that if I didn't give an honest answer that she could count on my husband to step in with one: 'There's nothing on the calendar, babe.'

He scooped another mouthful of stew into himself without even looking up from the bowl, which meant he missed the cocked eyebrow, the smirk. Lily told me she'd pick me up out front at 6pm and I nodded along like my insides weren't working through a wood-chipper.

Credit to her, though, there were times during our unexpected dinner date at home when Lily was so charming, so funny, so *normal*, that I felt it, too. She asked Simon about work and he regaled us all with tales of the latest client gone crackers. When that timed out, she asked Dawn about school – a narrative that lasted much longer than I think any of us were truly prepared for. Then her attention turned to me.

'It's been weeks, Ce, I must have missed *something* good at the office.'

I noted the specificity of the request; outside of the office, she must know that I'd been a fucking mess for weeks straight. 'I'm putting together a panel up north in a few weeks' time, that's quite exciting.' I leaned over to squeeze Simon's hand. 'I keep forgetting to tell you about that by the way,' then I pointed behind him, 'but it is on the calendar.' There was a note of spite in my tone that I think Simon overlooked, though I thought Lily was probably astute enough to catch my meaning. 'Honestly, things have been a bit mad with this wave of new clients. It's good for us all, though, really, because at least it means...' The words poured out of me like an uninhibited body of water and it hit me, only in those seconds, how much I'd missed Lily when she hadn't been around. And just like that, the wood-chipper in my belly cut out – a shorted fuse – and all I felt was gratitude – true, sincere gratitude – for having her there. There, in touching distance, where she'd always been when I needed her.

I flashed a tight smile when I'd run out of things to say. 'That's it.'

'Now,' Simon wiped his mouth cleans of gravy flecks, 'your turn.'

Lily glanced at me, then back to him. 'Nothing to report. It's business as usual–'

'Liar!'

'Dawn,' Simon cautioned her.

Leave her be, I thought, *the kid is switched on...*

Lily lowered herself down to be face to face with Dawn. 'What am I lying about?'

'There's *always* something exciting happening in your work.'

'That's not true.'

'Oh, it is *so* true.'

'Dawn,' Simon said again, though he ruffled her hair as he said it, too, as though trying to soften the edges of any reprimand. 'You can't hound people into telling you their business, Dawnie.'

'But that's what Lily *does*!' Dawn burst out in what looked to be genuine outrage.

No one had a straight enough expression to caution her this time, though. Instead, the three of us fell about in laughter and Dawn, dumbstruck, looked between us all, confused – as though she were suddenly the singular adult among three howling children. Our outburst had just about started to settle when Dawn collected up her cutlery and napkin, dumped them on her plate, and stood from the table.

'Where are you going without being excused?' Simon was pink with laughter.

'I'm getting ice cream,' she answered, her back to us. 'You're all being ridiculous.'

The second wave of laughter came, more furious than the first. The three of us managed to collect together our own leftovers and stand up, too, with Simon heading to the sink and Dawn still ferreting through the freezer to find whatever ice cream it was she thought she deserved.

Lily moved to start cleaning the table but I stopped her – 'You're our guest, you know the rules...' – and she gave in easily.

She pulled me to her, though, wordlessly, in a tight hug that she sealed with a kiss at the side of my temple. And when she released me I smiled and thought, for a wing-beat, perhaps my daughter was right; perhaps I was only being ridiculous.

Lily had said 6pm but I'd been hovering outside the front door since ten minutes to the hour. I shifted from one foot to the other to begin with but then ceased entirely, and crouched to a sit; then got up and started to walk along the road to the route I knew she'd likely drive along, to see whether I could meet her halfway. I was nearly at the end of our street when she turned into it; she flashed her headlights to catch my attention then pulled over.

'Get in, loser,' she said in her best American accent. It was one of our favourite popular culture references. 'What are you doing walking anyway? Bailing on me?' Her tone was light but I expected there was a serious accusation wrapped up inside it.

'I was getting nervous.' I decided honesty was the best policy, especially if I was expecting it from Lily. 'I thought if I started to walk we might bump into each other.'

'Ask and ye shall...' she answered. 'It's not a long drive but the neighbourhood isn't great. Sometimes these things can last a while, too, so I never like to walk home, you know? You never know who you'll run into.'

I bit back on a laugh.

But somehow she sensed it was there. 'Yeah, I heard it.'

The drive took just under ten minutes, and we were quiet for the most of it – apart from a few warm comments about Dawn and what a firecracker she was turning into. 'She'll be a handful,' Lily said, 'try to keep that.'

Then she abruptly pulled up against a kerb and cut the car engine. She was right; it wasn't a good neighbourhood – and I'd had no idea it was a such short drive away from my own. Lily nodded to the building outside of my passenger window and said that was where we were heading, so I unbuckled and followed her in. She moved quietly, and it was clear we were about to run a risk of interrupting something that was already underway. And I wondered whether she'd timed that deliberately.

The room was populated entirely by women. They were huddled in tight formations and there were conversations taking place in all pockets of the room, which made it impossible to pick out anything from any of them.

Lily didn't say anything, she only let me look about the space as though expecting me to spot something – and when I reached a tight-knit group at the back of the room, I found a sign that helped. *You're the woman from Lily's office.* Her face had started to heal and her hair had been washed, and she was wearing lighter coloured clothing, too – a gentle departure from the dark denims that had weighed her down when I'd seen her at Lily's the other day. She was buried inside a conversation with someone – a woman who didn't look quite as recovered from whatever trauma she'd met – and she didn't notice me, but from the strong held silence I thought Lily was aware that I'd seen her. Of course, now I knew there was the camera feed hooked up outside of Lily's office as well...

'You knew that she'd be here.'

She nodded. 'I knew that she'd be here.'

'And everyone else?'

She squeezed my arm. 'Give yourself a minute, Ce. Talk to some people.'

I didn't speak to anyone, though. When Lily abandoned me in the entryway and drifted further into the room, I found that I was lacking the confidence to do much at all. This was a strange space; the energy of it all unlike anything known or comfortable to me. But when a member of the group broke away from her huddle and looked as though she might be making an approach for me, I found that was encouragement enough to move from my spot and at least circulate.

No one stopped their conversations and I didn't feel that I could shoehorn myself into any of them. There were snippets that filtered up and drifted away, though, as I walked and I heard: 'I should have known this would happen... It was when he hurt Lauren that I realised... I'm *never* going to know who that man is... How do I know he won't do something like this again?'

Their words clung to my clothing like smoke in an early noughties nightclub and by the time I'd heard fractions from four groups I was cutting through the room at a diagonal to get back to the door.

'You found her, then?' a voice caught me. It was her – with the half-healed face. I could only nod.

'You look a little... Is everything okay?' She reached out to touch me but then seemed to think better of it before the contact landed.

'This is my first time here... I... It's a...'

'Of course it is.' Lily's arm reached around my shoulder and I fought the urge to turn and hide my face against the crook of her neck. 'Thanks, Zara, I'll take it from here.' Lily went to move, guiding me with her, but then glanced back. 'You're looking really well. I hope you're taking care.' She didn't wait for a reply from the woman; though something about her tone made me think she knew exactly how Zara was doing.

I gripped the doorframe to steady myself when we arrived back at the head of the room. Then I looked around the women again. Suddenly, like an origami time-jump, it all fell together. 'They're all victims.'

Lily dropped back against the opposite side of the frame. 'They're all women. Being a victim of a crime has nothing to do with who they are.'

'Lily...' The words caught in my throat but I knew, *knew*, that now was it; now was the time when I should be asking – and she was ready for me to, as well. I almost saw her brace for it when I said, 'Lily, are you killing people?'

She laughed – a hard-edged noise – and answered, 'Yes.'

Yes, as plainly as if she were answering a question about a dessert preference. *Do you want fresh cream with that?* A question of whether you'll be home for dinner; if you had a good day at school; whether you're getting along with a new client; if you're killing– I was crouched down, my fingertips touching the floor, the only thing holding me steady, and there was a trapped animal knocking itself from one side to the other in my chest cavity and Lily was–

'Gimme three things.' She crouched level with me. 'Three things, Ce.'

Three things I can smell: the staleness of the room; lingering tomato and herb and whatever else Simon had put in the pasta sauce for dinner that would haunt the kitchen for days; Lily's perfume. Two things I can hear: chatter from the groups who were none the wiser about what had just happened; my own heartbeat. One thing I can feel: Lily's hand against my shoulder, holding me steady. The same hand that she–

'Just breathe.'

'Lily.' I hardly even recognised my own voice when it came out; strangled with pain and heartbreak. 'Lily, you're...' I looked up at her and she, too, looked saddened by it all, as though she were expecting a better reaction. But behind her, blurred by the beginnings of tears, I saw the outlines of women huddled together in a safe space – a safe space they'd had to carve out for themselves, because someone had made the world unsafe for them and– 'Lily, do these women know?'

'Some of them do, some of them don't.'

'Christ, Lily, they could tell–'

'They won't tell the police,' she interrupted me, her tone level. 'They won't tell anyone.'

Another animal noise fell out of me; the panic had ruined my voice box. I stood, slowly, to level out the blood as it flooded from my ears to the right routes in my body again. The sound of my heartbeat died down, too, though I still needed the doorframe behind me to stay steady. 'How do you know?'

She smiled. 'Because their lives have only got better.' When she saw that I was steady she turned to face into the room again and rested next to me, our upper arms pressed together. 'Every woman in this room deserved what I gave them, Ce. They deserve more than what I can give them, actually. But what I did, what I do, it's a start.'

'Lily, this is fucking crazy,' I answered, though the life had been sucked clean out of my voice, leaving me flat. 'Those men... What they did...'

'I gave each and every one of them the chance for penance, Celia.' Her voice was hard. 'It isn't my fault that they didn't take the option when it came to them.'

Something clicked and whirred and fell together. 'Theo?'

There was a long pause before she answered, 'Penance.'

'Lily!' It was a hushed whisper, but I saw people turn. I moved, then, so I could face her and present my back to the onlookers. 'Lily, you can't decide this. You can't decide who lives and who dies and who's punished. You just... You *can't.*'

She lifted a hand to push a stray hair from my face and smiled. 'I already have.'

CHAPTER TWENTY-ONE

L ily confessed to murder with the same transparency that someone might confess to cheating. She told me how many men; where and why and whether she regretted it – which she told me plainly that she never did. And when I asked her whether she would stop doing it – 'For me, for Dawn. For the fact that you have a life to live that doesn't revolve around this... This fucking madness.' – she only shook her head and plunged her long spoon back into the sundae that was sitting between us. The ice cream bar had been her idea – 'You need some sugar after a shock.' – and I'd called Simon on the way to warn him I might be late home. And though it pained me to admit it, I also thought it wouldn't hurt for him to know my whereabouts, too.

Lily pushed a piece of brownie over to my side of the dish. 'Yours.'

'I don't have the stomach for it.'

'Don't be ridiculous. It's an inch chunk of brownie, I'm not asking you to throw back a scotch. Although if you think it would help...' She gave me a hooded glance, her face still angled towards the food in front of her. 'Never mind, I can have a scotch on my own when this is over with.'

'How can you drink at a time like this?' I nudged the sundae away. 'Or eat.'

'There's a lot of heavy-lifting involved. I have to keep my energy up.'

My fell face clean through the table and onto the floor. And Lily laughed with such an enthusiasm that a slim trail of ice cream came down her nose. She reached for a napkin and tried to settle herself. 'Okay, so humour isn't the way through this either.'

'How can you laugh at... Lily,' I lowered my voice, 'you're killing people.'

She matched my tone. 'I know.'

There was a long silence that followed while she ate around the brownie she'd left in the sundae glass. When it was the only thing still standing she said, 'Look, are you going to eat that or not?'

I speared it in half with my spoon. 'Of course I'm going to eat it.'

While I was preoccupied with chewing – though the sugar turned to grit on my tongue and I found that I was waiting and waiting and waiting still before I managed to even swallow – she used the quiet wisely.

'Ce, I get it, this is new information. But I've been doing this for some time now, so it makes sense that I'm a *little* more comfortable with it than you are. Though you have known for a couple of weeks already if we're being–'

'I didn't know,' I snapped, and she looked surprised. 'I guessed. But I didn't know.'

She looked down at the table like a scolded child. 'Because you didn't want to believe it, I'm guessing?'

'Would you? Would you have believed it of me?'

She laughed. 'No, you don't have it in you.'

I felt a knee-jerk need to defend myself somehow: I do *so* have it in me.

'That wasn't a criticism,' she added, as though sensing my offence. 'You're just... Honestly, Celia, you're a much better person than I am. That's why you don't have it in you. That's why I do.' There was another silence, then, while I forced down what was left of the brownie piece. 'I know we've covered a lot of ground already and it's *a lot* to take in all at once. But as far as our friendship goes, literally nothing has changed on my side. I'm still your best friend, I'm still Dawn's godmother, I'm still...'

She listed all the things that hadn't changed and I questioned her naiveté. *But is she really that wrong?* I chewed and thought and half-listened. Lily wasn't the most conventional godparent for my daughter anymore – but at least I knew my daughter would always be safe.

I sucked in a deep breath and asked the one question that had been stuck between my teeth all evening. 'Why did you start, Lil? I know there are hundreds–'

'I didn't say hundreds. And I haven't *killed* hundreds. Jesus, I'm not Harold Shipman. I've *dealt* with hundreds. There's more than one way to skin a cat, Ce. And not all of them deserved to die.'

'You don't have the authority to decide that *any* of them did.'

'We've been through that already.' And she actually sounded bored by the prospect of going through it again. 'If you want to know why I started then we need to get out of here.' She gathered up her phone and keys. 'Come on.'

'Where are we going?' I didn't love the idea of another scene change – unless the next setting was going to be Lily's car while she drove me the fifteen minutes back home.

'We're going to work...'

The office was a medley of stale smoke and Lily's perfume. It had been a long time since I'd last had reason to come into Lily's office – bar the recent attempt at breaking my way in, that is. Inside, though, everything looked a little different to how I remembered it. There was a sofa wedged into one corner of the room, separated out from the formal desk and chair arrangement on the other side of the space. I wondered whether that was to accommodate her whole range of customers, clients; whatever the preferred term might be. On the far wall there were three filing cabinets, too, the kind that require a key to get into, and a waist-high cupboard that could have housed anything from additional files through to an arsenal of guns – I wasn't ruling anything out at this point. Lily snapped on the overhead light and told me to make myself comfortable, which was such an inappropriate throwaway given the circumstances that I nearly laughed.

She disappeared through a door on the right-hand side of the room – the kitchen, I remembered, that also led to a closet bathroom – and when she came back seconds later she offered me a squat glass of wine.

'Look, you don't have to drink, but I'm certainly going to start,' she said before taking a generous mouthful from her own. I took the glass from her. 'Seriously, sit down.' She nodded to the sofa behind us. 'You're making the place look a mess.'

I followed instructions – I wondered whether this would always be the way around Lily now – and I took a seat out of the way. The wine I set on the small coffee table; I wasn't ready to lose total control of my faculties – or any control, come to think of it. Instead, I only sat quietly while Lily ferreted through her desk drawers.

When she came up for air she was holding something – a

key, it turned out, that she used to unlock one of the three cabinets. She reached to the back of the folders and pulled out one that looked well-thumbed; I could see the rough state of it even from this distance. *A cold case*, I wondered, *is that what started all of this?*

'Take your time,' she said, slamming it on the seat alongside me. 'I'm getting a top-up.' I hadn't even seen her neck the wine but her glass was empty and her face was hard. I didn't move until she was out of the room again.

The folder was a pale yellow, with Post-its and page-markers and torn corners sticking out from the lips of it. I heard the clunk of a fridge opening as I skimmed the first page – a woman's details, age, address, and a name – and the slam of it closing while I thumbed through to the next page: a mess of annotations in Lily's handwriting. The majority of the folder was made up of similar things, until I eventually arrived at something more official: a police report. Then another, then another, then–

'Thirty-two times she reported that man to the police.' She wandered back in; glass replenished. 'I have the other reports if you want them, but they're much the same. Turning up at work, flower deliveries, social media stalking, general stalking. He turned up at her office five times in the space of a month, and one officer told her that she should be flattered. Can you believe that?'

She perched on the windowsill and looked outside, and I wondered whether she was deliberately giving me the space. 'There was one officer at the station, someone who I was having a fling with, if you can call it that. He told the woman to come to me, to see whether I could help. I cornered him the day after, a day or two, I don't know, and I said, "What the hell do you expect me to do?" And he said, "I don't know. More than we can?"' She paused, sipped her drink and let out a sad laugh; it was more like a weighted huff. 'He was right.'

I hurried through the rest of file – more annotations, a redacted interview, more police reports and then–

'He killed her.'

'He killed her.' She drained the last inch of her wine in a single mouthful. 'I'm not letting it happen again, Ce. Not to a woman who I can help.'

'And you don't think there's another way to do that?'

'Drink?'

'Lily.' My voice was firm but I felt anything but. *Is there a word for when your insides quiver but your exterior remains perfectly still?* 'How far are you going to take this, Lil? When is this...' I gestured to the file, lifeless in front of me now, though I could still feel the weight of it. 'When is this going to stop?'

There was a long and uncomfortable pause; it stretched so far that I thought she mightn't answer me at all. But then, looking out into the hollow city like an anti-hero of noir, Lily asked, 'Are you going to try to stop me?'

I huffed. 'What the hell does that even mean?'

'You know what it means, Celia. Will you... Are you going to tell anyone about this?'

It was the first time since this big reveal had started that Lily both looked and sounded vulnerable. She wasn't an axe-wielding killer. *Does she even use an axe?* Instead, she was my best friend who'd slept with the wrong man, cheated on a test, binged when she'd told herself that she needed to diet. She was my best friend who'd made an honest mistake. But the comparison of all those things choked me. 'Lily, you're killing people.' I wondered whether saying it over and again would help one of us.

'You're right,' she answered plainly, the vulnerability suddenly gone. 'That's a certainty. What I'm less certain on is what you're going to do about it.' She glanced at her watch. 'Jesus, I had no idea of the time. Do you want a lift home?'

The turn was enough to cause whiplash. 'We're done here?'

'We're done here.' She knocked off the light closest to her; set her glass on the desk. I imagined her coming in the next morning and clearing away our remains. But she crossed to me, then, and grabbed the file; one thing she wouldn't leave for her future self to find. She took it back to the same cabinet it had come from and locked it away. 'If you're curious,' she threw the key to me, then, 'the ones in the top section are cases closed.' Then she tapped the drawer underneath that. 'They're cases open.'

'Fucking hell, Lily, you have– Jesus, what do you have, some kind of hit list?'

'I'm organised, sue me.' She shrugged on her jacket. 'I'll give you a spare key to the main front door but don't lose it, okay? I haven't got another. Come in, look around. I'm away for the next few days so you'll have the place to yourself.'

'Where are you going?'

But she ignored the question; let it pass like I hadn't said anything at all. 'Try to leave everything as you found it. I've got a system, believe it or not.' She laughed, flicked off another light, and then eyed the door as my signal to move. 'And if I can be so bold as to ask a favour?'

Am I in any position to say no?

I was close enough for her to pull in for an unexpected hug and I felt myself tense against her touch – which I hated. 'Before you make any decisions about whether I should stop, why don't you see if you can spot how many times Quen's name comes up in those folders?'

'Q-Quen... Parsons.'

She tucked her head against my collar and pressed the words into me. 'You weren't his last.'

CHAPTER TWENTY-TWO

Whenever I called Lily in the days after I got an international dial tone.

I risked a look at Quen's Instagram for long enough to know he was in the country, still – working at an office not a ten-minute walk from my own, if the surroundings in his lunchtime snaps were anything to go by – and the thought disturbed and comforted me in equal measure. Whoever she was going after, at least I knew it wasn't him – yet.

I distributed my own workload to the interns for long enough to buy myself two days out of the office and spent the time in Lily's instead.

I was surrounded by case files – the order for which I'd definitely lost, but I thought Lily knew me well enough to know that was an inevitable part of this gesture she'd made.

Ten folders in and I felt like I was reading the same words in bold print over and again, noting Lily's highlighted details, too, the glare of yellow and orange neon stripes pulling out words: rapist; beater; financial abuse. It was never-ending and rage inducing and–

My phone hummed across the floor: another call from

Simon. I couldn't answer. When he'd kissed me goodbye that morning, I could hardly stand for him to touch me. Seconds after the vibrations eased, another short burst of them came through to alert me to a new voicemail. That, I decided, I could manage. So I dialled through and put the call on loudspeaker.

'Hey, babe, it's me. Again. This is like, the third time I've called and... Look, I know you're not at work. Call me, yeah?'

I hit delete and pulled open the mouth of another file.

Two counts of assault. Neither pursued by the police. The third and final bout of assault involved their child – her child, not his child – child hospitalised – arm broken in four places – unlikely to heal properly. Her own jaw dislocated. Set. Healed. Still uncomfortable. No sanctuary housing. Financial constraints keep her at home. Arrange shelter? Research job. His not hers. Prone to working away – Isle of Wight?

Sometimes they were like this, this shorthand scribble in Lily's writing. Sometimes, they were official. Police reports and medical reports and financial statements and I wondered whether it spoke to the hierarchy of the cases. If they're written in great detail, does it mean she's nearly ready? Were the ones written in frantic and hurried notes ones that I didn't need to worry about yet? *Is there any point in worrying about any of them?* I shuffled papers as I wondered; the question felt two-fold. *Is there any point because what can I do? Is there any point because do these men deserve it?*

By the time I'd read through half the contents of the drawer – some folders thicker than others, some taking more and less of me to get through – I'd seen Quen's name three times. Twice for unwanted sexual advancements in the workplace, reported to HR but with no comeuppance; once for sexual assault. There was only a page of hasty notes made for this final claim, and I wondered what had become of the woman – what unwritten promises Lily might have made. And I'd seen the names of tens of men besides him who I wouldn't recognise if I walked past them in the street – despite how dangerous they were. The more I chased that thought around, the more I started to understand Lily's workload.

So I folded the information back into something that resembled organised and slotted everything into the drawers. I had decided before starting that anything that helped me to 'come around' to Lily's way of thinking wasn't worth it – even though I knew that was exactly what she wanted me to do. *Otherwise, why give me this?* I shoved another folder back in, forcing it into a space that was too small. I hung on to the back of the cabinet with one hand and shoved the drawer closed with the other and that's when I felt it – something taped to the back of the metal.

I pulled until the adhesive holding it in place gave way and I carried it to Lily's desk to pore over. It occurred to me this might be the clue to where she was; her most recent whereabouts stashed out of sight in case I– what? Reported her to the police? Jumped on a plane to follow her?

I landed heavy in the seat and let the folder fall open. There was a blank slip of paper at the front of it. I turned it and skimmed the information hidden beneath: bruising; bite marks; the address of Theo's first-year university accommodation.

It wasn't until I saw the names listed that I realised what I was reading. There they were; bold and highlighted like the rest of the men on Lily's wish list. And there I was at the end of page one; the unwilling centre of another folder...

Lily still wasn't answering her phone, though her dial tone was back to its regular ringer – so maybe she was home. But she wasn't taking her calls yet, either way. There was no one to talk sense into me. So I foolishly checked Quen's Instagram again, made a note of the food vendor's name in the background, took my own lunch early.

Less than ten minutes later I was standing not five metres away from him while he sat and filled his face at a table for two in the courtyard of a trendy lunch spot. This part of town was always packed with niche and independent traders. I wondered whether Quen thought he was doing something honourable by eating his lunch there.

It crossed my mind to approach him directly and– *What, Celia? What are you even fucking doing here?* But the nagging thought didn't come about in my own voice; it was Lily's loud and clear, as though she was an imbedded second conscience. And she was right – *I* was right. What did I think this was likely to achieve – other than to inflict a crippling physical ache in the bowl of my belly that left me reaching for a nearby seat? I pulled my vape from the inside pocket of my coat and feigned the appearance of a woman stopping for a lunchtime smoke.

But I couldn't take my eyes off him still. He shovelled bits of burrito into his mouth like it was the first food he'd seen in weeks but from his build it was clear that wasn't the case. Not that his build was a slovenly one. Instead, Quen was built like the archetypal man who spends evenings and weekends working out in the on-site gym that came complete with his overpriced city centre apartment. It was a reaching assumption, but I would have bet on it.

It caused a churn in me that he'd obviously got everything he fucking wanted.

He wiped his mouth clean, bunched together the napkin and leftover signs of dinner from the table and aimed for a nearby bin. The suit he was wearing was light grey with a black shirt underneath; an accompanying tie with a geometric pattern in different shades of grey, too. His hair was an expensive cut and his beard one that I imagined he might tweezer into shape every morning after his shower and I wanted to upchuck the slice and a half of toast I'd managed for breakfast. Instead, I pulled my eyes away and looked at the ground; counting street tiles along the floor while I forced vapour in and out of my lungs to try to regulate my breathing. I started to look for things to count, too, until–

'Celia?'

My whole body tensed. I thought of denying it; shaking off the accusation of my name. But then I was upright and looking him in the eye and I was back in the room and he was telling Theo–

'Like any of the other party-favours...'

'Celia, it is you, isn't it?'

'Are you ready to admit how you feel?'

'It's me, Quen Parsons. Jesus.' He pulled me into a hug and I wanted to die.

'Quen, wow,' was all I could manage. If you held my voice up to a bright light all of my panic would have poured through. 'You're here,' I stuttered, 'you're in the city.'

He gestured to the building across the road. 'I work here! I'm here most lunchtimes.' He laughed and I could remember the hollow knock of it from– 'I can't believe we're only just running into each other. This is wild. I haven't seen you since...' He petered out and narrowed his eyes and I was desperate to watch the weight of a memory hit him but instead he only coughed, then asked, 'Christ, did you hear about Theo?'

'Only recently, actually.'

'I remember you two were close in first year.'

My eyes were near slits while I inspected his words for signs of– something.

'Christ, it would have been the end-of-year party, wouldn't it, when we last saw each other?' The conversation turned again, and I wondered whether a memory had gripped him. He leaned closer and added, 'That was some night, right?'

What the fuck is happening?

'Jesus, Celia, I can't believe I'm seeing you again...'

Why doesn't he feel the shame of it? The weight of it?

'You work in the city, too, then?'

Why aren't you carrying it? Why can't I see the mark of it on you?

I must have nodded. He pulled a card from his trouser pocket. 'I'm in and out of the country a lot, up and down the country, too, actually.' He laughed and rubbed at the back of his neck, as though embarrassed to admit his obvious success. But he wasn't; he wasn't embarrassed about *anything*! 'Why don't you give me a call some time, we can get something set up?'

I must have taken the card.

'Great to see you, Celia, really, you're looking so well.' He shook his head and smiled. 'Helluva night,' he said, more to himself, as he walked away.

And I must have numbed by then. I must have just stood there.

I went to Lily's – because where else could I possibly go? I rang her buzzer over and over and– She didn't answer through the intercom. Instead, she came down to see what lunatic was responsible for sending such a frantic chorus through her otherwise quiet apartment. When she pushed the door open, I was so full of tears that I almost didn't recognise her through the blur of my vision. But when she spoke – 'Celia, what in God's green...' – I rushed up the few steps that were between us and collapsed against her. It was like a re-imagining of that very same night; the poor man's remake.

After, I'd rushed home and found Lily already there. She must have left while I was– But now she was hanging out of her bedroom window, smoking a joint that she'd no doubt stolen from one of the boys that had hit on her during the party. She enjoyed smoking it, but she'd never kept any in the house on principle. She'd looked out of the window, still, and offered me a toke, and it was only when I didn't answer that she turned to look and found me torn and bruising and–

'Is that blood?' I could remember her asking, though I couldn't remember being aware of the slow river bleeding down me from a gash on my cheek; from a slap; from having– *No*, I corrected the memory, *no, I hadn't fought.* Barnie had only hit me because he could – and because none of the others were prepared to stop him.

Now, Lily was crushed under my weight. Her legs buckled as we both fell to the floor like small paper dolls being folded back into each other. 'Celia, love, tell me what's happened?' I sobbed against her until her white T-shirt was tie-dyed with whatever mascara I'd plucked from the bathroom box that morning; I had so many half-finished ones, but sorting through them no longer seemed like an important thing on my to-do list. 'Celia?' She pushed damp hair out of my face and I sobbed more and my breathing got caught in my throat like a dry meal and–

'Quen,' I managed, and I felt her chest empty in a sigh.

'Celia, why?'

I shook my head. I shook my head and let strangled sounds fall out of me as though I were gutting lumps of feeling, until I eventually managed, 'I needed to know– I needed to know who he is– who he is now.'

There was a long pause. Lily didn't want to remind me, of course, that from her own files – from her own long conversations with local women who'd been unfortunate enough to need protection from this very man – she didn't want to remind me that she already knew. Instead she only asked, 'And?'

And nothing, I thought, though I didn't admit it aloud. There was no reason to. Lily could see from the mess of me what I was thinking – what I was feeling towards him. I don't know how much time passed before she ushered me inside and cleaned me up again – as she had done on the night that it happened.

She wiped panda prints of black from around my eyes, kissed my forehead, and helped me to apply enough make-up so that Dawn wouldn't ask why I'd been crying – she was always the first to notice these things – when I eventually arrived home.

She kissed my forehead and told me inane details about her trip – and I said nothing at all about Quen; nothing at all about stopping her.

CHAPTER TWENTY-THREE

S imon stood behind me in the mirror and took the ends of the necklace from me. When he hooked the jewellery together, he let the chain fall and wrapped his arms around my midriff instead.

I was wearing a fitted black dress with a plunge neckline, but nothing too deep because this was a dinner with the in-laws after all. Simon was wearing dark blue jeans and a plain white shirt, with a skinny black tie that was befitting of his teenage self – if the pictures I'd seen were anything to make a judgement by.

He kept hold of me for a long time and watched my reflection; our eyes were tied in the glass until eventually I cracked with a smile and shrugged him off. I still needed to finish getting ready, and it wouldn't be long before Lily arrived. She was coming over to watch Dawn for the evening while we helped Simon's parents celebrate another year of wedded bliss; if you could call 'not being willing to admit defeat' such a thing.

Simon landed on the bed and watched while I drew a neat line of kohl pencil along each eye. He looked enamoured, though I couldn't work out why; he must have seen me do this a hundred times and more for one dinner or another. I smiled at him through my reflection and then swapped to the task of choosing eye shadow: a bronze-gold shade, with just enough sparkle to hide the fact that I hadn't slept properly in weeks.

'You're as beautiful as the day I met you. Did I ever tell you that?'

I smiled. 'That's an old line. You can do better.'

'I'm being serious.' I watched as he moved to lean forwards, his arms against his thighs but his head angled to hold my stare. 'Everything about you, Ce, it's all so... You.' He laughed. 'That makes no fucking sense but I know what I'm trying to say. Maybe I'm heady from the fumes of Mum and Dad's open bar already.' It was their sixtieth celebration and they were hellbent on making a splash. I wondered how many people would make the 'you'd get less for murder' joke before the night was out. 'I'll try this again when I've got a stiff drink in me.'

I reached for the mascara that was lying on the dressing table. I'd had a clear-out; I was down to a favourite two now, and I went for the waterproof. 'I think you're trying to say that...' My mouth bobbed open and closed as I applied the make-up. 'I think you're trying to say that you know me.' I smiled at his reflection. 'Right?'

He nodded. 'Inside and out.'

I'm glad one of us does, I thought as I applied mascara to the other eye. *Because I haven't recognised myself in weeks*. I hadn't since–

The front door cut me off.

'Lily's here!' Dawn's excitement travelled up the stairs to us.

'I'll go.' He stood and snuck across to plant a kiss on the base of my neck. 'You take your time; we've got ages.' He left before I could answer and seconds later I heard a cheerful, 'Lilith!' as he plodded down the stairs.

Lily and I hadn't seen much of each other again – but if anyone asked, we had. She told me she'd never needed an alibi –

'Though it doesn't hurt to have one in your back pocket.' – but that if I really was determined to be involved in what was happening, knowing she could count on me for her whereabouts, should anyone ask, was a good piece of insurance to have. It hadn't even crossed my mind to say no. And I wondered what that said about me now.

I smudged eye shadow over my lids and applied a gentle shade of pink to each lip, before giving myself a pucker and a practice smile. *No one will know what you are*, I thought as I stared myself down. She hadn't given me details, but there had been two nights in the last five weeks when she'd text in the early hours – 'Party-party.' – and I'd known. I'd lay there and stared into the judgemental dark of my ceiling, with my husband sleeping soundly next to me and my daughter, two rooms away, dreaming of nothing and everything all at once. And I'd known that there was a man dying, somewhere. And it had somehow felt just fine.

'Babe!' Simon's voice snapped me out of the medley of memories. 'Taxi!'

I grabbed my bag and switched the bedroom light off on my way out. Lily and Dawn were waiting for me at the bottom of the stairs.

'Get a look at you, beaut.'

'Yeah, Mum, you look amazing.' She enveloped me in a hug. 'Daddy's too scruffy to be a prince but you're definitely a princess, I think.'

Lily and I locked eyes over the top of Dawn's head. She leaned forward to kiss my cheek. 'I don't know, Dawnie, villains can be quite beautiful, too.' Some understanding passed between us as she pulled away, and despite the shady comment, I found that I left the house smiling.

When we got home hours later Simon was merry-tipsy. The kind of tipsy that, had we not had Dawn and Lily to consider, would have led to loud sex in every other room of the house while we drunkenly made our way to the bedroom. He kissed at my earlobe for much of the taxi ride from party to front door, and I knew he shared the memory of those times, too.

While he fumbled with the front door key, I felt a swell of love for him – this safe and wonderful man who I could trust, wholeheartedly. I snatched the key from his hand, backed him against the bright blue panelling of the door, and kissed him like we were teenagers in a hurry. Simon's hands grabbed at my ribcage as though ready to lift me up to him and for a second I thought, *if he does, I'll let him. I'll have sex with my husband right against this front door.* But he thought better of it, and broke our kiss open with a smile that started slow but soon overtook him.

'Where did that come from?'

'Do I need a reason?' I scooted round him to the front door and unlocked it myself. 'Maybe I just wanted my husband. Is that a crime?' He kissed the base of my neck as I pushed through the door. 'Besides which, even if it were a crime I reckon I'd still give it a go.'

He slapped my backside as we walked into the hallway. 'You're a rebel, you are.'

'Oh, you've no idea.' I was heading for the kitchen. 'Drink?'

'Give me a minute to kiss her goodnight.' He had a foot on the stairs. 'I'll make drinks for all of us when I'm down.' He started to climb, then, but threw down, 'Why don't you ask Lil if she wants to stay? It's late for her to be out and about.'

I smiled – in part at his generosity; in part at his naiveté. 'I'll ask.'

Lily was sitting in the garden, leaning far back in a garden chair with her feet on the table in front of her. They were bare, and I loved the comfort it implied. She lifted a cigarette for a deep drag on it and I took a greedy inhale of the second-hand smoke before leaning over and taking it from her.

'Hey,' she turned, 'you're not meant to be smoking.'

I landed heavy in a seat opposite her. 'It's a treat for good behaviour.'

She smirked. 'Is that what we're calling it?'

'Calling it by its actual name might make me think twice.'

Her tone changed to something more serious, then. 'Are you struggling, Ce?'

Lily had started to ask this regularly – over the odd text exchange or even the occasional worried phone call, usually if she hadn't been able to get hold of me for something – and I saw the worry in her, then, that she thought this would all get too much. But it worried me more than it wouldn't. It worried me that even after Quen, even after the rest of them, none of this would stop – I would still be in this.

'Now isn't the time.' I nodded to the house behind her. 'Ears.'

'Dawn is flat out,' she answered, and leaned forward to take back the cigarette. She spoke through smoke, then. 'I'm going away in a week or so again, work stuff.'

'Work stuff that I need to know about?'

'Not yet.' She shrugged. 'Maybe soon?'

I leaned forward and lowered my voice. 'Is it him?'

'I said I'd tell you when it was.'

I was impatient for it and I'd made no secret of it, either. Seeing him had lit a fire of something in me; something I didn't recognise, but also didn't feel inclined to put out. Still, Lily had explained that there were other jobs to contend with; timelines to stick to; opportunities she couldn't afford to pass up.

She'd also told me it wasn't always death: 'Sometimes it's destruction, and that can take a little longer.' But she didn't need to give me the gory details; I'd seen them all a first time already in the files I'd filtered through. There were men in there who'd been bloodied and beaten, either first-hand by Lily or by an unnamed friend who happened to owe Lily a favour. Her pool of resources looked to be limitless and not for the first time I wondered how she'd managed to keep this a secret at all. But I wasn't keen for secrets any longer. I wanted to know when. But not for all of them; only for him.

'You're pushing too much for it.'

'Because I want it done,' I snapped.

She watched the end of her cigarette burn for a second longer before stubbing it out on a saucer that she must have brought out with her, too. She didn't answer for a second, but she did pull out a packet of Mayfair. She lifted the lip of the cardboard and offered me one, which I took. I could blame it on the drink in the morning, I reasoned, as I took the lighter from her, too.

'If you rush, you make mistakes.'

'How is it rushing after this long?'

She shrugged. 'Quen, he's a hard man to get close to. The others are easier.'

'And what if I get close to him on my own?' Though I couldn't believe I'd asked the question, I wasn't shocked enough at myself to take it back either.

'Then you'll be doing me out of a job. And landing yourself in prison.'

A huff of air escaped me.

'Oh, because you won't get caught?' Lily snapped.

'Get caught doing–' Simon's question broke off as he gasped and threw a hand to his mouth. 'You naughty little shits. Give me one.' He snatched at the packet, then clicked his fingers fast for a lighter. 'Drunk smoking without me, Christ, I expected better.'

'I know,' Lily smirked, 'just imagine what else we get up to.'

Simon held his hands up in surrender. 'Celia has told me that's not a thing between you two, so I think it's best that I don't entertain the idea for too long.'

The three of us shared in childish laughter but when it was over Lily looked at me over the smoke that the three of us were stirring. While holding my gaze, she spoke to Simon. 'I was actually just telling Celia I'm planning to steal her for a weekend, if you and Dawn can spare her.'

'Hm?' Simon answered, his tone so mellow that he almost seemed disinterested in what was being said.

'I've got this work thing in Leeds. I've heard there's a pretty good literature festival there and,' she snapped her fingers, 'what do you know, I just so happen to be looking into one of the event organisers.' She was talking to both of us now. 'His wife thinks he's actually there for a weekend with someone so...' She shrugged. 'It's easy money for me, but could be a good chance for Celia to hand some cards out.'

'And have a cheeky weekend away while she's at it.' Simon moved behind Lily and squeezed gently at her shoulders, with the cigarette dangling from the corner of his mouth. 'I know your game, Lilith, I know your– Shit, I said I'd do drinks.' He made for the door. 'Lily, you'll stay over, won't you? Two fingers of scotch, no ice?' He asked both things as though they formed part of the same question, then disappeared through the door back into the house.

'You'll stay over?' I asked again.

'You'll come to Leeds.'

I couldn't understand where the offer had come from – or whether her reason for it was sincere, or just a well-timed lie. 'Why am I coming?' I asked, and Lily smiled.

'Because I want you to see how it's done.'

SHE

She packed two lots of ID cards inside the side pocket of her travel case: one set that boasted a dated picture of her, though one that was still passable; another that boasted a picture of Celia, pulled from the back catalogues of their friendship folders.

For two full days they would be completely different people. It was probably something she should have warned Celia of, but it would be one of many surprises for the coming days – and a relatively low-key surprise at that, in comparison to some of the other things that could happen.

She zipped the compartment closed and wedged her clothes into the bottom of the bag: black jeans; black T-shirt; black everything. Apart from a postbox red dress that she planned on wearing when she took Celia for dinner on the Saturday night. It had been a long time since they'd had a girls' night away, and even though it was a working trip, she thought they should still make the most of some uninterrupted time together.

Besides which, this would be her first real opportunity to see how Celia felt about all this madness. It was one thing to idly agree to the prospect of a major crime; it was another thing to agree to stalking and intimidating a man, when his case folder was lying limp and open in front of you on hotel sheets.

She planned to give Celia the folder on the drive up there. She'd already collected the car – her usual firm, booked under a fresh name that they didn't recognise but wouldn't question, because they never did – and she planned to give Celia the folder when they hit the motorway, so she had time to read the allegations made against the man.

Everything was fairly low level for this one, though, and deliberately so. She thought it would tip the scales unfairly if her first ask of Celia was that she sit on a man's chest long enough for Lily to tie his hands. Besides which, she didn't think she could rely on Celia to get that job done. It wasn't a comment on her strength, or physical abilities.

She smiled. 'It's only that you're too good a person, Ce.'

She wedged her own file down the side of the bag, where Celia wouldn't easily spot it. Then she placed the one for Celia loosely, on top of the packed clothes. It would be easy enough to reach behind the seat while she was driving to grab it and gift it to her friend.

The front doorbell to her apartment chimed and she checked the time. Of course, the first time Celia happened to be on time for anything it would be this. She hit the button for the intercom – 'I'll be down in a second.' – and did a final sweep of the flat before grabbing her bag and hitting the stairs. When she pushed through the main door, she found Celia sitting on the steps to the building, pulling in a long breath from her vape while still exhaling the previous one from her nostrils.

'Nervous?' She dropped down next to her. 'You can still say no to this.'

Celia huffed. 'Yes, I'm nervous.' Then there came another pull. She thought she could smell vanilla, or maybe it was custard, when her friend exhaled. 'No, I'm not saying no to it. Where's your car?' Celia looked around the length of the street.

She pulled the keys for the Volkswagen Polo from her jeans pocket and hit the unlock. Celia's head snapped around at the sound of the vehicle springing to life.

'That isn't your car.'

'It is for this weekend.' She stood and took her bag across the street with her. Celia didn't move, though, and it crossed her mind that maybe, just *maybe*, she still wouldn't come. 'You can still–'

'No,' Celia cut her off, stood and crossed to her friend, 'no, I can't.'

She opened the back door for Celia to throw her bag in, then added her own. She said nothing as they piled themselves into the car, clicked in seat belts, and Celia began to fiddle with the settings for the radio – as she always did during a long drive anywhere.

Lily said nothing as she geared the car into life and pulled away from the kerb. To herself, though, she smiled and thought, *Atta girl*.

CHAPTER TWENTY-FOUR

The news reader was hardly a mouthful into the announcement when I punched the radio quiet and stared across at her. Lily wore a blank expression, as though nothing at all had just happened, but there was no way she didn't know the significance of it, too.

'Who was he?' I asked, and I wondered whether she'd lie.

There was a long pause before she answered. 'I didn't want to throw you in at the deep end for your first time away.'

'So who the hell was I watching on Friday night?'

Lily smiled. 'He's a legitimate case. He's just not someone we're going to hurt.' She hesitated before adding, 'Actually, we will hurt him but it will be more of a financial thing. I thought he was away with another woman for the weekend. And thanks to your handy work, I now know that he was.'

She sounded far too fucking pleased with herself and quite unexpectedly, an anger surged up in me like a small wild thing. 'What the hell is the point in doing any of this if you're just going to take my choices away?'

'I beg your pardon?' She sounded affronted now, much less

sure of herself than she had some seconds ago. 'How exactly am I taking choices–'

'You lured me there under false pretences.'

'I *took* you there to watch a man. You watched a man.'

'While you killed another!'

Lily pulled into the motorway lay-by at a dangerous speed and banged the hazard warning lights on with a hard fist. 'Let me get this straight, Ce. You're sad because I *didn't* let you murder a man? Is that the conversation we're actually having here?'

I repeated her sentence to check it over because when I heard it from her mouth I realised, too, how ridiculous my gripe was. But– 'Yes, yes I'm sad about it. No, I'm not sad. I'm something else. I'm... I'm hurt! That's what I am.'

'Hurt,' she parroted, again making the scenario seem a ridiculous one.

'Lily, I just thought–' I cut myself off. *What did I think, exactly?* That she was going to let me tag along as a little mini version of herself; a Dawn figure, who might stare wide-eyed from the sidelines and watch while she, the expert, set about her work – undistracted by the fact that she suddenly had an audience to perform to. It was absurd and I knew it. But there was still something about how the weekend had rolled out that didn't sit right with me – and I was shocked to shame in myself that the murder *wasn't* the part that felt wrong.

In the end I could only quietly admit, 'I thought this would work differently. I thought I'd be more than a... than a ride-along on the cases that you don't want to be doing for yourself.'

'And you think that's what Friday was?'

'Christ, wasn't it? You can go and tell that man's wife that she was right to suspect the cheating bastard. You can tell her exactly where he was, because *I* was watching him the whole time. Meanwhile, you're telling me that you're waiting to see if he turns up somewhere else, when actually you were out there killing this...' I gestured wildly to the radio; I'd lost the murdered man's name already, but I was no closer to losing my spark in all of this. 'This– What was he, even?'

She looked out the window, then, and focused more on the speeding cars. An uncountable amount had passed when she finally tipped her head back against the car seat and spoke to the ceiling. 'He was a child pornographer. The woman who told me about him, she told me because...' She pulled in a greedy breath and spoke around the exhale, 'Her daughter told her that the guy had asked her to do things. She'd done them, thinking it was okay, because he was an adult.' The speeding cars took her attention again, then, so I couldn't see her face. 'That's who I was with Friday night.'

With her faced away I finally had guts enough to ask the real question I was longing to hear answered now. 'What did you do to him?'

Lily's head snapped around. 'Celia, who *are* you?' Her face broke into a smile, then, but I knew her well enough to know the question was a sincere one. *Mind you*, the thought arose, *you don't even know much of yourself at the moment, do you? So how well can you even know–* 'First you're not on board, then you are. Then you want to know how it's done, but you don't want the dull cases. Now you're asking for the dirty innards of... this guy.' She also gestured to the radio and I wondered whether she'd forgotten his name, too, or whether she just didn't want to use it. 'I've gotta say, Ce, all of this smacks of some kind of crisis.'

'Crisis?'

'I said what I said. You can't go from zero to a hundred without there being problems somewhere along the line. And how do I know...' She petered out, as though scared to finish the sentence – or rather, scared to make the accusation. But somewhere in my belly I knew what her worry was; it was the same, I think, as what my own worry was sometimes, still, in the dead of night when my husband was sleeping soundly against me and I was wide awake counting the list of things I had to lose in all this.

'You're worried I'll go to the police.'

She let out a pained sigh. 'Celia, *of course* I'm worried. And no,' she reached across and took my hand, 'that isn't a reflection of my trust in you. I trust you more than anyone I know in the goddamn world. That's the only reason you *know* this stuff is happening. But you're also one of the kindest people I know in the world, too.'

'Maybe I'm not that kind anymore.' I snatched my hand away as though the gesture might underscore my point. 'Maybe I'm more brittle than you realise.'

She smiled and reached out to push back a few strands of hair that had struggled free from my updo. 'Lovely, lovely Celia.' If we hadn't been best friends, if the option hadn't been an entirely ridiculous one, I would have accused Lily of looking at me with a kind of longing in the seconds that passed, then. 'You just aren't.'

Lily turned and started the car again, then, and checked her mirrors before pulling out. 'I'm not letting you jump in at the deep end. I'm just not.'

I waited until she joined the traffic to talk. 'Then give me the shallow end. Tell me what you did.'

I spent the final two hours of the journey home listening to Lily talk me through murder, while I quietly pretended not to panic. *Three things I can smell: petrol fumes from Lily over-revving; Lily's perfume; the air freshener hanging from the rear-view, placed there by the car rental company that knows Lily's real name but also knows never to use that because—*

'He started to cry and tell me that he didn't even think he'd done anything wrong. I couldn't prove anything, yada-yada.

Then bam, I hit him with the proof.' *Two things I can hear: the radio playing the best of the 1990s as a low hum percussion to Lily's confession; oh, Lily's confession.*

'I'd already got everything I needed at the place where I took him to. It just makes sense to have everything there and ready. Plus, it's a good precursor for them. They can take a good guess at where it's all going, I suppose.' *One thing I can feel: cold steel buckled around my wrists and clipped into place by a man wearing a police officer's streetwear uniform but maybe it isn't cold, maybe it's warm from having been recently pulled from wherever the officers are told to keep them and–*

'Sorry, I know I rattled through that. Have you got any... I don't know, questions, comments? I realise it isn't really that sort of discussion.' She laughed, and I tried to force a laugh, too, but all I managed was a soft noise that brought back with it the taste of whatever I'd eaten for breakfast. The morning seemed so long ago now.

'Can we stop at the service station, please?' I managed, as we drove by the sign for it. And I didn't speak again until we'd stopped, and I'd used the bathroom, and I'd managed to get back in the car. Lily bought cigarettes while I was in there, and I took one when she offered the packet to me. I hoped it might cover the smell of upchuck that I thought would pour out when I spoke again...

I declined Lily's offer of dinner when we got back into the city. I wanted to get home to shower away all the information that clung to me like old lint from the car journey. I wanted to burn my clothes, hold my husband, promise my daughter that nothing in the world would ever hurt her – though I wasn't entirely sure what it was that I thought I'd be protecting her from. I might have been unsettled by Lily's confession. But Lily was also the only person I'd ever met who was making such a swift job of cleaning up the badness in the world for girls like Dawn. *For girls like me*, I thought, as I hauled my bag free of her back seat.

'Hey,' Lily called my attention before I could shut the door, 'we good?'

I shrugged. 'I don't know.' It felt like a betrayal had taken place somehow. I thought doing this with Lily would give something back to me – some control, over what had happened – but now, knowing that I'd slept in a twin bed next to her hours after she'd finished pulling a man apart, everything felt different. Though that was probably an entirely normal reaction, given the circumstances. *Though a normal reaction might have been to go to the police in the first place*, I thought as I closed the door and turned towards home. I couldn't give her any more than that.

I walked into the house with the same level of trepidation that I imagined soon-to-be-victims must enter a house in a horror film; unbeknownst to them there was already a killer waiting for them inside. It somehow felt like the most and least appropriate comparison I could have made.

There weren't any lights on in the living room. But the open-plan wind of the downstairs made it easy to spot a low glow coming from the kitchen. I hadn't realised the time, or the darkness that had fallen between the final few junctions of the motorway journey. I hadn't let Simon know when I was nearly home, either, though I couldn't believe the gloom of the house was anything much to do with the burnt dinner I might be about to walk into.

When I rounded the corner I found my husband, tired and weary and waiting. There was no sign of Dawn, though, even though this was still a respectable enough hour for her to be up

– and I'd expected her to be, too, for the grand homecoming. The oven was dead, and there were no smells – burnt or otherwise – that might imply dinner was waiting, had been waiting. *This can't be over dinner...*

'Tea?' he asked when he saw me creep in. His voice was hard around the edges.

'I can make it.' I tried to overcompensate his flatness with my own cheer. 'Will you have one?'

'Sit down, babe, I'll make it.' He stood and crossed to the kettle, tap, cupboard. Even though he'd use an affectionate term, it was still uncomfortable in the room; the humid weather that comes after a heatwave. The atmosphere made me want to open the doors, throw open the windows, tumble out into the garden. But instead I followed instructions and sat, silently, while my husband made tea for me. All the while thinking, *Well this isn't awkward at all.*

'Good time away?' he asked as he set the mug down.

'It was okay, thank you. You know what Lily is like, work, work, work.' But then I remembered *I* had been there for work, too, as far as Simon knew. So I stitched the lies together to cover the cotton ball insides. 'I met the client she mentioned,' I shook my head and made a grimace, 'not sure he's the type I want to be working with, really. I took his details in case anyone at work wants to pursue it, though.'

'So not a totally wasted trip?'

'Not a wasted trip at all.' I smiled. 'It's always nice to have a break, isn't it?' *A break with your best friend the serial killer.* I took a large swig of tea even though it was still too warm and rinsed it around my tongue and teeth like it was mouthwash; as though I might wash the worries away. 'How have things been here? I didn't expect Dawn to be in bed quite so early.' I turned to glance behind me like she might come rushing down, having heard her cue to surprise me.

'I put her to bed early.'

'Is she okay?'

He made a noise that I took to be a yes. 'We had a pretty good weekend, even though I've watched *Frozen* two and a half times while you've been away.' There was a crack of normalcy, then, and I felt a tide of gratitude for it. *Maybe he's tired*, I thought, *maybe Dawn has been a lot, and he's tired and–* 'Of course, it put a bit of a dampener on things when the police turned up late afternoon today.'

I spat my tea across the kitchen table. 'I'm sorry?'

'Don't be, I'll get some kitchen roll.' He moved away from the table to grab tissues, then, without saying anything more.

'Simon, that's not what I mea–'

'I know.' He wiped over the table with such a stern expression, anyone might have thought the wood grain had done something to personally offend him. 'They said they were sorry to trouble us at home, on a weekend. But there'd been another death and they were keen to talk to you about it, especially after the first one.' He sat back down with a heavy thud. 'So which part of this story do you want to explain first?'

I shook my head and tried to blink back what felt like tears, though I couldn't understand why that would be my reaction to this. 'I can't explain this second part,' I admitted, because it felt easier to start with a truth.

'Then I guess you'd better start with the first.'

CHAPTER TWENTY-FIVE

The following morning, Simon and I went about our business like nothing at all had happened.

He and I had breakfast with Dawn; Simon volunteered to take her to school on his way to see a new building site; I volunteered to make dinner for everyone – 'Tuna pasta bake, please,' Dawn commanded on her way out the door – and I promised to be home at a reasonable time to make it and eat it and watch something other than *Frozen*.

'I didn't agree to those terms!' she shouted back into the house.

Simon leaned forward to kiss me goodbye; a soft and gentle peck, tender like he was on any other morning. I waved them into the car, locked the door and went back to the kitchen to tidy up from breakfast. But instead of recycling porridge pots and scrubbing crumbs and marmalade clean from plates, I found I was leaning over the kitchen sink instead, my insides becoming my outsides; my porridge reappearing and smelling too sweet as it had when I'd eaten it.

I groaned and slammed the tap on to start washing the remains away. Then I collected the breakfast things, washed them, left them to drain; I ran on automatic until it came to collecting up my work things. My briefcase and laptop bag were already waiting for me by the front door – where Simon had wedged DS Allen's business card. I had promised I would call.

I'd thought of calling Lily the night before, when Simon had finally dropped into sleep – albeit a restless one. I thought of dialling her number and whispering a confession into the speaker: 'Simon knows something,' I wanted to panic it out, 'Simon knows, I know he does.' But I'd resisted the urge for a bushel of reasons: sweet ripe and shiny reasons, like the police being able to trace when phone calls were made; like Simon waking up and overhearing something; like Lily, calm and deadly Lily, deciding I wasn't fit for this role after all.

But you aren't fucking fit for it, I thought as I pocketed the business card, slammed and locked the front door behind me. I walked to work. I needed the grit and dirt of the city to replace the grime of the weekend that I felt I'd brought home; despite showering three times in the thirteen hours I'd been back.

The office was uncharacteristically busy for the time of the morning when I stepped in. But I was glad for the clutter of it. Rory looked to be herding strangers from one desk to another while Clive was clicking his fingers, trying to get anyone's attention on their way past him. When he saw me he made a hand gesture that looked like writing – 'Pen?' he mouthed – and I reached over to grab one from the far corner of his own desk, which I passed to him. He rolled his eyes – 'Sorry, Ce.' – then went back to whatever conversation had him ruffled.

Lou was depositing cups of coffee at every other desk around the place, too, and I felt a disproportionate disappointment that I'd missed the Starbucks run. Though it would at least give me an excuse to get out of the office.

I dropped into my chair without being accosted by any other colleagues. But soon Lou appeared at the corner of my desk anyway, and gently placed down a brilliant white takeout coffee cup with a big and swirling C on the side.

I groaned, half-laughed. 'How did you know?'

'It's Monday.' She laughed, too, then went to finish her rounds.

The space was the perfect excuse not to call the detectives back. There wasn't enough quiet, nor privacy. So even though I'd promised Simon I would, I had ample excuse to just... I slipped the business card out of my back pocket and shoved it in the centre drawer of my desk, then dropped a small and bubble-like paperweight down on top, as though the card were such an independent force that it might climb free if I left it unattended for long enough. I slammed the drawer closed, then, and set my laptop to turn on, then the main PC, then anything else I could think of to busy myself with. But after turning everything on, finding my diary, checking my meetings, I found the laptop boasting 'Please wait...' underneath the loading screen. Meanwhile, the decrepit PC monitor hadn't even managed to bring a bulb of light to the table yet.

I knew Lily's work number and mobile number by heart. She and Simon were the only people in the world I was equipped to call in a crisis if I didn't have my phone with me. Though of course, this wasn't Simon's fire.

I punched in her office number and waited for it connect, ring once, twice. Then I slammed the receiver down. *Would they check my office phone?* I forced out a long stream of air and clenched and unclenched both hands to try to settle the start of their shakes. *Three things I can smell: twelve different types of aftershave because the men in the office know nothing of moderation; coffee; the promise of rain creeping in from an open window. Two things I can hear: Clive trying to calm down whoever he's on the phone to; Lou explaining to Rory that she's allowed to forget minor details of coffee orders. One thing I can feel: a deadening in my legs as though the vein structure has been replaced by strings of lead.* I pushed out another breath. It was entirely reasonable to think that I might call a friend from my work phone. Before calling the police.

I didn't know whether that was true. But I dialled Lily's number, her mobile this time. When she answered it was clear that I'd pulled her from sleep; her voice was thick with an overnight build-up.

'Can you talk?' I asked.

'Of course I can talk, beaut. What's shaking?' Her voice still sounded thick. I imagined her stretching her body out, her phone wedged against her ear while she star-fished across a bed that was too big for a single occupant. It had been one of her favourite purchases since she bought her own place. During moments like that, when the gentle memories stepped in, I realised this was still Lily. *My* Lily. 'Hey, you there?' Kind Lily. Supportive Lily. Killer Lily.

'The police came to the house while I was away.'

There was a long pause, and I expected panic to come at the end of it. Though she sounded more awake, there certainly wasn't the knee-jerk worry I'd been expecting. 'I assume there's more to that?'

'They want to talk to me about a dead man.'

'Ce, I'm not a fan of this stop-start storytelling.' I could hear her moving around. I wondered whether she was bolt upright now, suddenly paying attention. 'What actually happened? Start to finish.'

I forced a long stream of air through the O of my lips. 'DS Allen and DC Moss came to the house yesterday while I was away. They told Simon they wanted to talk to me about another murder that had taken place, that they thought might be related to the first.'

There came a sharp intake of breath. 'And you didn't tell Simon about the first?'

'Well, no.' I hesitated. *Had she missed the point of this entirely?* 'Lil, that's not really the thing I'm most worried about.'

'Did they leave a card, or did they say they'd come again?'

'They left a card but—'

'Did you call them yet?'

'*Yet?*' I parroted. 'No, I didn't call anyone. I called you!'

'Call them.'

'And it's that simple?'

'It's *that* simple.' She sounded so confident that I almost believed her. 'What did you tell Simon?'

'So we're totally done on that police talk, then?' I was stunned. How often must this have happened to her already? Was this a *regular* occurrence? Would I be *known* to the police now? I rattled through questions quicker than I could speak them, and then it occurred to me that Lily hadn't even answered the first one. 'Lily,' I urged, 'help me here.'

'I am helping you. I just gave you quiet time to panic.' There came another flurry of sounds; a groan that I thought must accompany a stretch. 'Now do you want to talk about Simon?'

When he sat across the table from me, giving me the same hard stare he would have once given a three-year old Dawn for eating biscuits when no one was looking, I'd wanted to tell him everything. *Lily killed a man this weekend*, I wanted to say. *She killed a man while I watched another; it isn't the first time and it won't be the last and I know the first man who was murdered because*— and the panicked confession broke off there. Simon didn't know; I had never wanted him to. Instead, I'd told him the minimum amount that I could and relied on the harsh reality that lies by omission sometimes have to be okay.

'I told him Mitchell and I went to university together and that he'd been searching for me on social media. That's why the police got in touch. I said Mitchell hadn't actually contacted me, though, so I hadn't been able to help them, and I couldn't shed any light on why he might have been looking for me.' I paused to steady myself with another breath. 'Then I told him I had no way of knowing anything about this second murder. The whole thing was news to me.'

She lingered for a second then said, 'Well done.' Short and curt and neat. I thought that if I'd been in front of her she might have patted me on the head and given me a treat. 'Now call them.'

'Lily,' I lowered my tone, though anyone who had listened to the conversation so far had certainly heard enough for office gossip to take off, 'do you know anything about this second man?'

'Ce,' she was near laughter, 'at this point, I literally know as much as you.'

CHAPTER TWENTY-SIX

L ily gave me strict instructions: call the detectives; do not call her. She said she didn't know what or who they wanted to talk to me about – and I had no reason to disbelieve her. *Apart from her being a cold-blooded killer and all*, I thought as I shifted awkwardly on the steel seat that was designed to keep suspects uncomfortable, I guessed.

It was every bit the police drama space, right down to the mirror I wanted to stare hard into in the morbid hope there might be someone on the other side.

I brushed away the negative thoughts of Lily – something that had been increasingly difficult since her swap-out at Leeds, but still – and stared around the room like someone who didn't have the time to be there. It was hard to act like I didn't care when there was a kick-drum chipping flecks of bone off my ribcage. But DC Moss had escorted me here with a smile and no handcuffs, so I had to take that as a good sign. Even if my watch was ticking louder than it ever had before, signalling one minute, then two, then–

'Celia.' DS Allen stepped into the room with a smile I couldn't read. Moss trailed behind her. It hadn't struck me until today just how young he was. *But old enough to be a* real *detective?* I thought as the pair of them took their seats. Although perhaps the voice of inexperience would work to a criminal's advantage. *If a criminal were here; but you aren't a criminal, remember?* It was Lily's voice, not mine.

I flashed a tight smile at the senior detective.

'Thanks ever so much for lending us some of your time on this.'

'It's no problem,' I lied, and I thought my tone had likely given it away. But I could pass the hesitance off as anything: a hectic workday; a pile of paperwork; knowing what Lily was doing last weekend. 'What can I help you with, exactly?'

'Straight to the point,' Allen said with what sounded like the beginnings of a laugh. As though taking a cue, Moss opened a folder out onto the table. It looked like the same cardboard files that Lily used for her cases, and I suddenly imagined a warehouse full of the things. Empty, save for the details of criminals and live cases and other wild and ridiculous stories that hadn't crossed my mind until all of this had started. Yet now my entire life looked to be revolving around those damn folders and– I forced out a long breath. *Three things I can smell: cleaning solution rising up from the table; perfume, which I guessed belonged to Allen; though Moss didn't smell bad either. Two things I can–*

'We wanted you to have a look at this man for us.' Moss pushed a photograph towards me.

The image showed a man in his mid-thirties, I guessed. It looked as though he was in a bistro; somewhere upmarket enough to have exposed bulbs and copperwork pipes everywhere for aesthetics rather than anything practical. He was wearing a white shirt that made me wonder whether he was trying to impress someone that night; the person taking the picture, maybe. There was a floral trim around the edge of the shirt, too, which I only noticed with a squint. Light and royal blue, one then the other around each cuff. His hair was a deep brown and his eyes a kind of honey and there was nothing familiar about him at all.

I breathed a sigh of relief, though I hoped they might misread it as impatience. 'I don't know that I've ever seen that man before, no. Should I...' I glanced up and looked from Moss to Allen to the image. 'Sorry, should I know him?'

'There's no real reason why you would, necessarily.' Allen pulled the image back and filed it somewhere behind the rest of the detritus that had spilled out of Moss's folder. But she pulled out another picture in its place. This one showed a building; this one, I did know. 'Does that ring a bell?'

'I used this place for a photoshoot about...' *Think, Celia, think.* 'Six months ago, maybe? I can find the exact date on my work calendar. I had a new client at the time who was promoting a series of gritty crime novels that he was having reissued with a new publisher. We thought it was a good spot for something...' I laughed. 'Well, gritty.'

'Did you gain permission from the building owner to do that?' Moss asked.

There was an opportunity to play stupid here, I felt it, and I leapt on it. 'Oh shit, is that the man in the picture? I co-ordinated with a colleague on this whole thing, he's the one– I mean, obviously *I* could have checked on him but I didn't think I needed to, you know?' I deliberately looked at Allen. 'Is that what this is about?'

She smiled. 'We're not investigating whether the photoshoot was above board, don't worry.' She re-filed the image and closed the gaping mouth of the folder, then, and I was relieved that must mean there weren't more pictures coming. 'The man in the picture, his name is Kyle Rox. I know the picture didn't trigger anything, but did the name...'

I shook my head before the question was out and her face dropped into something that looked like disappointment. 'He was murdered five days ago. The building, the one from the photograph, it was where we found him and... well, it's not like this little corner of the world to have two murder victims so close together.'

'You think he...' I swallowed hard to try to clear a lump that was gathering. I imagined all my words rolled in egg white and flour. 'Sorry, do you think he has something to do with Mitchell? With what happened to Mitchell?'

'We're considering the possibility,' Moss answered. 'Though we can't rule anything out at the moment, one way or another. Which is why we thought it would be worth having a chat with you about it all. Especially as the link between you and Mitchell was so...'

'Odd,' I finished her sentence, and she huffed a laugh.

'Well, maybe not odd, but certainly a little precarious.'

'I wish I could help you,' I looked between them both again, 'I really do.' *But I'm relieved to my fucking core that I actually can't.* 'But there's nothing I can tell you about this man, this...' I waved at the flattened folder. 'This business. Honestly, this is a world so far removed from my own.' A nervous laugh fell out of me and I thought it might have been the most sincere thing to come out of my mouth since my arse had touched the seat. 'I wish I could help more.'

'Your husband,' Allen started. If I'd been a wild animal, the fur on my back would have gathered at the mere mention of Simon. 'He didn't know Mitchell?'

'He didn't even know *about* Mitchell,' I answered.

'Ah.' She pushed back from the table. 'I hope we didn't cause any trouble on the home front.' It felt as though she'd paused for an answer but I only smiled. I wasn't there to discuss marital imbalances and, given that I wasn't there to talk about a crime either, stringing the conversation out with niceties seemed like the worst idea I could have. When I didn't answer, she stood, and Moss followed suit. 'Thanks for coming in, Celia, we really appreciate it.'

I followed their move to leave the room. 'Any time.'

Moss escorted me back to the station entrance like the young gentleman I guessed he was. He said a polite goodbye and kicked me back into the glaring sun, where I could gulp in air like a fish that had escaped a line. I walked towards home with my legs on automatic; my main focus only keeping my breathing steady, and making the most of the adrenaline surge that I hoped would carry me through the evening.

I would go home and kiss my husband and enjoy a dinner with my family. I would drink wine and watch television. I would go to bed. I would not call Lily.

***

It was a normal evening through until bedtime – and that's when he asked. I was staring down a reflection that I hardly recognised. There was a change, I was convinced of it, though I couldn't put my finger on what it was. Still, my reflection and I were brushing our teeth. Simon came to a stop in the open doorway and leaned against the frame, casual and unconcerned. He waited until I dipped to spit a mouthful of foam into the sink; I heard him take such a deep breath that I worried if I rose, I might find there wasn't enough air left for me.

'Did you call the police?'

I looked at him in the mirror and nodded. 'I saw them.'

'Today?' He looked irked, then, and I wondered whether this was something I should have mentioned earlier. Not that there was a protocol for this. When Simon and I had decided on the ground rules for our relationship a hundred years ago, no one had thought to mention how best to handle one of us being questioned in murder investigations. *Funny that*, I thought, still brushing, though I nodded again.

'Are you going to tell me what happened?'

I hit the cold water tap to turn on and buried my mouth beneath it. When I was clean of foam and whitening grit, I looked at him through the mirror again. It felt like a conversation best had through a looking glass, somehow, as though the mirror version of me might be more convincing than the version who was already wondering how many smells she could count to ground her.

'They asked me about another case. I couldn't help them.'

'Couldn't help them, meaning?'

I shrugged. 'Meaning, I don't know anything about the man that was murdered.'

'*This* man?'

'Yes, Simon, this man.' I grabbed the mouthwash. 'I can't help them with the other man either.'

'The one you know?'

'Jesus, what is this?' It wasn't anger. But I felt something flare up from the well of my belly. 'I knew him a hundred years ago, I didn't know him when he died.' I uncapped the bottle and upended it without using the lid to measure it. It was a spiteful domestic jab, but I knew he hated it.

'I still don't understand why he was looking for you.'

I made him wait a full thirty seconds for an answer; I counted them evenly in my head. We had never been this couple before, and I didn't like the outfit on us. I spat hard into the basin and a spatter of bright green flecked onto the shelf behind the sink unit. I knew he'd hate that, too.

'You'd have to ask him.'

He huffed and shook his head, then went to move away.

'I'm telling you as much as I know, Si.' I turned and reached for him. 'I'm sorry I didn't tell you to begin with.' Whatever the mirror spell was, it was broken. Once I was face to face with him my resolve was broken and he was my Simon again; *my* Simon, who I loved and wouldn't hurt and would never lie to. Only I already had – and I still was.

But at least I could end on a truth: 'When the police turned up to ask me about Mitchell, I honestly had no idea what was going on. I hadn't spoken to him in literally years, and he certainly hadn't been in touch. It was news to me that he was even looking for me.' I was careful with my words. I avoided, *I don't know why he was looking for me.* I avoided, *There's nothing more I can tell you.* When I stepped forward to pull my husband into a hug, I felt the tension of him slip away as he relaxed into the gesture and held me in return.

'It's unsettling, Ce, that's all, and I wish you'd told me.' He spoke into my neck. 'But there's nothing else?' He pulled away once he'd asked the question and held me at arm's length; it felt like a dare, or a challenge.

And I had to lie.

CHAPTER TWENTY-SEVEN

I t had never occurred to me before how often Lily tumbled off the grid. Her unexplained absences were always attributed to work which was, in many ways, a true excuse. Only now I knew what her work entailed, there was something more unsettling about the times I couldn't get hold of her – or the times when I was patiently waiting for her to get hold of me. It felt as though my agency was slipping away, though, and I didn't take kindly to the sensation.

Since speaking to the detectives, I'd dutifully followed her instruction not to call her, on the misguided assumption she might call me. Better yet, maybe she'd arrive at the house; play with my daughter and joke with my husband; tell me about her latest murder while Simon put Dawn to bed. But she didn't do any of that; nor did she get in touch.

Days ran into just over a week and I cracked, only once, to be greeted with the voicemail system at her office. I was too nervous to call her mobile, though I hadn't ruled out turning up at the apartment. Not that any of it would have mattered, I managed to reason with myself, sometimes, given that she was my best friend, and I was therefore more than allowed to call her. *But what might you be giving away? What might they use against you, if you do call?* The paranoia bubbled in me like pasta on too high a heat.

I was facing the garden, waiting for the kettle to boil, when I pulled in a greedy breath and considered– *Three things I can*–

'You look miles away.' Simon wrapped his arms around me from behind and kissed the back of my shoulder. 'Everything okay in that big beautiful brain of yours?'

I laughed. 'I'm running through my to-do list for today.'

'Well,' he kissed me again, this time on the base of my neck, 'don't forget to add Mother's Meeting to the end of it, will you? I'm not stepping in again.' It was a not-so-subtle reminder that I'd missed the last meeting without even realising it. When they couldn't get hold of me, they called Simon – who happened to be working at a shared office space in need of structural renovation, only a short walk from where the coven had gathered. He could have said no, of course; he could have said, 'This doesn't count as an emergency phone call.' But he hadn't – and it was time for me to pay him back for it.

I groaned in a playful way. 'Do I have to?'

He turned me around and kissed my forehead. 'Yes, yes you do. Kettle's boiled.' He grabbed his cup from the steel tree that held them and set it on the counter. 'Coffee, please. I need to be wiiide awake for today's meetings.'

'Post's arrived!' Dawn announced as she strolled into the kitchen, proudly holding a bunch of brown and white envelopes. 'Should I–'

'Bills are for grown-ups and they're certainly not for mornings.' Simon snatched the bundle from her and set it on the far corner of the island. 'What does Dawnie want for breakfast?'

The domestic unfolded around me. We listened to the radio while we made porridge, drank tea and coffee, talked about our plans for the day. There were no announcements made about recent murders.

While Sasha ordered flat whites and Flora, Dolly, and Veryan discussed the structural integrity of the school's roof, it struck me like a blunt force trauma to the back of the head how hard these normal things had become.

They'd always been hard, in a sense; hard because they felt like a waste of time, or hard because beyond Sasha I had nothing in common with any of the mothers – and Dawn didn't even like their kids, so there was no hidden reason there for keeping on anyone's good side. But now it was a different hard. Like the innocent woman in a cheesy noir, I felt as though I'd seen the greyscale underbelly of the world.

No, I corrected myself, *I hadn't seen it; I'd been living with it.* Lily *was* the greyscale underbelly; she *was* the person people made news reports about, if only they knew it. And this newfound awareness of what was happening behind the scenes made it harder to play nice with women whose main concern looked to be how many inane things they could find to fill their days.

'Celia, are you with us?'

No, I wanted to answer. But instead I smiled and set down the napkin I'd been folding and unfolding into even squares since the conversation started. 'I don't think it should rest with us to monitor the building's upkeep. Aren't there people actually employed by the school to be doing this?'

'I agree with Ce.' Sasha leaned over me to set my drink on the table before scooting around to a free seat with her own. 'I understand it's a concern and all. Kids' safety, yada, yada,' she waved it off like it was nothing, 'but I've got bigger worries regarding my kid's safety, if I'm honest.'

There was an instant hush around the table. I glanced up in time to watch the perfect mothers swapping glances and, as though some quiet nomination had passed between them all, Olive was the one to lean forward and ask, 'Has something happened, Sasha? You sound troubled.'

Sash laughed. 'Do you listen to the news? On the way here I heard a report about *three* kids going missing, girls, all of them, somewhere up north. Hardly into their teens and bam, just–'

'Yes, well.' Maria cut across her. 'We're all aware of the dangers of the world.'

Are we? I sipped my coffee and thought again of Lily.

'So, the roof,' Olive finally said. 'Should we take it up with the headteacher?'

'Agreed,' Sasha snapped. 'What's next?'

'Some of us have been thinking of a mother's– Sorry, parents' away day.' Dolly looked far too pleased with the suggestion, and I wondered whether mine and Sasha's deadpan expressions were enough to counteract her obvious glee. *Imagine this*, I found myself thinking, *imagine all of* this *being all you have...*

And somehow that single thought scared me more than anything I could imagine Lily might have been doing at that moment.

Dawn was walking me through a science project that I didn't understand the mechanics of, but I was forced to nod along in the way that parents are. I made noises in all the right places, and occasionally I would rope Simon in – 'Babe, are you hearing this?' – to make sure I wasn't the only dunce in the room with my child. His stock 'Mhmm' response was all the reassurance I needed that he either wasn't listening or didn't understand. It was a comfort.

He was stirring garlic into shop-bought mayonnaise – Simon's version of homegrown – and there were home-made pizzas in the oven, too.

After the horror of the mother's meeting, I'd bought dough, tomato sauce, and more topping options than the three of us combined could possibly ever want while I was on the journey home.

I also bought two bottles of white wine, one of which was already chilling in the fridge. I was waiting for Simon to suggest it first, though I'd set a timer on it, too; if he hadn't offered me a glass of wine by dinner, I would instigate it. The least I deserved was half a bottle of wine after two hours – *two* hours – of talking about the general running of the school, and how far the mothers thought their power should reach in that. Thank God Sasha had been there to buffer the blow of some of their comments.

Though even she hadn't been able to dissuade them from the idea of a parents' trip away. 'It's not like we have to fucking go,' she'd said as soon as we spilled out of the coffee shop, leaving the others behind.

'Why don't we both go?' Simon asked, then, during a small lull in Dawn's teachings. I wondered whether he'd been listening in on my thoughts – or, the more likely explanation, he hadn't got over the shock of the suggestion either. 'Rather than throwing one of us under the bus, we could *both* go.'

'Are you talking about what I think you're talking about?'

He laughed. 'I think it would be good for us to have time away.'

I lowered my voice to speak to Dawn. 'Honey, do you want to eat outside tonight? Maybe you could go and get the table ready out there?' Her eyes lit up; Dawn had always thought eating in the garden was an extra special treat, although I'd never been sure of why. Still, it was an easy way to get her out of the way for a minute or two. I crossed the kitchen to Simon, then, and leaned back against the counter to speak to him while he stirred. *He's making too much of a meal from that job*, I thought, eyeing the sauce. *What's he distracting himself from?* 'Do we need time away?' I asked.

'I just think things haven't been great.' He sighed and dropped the spoon. 'That's me being over-dramatic.' He stood in front of me, a hand resting on each of my hip juts. 'I feel that there's been a disconnect between us lately. I feel that you've been working a lot, and when you haven't been working, I feel that you're quite distracted by work still, and I feel–'

'I get it, babe, you're using your counselling tools,' I said to break the tension.

Simon smiled and leaned forward to kiss my cheek. 'I just think it might be good for us to reconnect a little. But I also one hundred per cent agree that a parents' what's-it maybe isn't the place for it, I don't even know why I said that.' He laughed. 'Forgive me? Maybe you could ask Lily where she's been lately, she's always good for a bit of travel inspiration.'

The timer sounded and Simon moved away to grab oven gloves. 'I tried to work out where she was from the postcard that came this morning but I'm clueless. Mind you, it's probably written on there somewhere and I'm just– Christ! Bloody glasses.' The oven had ejected heat enough to cloud his vision, which I hoped might mean he couldn't see the panic I'd tumbled into.

'I didn't even know she was away,' I forced out, trying to sound more level than I suddenly felt. 'Where's the postcard, babe?'

'It's just on the side.' He gestured behind us. 'Island, somewhere.'

I ferreted through the pile of post that Simon had skimmed, half-opened and then discarded again. Then there, midway down the pile, I found the brilliant bright blue postcard he'd been referring to: somewhere in the Isle of Wight according to the text in the corner. There was a beautifully violent ocean wave on the front being ridden by a surfer: male and smiling. I turned it over and found a bittersweet message in Lily's wild scrawl: 'Wish you were here. Lx.' and at once, without any further prompts needed, I remembered: *Raff*.

I thought back to Theo, then, and how she'd done the same thing while watching him, and I wondered how much of a paper trail I already had for Lily's killing career, without having known it all at the time.

CHAPTER TWENTY-EIGHT

A nother two days rolled by without any contact. Post-postcard, I became even more nervous of calling Lily's mobile. There was still no answer at her office.

But there also weren't any news reports detailing suspicious deaths of local surfer types, so I thought for the time being that must mean Raff was safe.

After the Leeds trip, I didn't think she'd go after anyone without me; I trusted her for that. But I imagined her watching him, learning his behaviours, doing all the things that serial killers always did in the Netflix dramas; which were, as is the case for most people now, my main source of reference for these things.

Lily hadn't exactly walked me through how she did it all – whether she watched, whether she paid someone else to. There'd been enough information in her files for me to guess that there was some spectator work involved, though, and there'd been notes in some of them written by another person, too. And then there was the time when she knew I'd visited Mitchell Webster's widow without my telling her about it...

There was so much I still didn't understand, and the

thoughts of it were enough to cause a spiral. So instead I did the only sensible thing I could think to: I acted normal. I made promises to Simon that I didn't know I could keep about spending more time together – 'Quality time,' I reiterated with a forced smile – and I promised, too, that we'd find time for a trip away somewhere, just the two of us. Though of course, small ears meant that I then had to make a similar promise to Dawn, who had overheard half of the conversation between me and Simon. There would be a family holiday, and couple's getaway, and I would plan both – I offered too readily, but it gave me something substantial to put at the top of a to-do list.

I populated it with small and large tasks alike: call Vita and India for dinner; start thinking about Christmas presents (no matter the month, it was never too early); plan dinner for this evening – and tomorrow evening, or the rest of the week, even; make time for a food shop; write a shopping list!

Where I could, every entry on the list was given its own list of smaller parts. The shopping list kept me busiest, though I found I'd populated it with things we hardly ever had, and definitely didn't need. But it had been an exercise in distraction if nothing else. And besides the list-making, I counted every smell, every sound, and all the touch contact that I could manage. It was a busy week at work, which made it easier still, with emails and phone calls and–

'Celia, do you represent anyone who might be good for this? We're a body short.' Lou pulled up a spare chair and dumped herself next to me at my desk. 'It sounds like something you'd enjoy coming along to as well, actually.'

I snatched at the paper she was waving. 'Well, gimme the goods.' I kept my tone light and my smile wide and my heartbeat erratic as I eyed in the details of the event: it was a crime writing panel discussion, part of a festival on the Scottish border. And my stomach turned over in embarrassment and excitement intertwined at my immediate thought that this could be a helpful alibi to commit to. I had no idea what Lily might have planned. But I reasoned that pencilling in nights away on the kitchen calendar mightn't be a bad idea given that these days I needed better and improved excuses to slip away into the night.

'I have someone for this.' It was a partial lie. I couldn't think of a name off the top of my head, but there was bound to be someone. 'Let me pull some names.'

Lou and I spent the next hour sifting through my clients' files. *Because apparently this is what I do now.* I shook the thought away and clicked from one name to the next while we weighed up who had publication days coming up, who'd been off the grid for too long, and who was likely to be a pain to work with. By the end of it all, we decided on a young female crime writer from Northern Ireland. She was calm and kind and–

'She won't drive me fucking mental alongside a panel of blokes,' Lou finished. She stood, then, and crossed to the outer side of my desk and I knew my time with her was drawing to a close – which meant I'd need more work, now, another distraction, another folder to open. 'You'll come up, won't you? Can you take the time?'

The same stomach churn as before rolled through me. 'I'll do my best to, absolutely. I don't think there's anything else in the calendar for me that week.'

'Beautiful. First round is on me. I owe you.' She gently tapped the top of my computer monitor and then turned to walk away. But she quickly spun back around and added, 'Christ, don't look too obvious with it, but a beautiful man has just walked in.'

I laughed and took a not-too-obvious glance in the direction of the office entrance. And there he was: expensive haircut; black suit; geometric tie. *Three things I can smell: gym sweat clinging to Lou; someone's microwavable lunch wafting in from the kitchen; city smoke pouring in through the window. Two things I can hear: frantic tapping while everyone around me pretends that a rapist hasn't just walked into our office; Theo's shaky voice telling me he doesn't love me. One thing–* I jerked my head as though shaking away a hovering wasp. *I'm doing it wrong.* But there wasn't time for me to start again because Quen was walking towards my desk.

'Celia, is this one of yours?' Lou asked in a quieter tone.

As he closed the space between us, Quen smiled over at me like we were old friends. 'I'm glad I caught you at your desk.'

'You're here.' My tone gave away my surprise.

Lou turned back to face me. She raised her eyebrows in a gesture I recognised as a friendly one; the kind you would do on a night out if an attractive man approached you with a slick smile and an offer. But we weren't on a night out. And he was a fucking animal.

I stood and smoothed down my skirt and tried to swallow the flashback that came with the gesture. 'What are you...' But another thought intruded. 'How did you find out where I work?'

I imagined him with his own file room: one for every woman. There had been a handful of others in Lily's folders; some had made allegations of sexual abuse; some had only reported him to be a persistent and ignorant arsehole they wanted rid of. I knew both character accounts to be true of him...

'LinkedIn.' He smiled. 'Is it weird that I...'

Yes. 'No.' I tried to force a laugh. 'Persistent.'

He held my stare for a moment and I felt something sordid and soiled pass between us. 'Well, you know me.'

'I'm sorry, I'm a little... Well, I'm taken aback.' *I'm safe,* I tried to remind myself, *in an office full of people, I am present and I am safe.* 'I was going to call you but–'

'My God, it's no worries.' He gestured to the lively office

around us. 'You've been busy. I just– Christ, tell me if this is weird, Celia.' I didn't need to hear anything of what was coming; I could already answer for him. 'But I just think... I don't know, after losing Theo how we did, and then losing Mitch so recently, too, in fucking dreadful circumstances as well, and then us running into each other. It seems a weird coincidence, don't you think?'

I wanted to protest but the words knotted and expanded in my throat.

'And I just think– This is so cheesy.' He rubbed at the back of his neck, avoided eye contact but flashed a two-grand smile. There was nothing about his appearance that didn't look auto-tuned for public consumption – including his sincerity, his nice guy demeanour. 'I don't know, maybe the universe is giving us some kind of sign? And I know I gave you my card and you didn't call and you've been busy, I see,' again he paused to gesture to the room, 'but you must have a lunch break, right?'

He looked at me, then, full on and held my stare. *You're here to catch me at a convenient time; at a time when you think it's hard to say no.* I could have grabbed the nearest pen and stabbed the nearest limb.

'Not on days like today,' I answered and forced a laugh along with it.

There was such a swell of discomfort in my lower abdomen that I felt worried to look down. I was convinced that the memories and the howls and the lies, and the hours of private paid-for counselling for the sake of keeping it all quiet... I was convinced they were all *there*. A cat's cradle of trauma wound inside and outside itself to form an observable bulge that anyone might see.

Instead, I looked at him. I couldn't hold his sightline for fear that I'd either turn to stone or collapse in on myself like poor origami. But I looked just below his chin – at the perfect pruned beard – and I mustered a smile. Because Quen was, I thought, maybe right about one thing in all of this: sometimes, the universe gives you some kind of sign.

'Well, hey, you've got my card,' he answered, though he didn't seem at all rebuffed by my own comment. 'Like I said before, I'm in and out of the city quite a lot. But you'll always catch me for a coffee.'

I said nothing of the contradiction in terms; he was clearly boasting success again, and given that I was still thinking about grabbing a pen and aiming for something – this time an eye, maybe – I thought Quen's calendar was the least of my worries at that moment. Though I had a feeling it would become more important in the coming weeks – if I had anything to do with it. 'You'll call?' he pushed, then, when I didn't answer, and I made a noncommittal noise. 'Brilliant. In which case, I'll let you get back to work.'

'Lots of planning to do around here,' I said with a smile. I hoped it was a believable expression, though I wondered whether he was astute enough to notice the authenticity in anything a woman said or did towards him. *How many hints must you have not taken, Quen? How many women–* 'Thanks for stopping by,' I managed, 'I'll definitely call.'

Quen mustered an enthusiastic goodbye in response. He was hardly halfway to the door and already Lou was flapping her hands about and making cooing noises and I wanted the building to crack through its core and swallow me into the foundations.

'I know you're married, Ce, but I'm not,' she said, pulling up the same chair as before, 'dish the dirt on tall, dark and charming.'

He's an animal and a liar and abuser. The words were knocking against my teeth. But instead I forced the same smile

I'd given to Quen and said, 'He's an old friend from university, that's really all it is.'

'This old friend have a name? Or a wife?'

'I have no idea whether he has a wife or not.' Though of course I did. No wife, no children; no one, in theory, who would miss him if he slipped out of the city and off the face of the earth.

'And a name?' she pushed.

I hesitated over using it. It wasn't just the upset at having his name in my mouth, but something much more practical. I didn't want anyone to know he'd been there, I realised, just in case. I didn't want a trail leading Quen to me or vice versa. But I corrected the thought quickly enough: it wasn't a just in case that I was worried about, it was a *when*.

'His name's Patrick,' I lied, 'and he really is no one.'

Or at least he will be no one, soon.

SHE

She'd been carrying the Quen file around since the Leeds trip. Ideally, she would have been able to give it to Celia then. But nothing had gone to plan while they were away – including how much Celia knew of what had happened.

On the journey up there she'd expressed so many doubts over what Lily was doing, it became impossible to know how serious she was about helping at all. Though Lily didn't judge her for it. Celia had handled the news of a killer best friend better than Lily could have hoped she might – although, ideally again, she'd hoped that Celia would never find out at all.

She was in the thick of it now, though, with the police calling not once but twice. Lily had avoided her since then and it was in part to make sure there weren't too many emergency phone calls passed between them, in case the worst should happen and their call records were ever called onto an investigation. With a great measure of intrigue though, she also wanted to know how Celia would react – when she'd been told not to call, when Lily wasn't calling her, when there wasn't a life raft to jump onto and guide her on how to be. Lily was keeping an eye on her, of course, so Celia wasn't entirely alone – but it was important that she spent a day or two thinking she was. Quen was an important case but he was also one of many. There were times when Lily really wouldn't be around for prolonged periods – and she needed to know Celia could handle herself through it.

She added the latest printout of Quen's diary to the bulging folder on her work desk. He had more trips out of the country planned for the coming weeks and months, but she wasn't sure that they could wait that long. So she'd gone to the trouble of highlighting the most feasible dates when he would be out of the city, within a decent driving distance. It would be harder for Celia to get away, she thought, but at least there were options for when one or both of them felt ready. Though Lily had been ready for years...

Her work phone started to chirp on the corner of her desk but she let it ring out. There were other things she wanted to get ready for Celia, before gifting the folder to her at their next meeting. She had a speech prepared, too, something about there being no rush, something about there being a chance to practise. Although she couldn't second-guess how Celia might feel about the test run of another man before Quen; even if she had been disappointed at the missed opportunity in Leeds.

Still, there wasn't exactly a manual for teaching your best friends these things, even though Lily would have highlighted, colour-coded and tabbed the book's pages if such a thing did exist.

The phone call died out but her answering machine flashed to alert her to a new message left behind, so she leaned forward and pressed the speaker button.

'Lily, it's me.' Her head snapped up at the sound of Celia's voice. There was something hurried about it; the anxiety came through the speaker in cartoon waves. 'I don't know where you are, or how long I'm meant to play the waiting game or– Fuck, I

hardly know anything. Apart from I'm ready, Lily. I don't need–
I don't *want* others, I just want him, and I just want to fucking–
I'm coming to your office. I don't even know whether you're
there but I'm coming over. I'll be there now.'

The line went dead.

She opened the top drawer of her desk and pulled out a
spool of red ribbon. She didn't know what had happened,
though something obviously had. And whatever it was, she was
determined to balance it out with the best gift she could possibly
give her best friend – a light brown folder bursting with
information, tied together with a cherry red bow.

CHAPTER TWENTY-NINE

I sprinted the stairs to Lily's office and found the door was already wide open. On the walk there I'd nearly talked myself out of going at all. *She would have answered if she was here*, I thought, but I saw now that that wasn't true. She was there, sitting at her desk as though waiting for a client to stroll through: *Is that what I am?* Her feet were propped up on the desk and she looked to be skimming through scribblings and note-takings on different coloured Post-it notes. I wondered whether there was a system to them – or whether there was a system to any of this.

'What happened?' she asked, without looking up.

'He came to my office,' I answered, plainly, my tone flat and lifeless. From my office to Lily's, I wondered how the weight of the admission would hit me when I could say it aloud to someone who would understand the horror of it. I flashed back to the night it all happened, when I had deflated on the living floor room of our apartment, told Lily the jagged details and begged her not to confront them.

No, I remembered, *it wasn't that I didn't want her to confront them*. I only hadn't wanted her to leave me. Weeks ago, after seeing Quen for the first time, a similar reaction had overtaken me. Now, things were different. Though I wondered whether it was things, exactly – or whether it was somehow me that had changed.

She dropped her legs and leaned forward. 'That fucker. What happened?' Her voice was hard-edged and I saw a lick of fire-like anger emanate from her.

'Who's Kyle Rox?'

I realised, then, there were more people than Quen to deal with. And if we *were* going to deal with him, there were things I needed to know first – things I needed to know more of. Lily looked back at me with a blank expression and then a small laugh tumbled out of her.

'Fuck if I know, why?'

'That's the man you told me not to talk to the detectives about.'

'Hm.' Her legs were back up, then, and she looked... relaxed, I thought. 'I didn't tell you not to talk to them about him. In fact, I think–'

'Lily, don't,' I cut her off, and she looked surprised at the interruption. 'I'm sick of bullshit, I'm sick of all of this already. Who is Kyle Rox; and why do the police think I know something about him? Why do they think he's linked to Mitchell?'

'Ce, I genuinely have no idea.'

'He isn't...'

She shook her head and flashed a downturned smile. 'He isn't one of mine.'

The words landed like small marbles on my forehead and there was suddenly an ache in my temples. I closed my eyes and rubbed hard at the lids. 'It's a coincidence?'

She shrugged. 'Call it whatever you will, beaut, but he wasn't me. Now what's your next question?'

'How do you kill a man?'

'What, do you want like a diagram?'

'Lily!' Her eyes stretched wide at my raised voice. I walked closer, then, and took a seat opposite her. I wanted to knock her legs off the table, shake her by the shoulders, shout in her face. There were waves of something moving through me that I didn't recognise as my own feelings – but they needed to go somewhere. 'I'm being serious, Lil. You can't do this on your own. You can't keep taking agency away from people like this.'

The accusation was out, then, and she looked as though I'd slapped her one cheek then the other with every word.

'I beg your pardon?' Feet down again, she leaned forward on her elbows, as though to crouch over the top of the table. 'Agency?'

'Agency,' I parroted. Everything in me wanted to lean back in my own seat to create a greater distance between us, but I tried to swallow the rise of nerves and focus instead on the rage – on the flame of it. 'You're a predator, Lily. Look at what you do, what you've been doing for... for however long you've been doing it.' I tried to keep my tone level, and I tried to hold her stare. But it was a hard task when she looked as though she might collapse in tears or flare up in fury any second; it was impossible to know which side the coin might land on. 'You took other people's pain, Lil. I'm not saying it was a bad thing...' I petered out and half-laughed. 'Murder is always a bad thing. But how you're doing it, Lily, you're taking from people. You–'

'Let's get one thing straight,' she started, and I saw the fury.

But I had my own to exorcise. 'Yes, let's. You think you're helping people and maybe you are. Maybe the people who come to you really want someone else to handle their business. But some of us don't. Some of us want the opportunity to level the score for our-fucking-selves. You're taking *my* agency, *my* pain.'

'So *I'm* the bad guy here, am I?' I saw a sparkle of something; a tear ready to creep out of her eye, I thought, but she scrunched up her expression in something like confusion and ironed out the tear along with it when she straightened her face again. 'I can't fucking believe this, Celia, I can't.' Dumbstruck was exactly how she looked, too, like someone had put linear equations and hieroglyphics in front of her and told her to work it out alone.

'Lily,' I tried to lower my tone into something softer. I was furious, still, but it was impossible not to feel something for her, then. She was Lily; *my* Lily. But– 'Look at what you've become with this, Lil. Look at what you've done.'

'Please. I'm no bad guy, Celia. Besides which even if I am, what does that make you? The sidekick? And these men,' she huffed a hard laugh, 'they're hardly even human.'

'And you'd treat an animal like this, would you?'

'I would if it were dangerous and couldn't be contained.'

Is this what I want to be? I thought, then, in quiet answer to her own question. I was making accusations and brewing rage into a Molotov cocktail to throw at the one person who knew me – who knew it all. But what was I criticising, exactly: the fact that she was killing people; or the fact that she hadn't yet helped me to?

In the lull between us while I was trying to find an answer worth voicing, Lily yanked open a desk drawer and pulled out a thick cardboard folder tied together with a bright bow. It landed with a weight on the desk; she'd nearly thrown it, letting it drop more my side than hers.

'There's your agency, Ce.'

I reached forward with a hesitancy, as though the papers might slash me to ribbons. No sooner had I pulled the folder towards me and Lily followed it up with a second thud on the desk: an old model of iPhone.

'That's clean, the number is registered to a fake name and the phone means nothing. If you need to talk to him,' she huffed, 'for the purposes of getting this done, I mean, use that. You can scrap it when you're done.'

I pulled the folder onto my lap. 'What are you giving me?'

She pushed away from the desk and walked to the open window at the back of the room without answering. A threatening quiet elbowed between us both while Lily freed a cigarette from the packet that must have been on the windowsill. She lit up and pulled a drag so hard that I thought I heard the paper burn down. She answered on the exhale with a plume of smoke following her words.

'It's everything you'll need.' She took another drag and this time exhaled through her nose. She looked like a creature from the books I read to Dawn – snippets of Greek myth thrown into modern-day writing. Lily was dressed top to toe in black, apart from a deep red belt that scored her around the middle; the colour on her lips matched it. When she exhaled another stream of smoke through her nose, then, I re-imagined her as a bringer of justice; the kind of creature with talons and an agenda, and I wondered whether that's how she saw herself.

'It's taken a while because he's hard to get close to. And it's close, still, to when Mitchell died.' She spoke without looking at me, and I thought there was a tinge of disappointment to her tone, now. 'I wouldn't normally go after two people so close together when there's a link between them both but– But then there's an exception to every rule, isn't there?' Her head snapped round and she flashed a sad smile and my stomach dropped. *You've been getting him ready for me*, I realised, and somehow, for a second or two, I shared the disappointment that I thought Lily must have been feeling in me. Imagine trying this hard for someone, for them only to tell you what a monster you are at the end of it all...

'Lily–'

'Read the file,' she interrupted, 'let me know what you want to do.' She paused for another inhale. 'Take your agency. It isn't like you haven't waited long enough for it.'

'I'm sorry for what I said,' I blurted out, without knowing whether it was true.

'Don't be.' Her smile relaxed a little, then. 'Everyone is a monster some time or another, Ce. I've made peace with it.'

'I didn't mean–'

'You did. I am.' She shrugged. 'But so are they. And when I go to bed at the end of every case, at the end of every *day*, I know I'm on the right side. You don't have to even pick a side. That's all...' Her sentence drifted off and she looked back out into the city rather than at me before she finished, 'That's all I was trying to give you. You don't have to be this person; you don't have to carry this. Because let me tell you a thing or two that you might like to know before you settle in for this, beaut. I might have made my peace with this now but it didn't come easy. Of course I felt guilty; of course I questioned it all. The conversations you're having with me? I had them with myself, every fucking day.'

'But you decided to do it anyway?'

'I decide, every time, to do it anyway.'

I shifted the folder back onto the desk and walked over to her. She was dubbing out her cigarette as I pulled her into a hug. I wrapped my arms around her neck like a small chimp clinging to its mother.

'Take your time; take the file.' She spoke into my neck. 'Decide who you want to be. You don't have to be the victim turned bad guy. You're allowed to be something else.' A long pause rolled by, though it was at least a more comfortable one, before she added, 'You're allowed to choose what happens to you, Celia.'

CHAPTER THIRTY

Simon and Dawn had disappeared mid-morning for a parents' and kids' swimming club. They'd invited me along, but there was so much to do around the house that I'd declined in favour of making the most of the quiet.

I needed to arrange final details on both holidays – one for me and Simon; one for the three of us – and the kitchen needed to be decorated with bunting, and the food needed to be cooked and– There was no occasion. But somehow it felt like readying myself for a last meal. I had encouraged them out of the house so I could cook their favourite foods: pizzas with all the toppings; punnets of ripe raspberries, strawberries, anything Simon might want to blend and add ice cream to; baked goods that needed to be warmed through still.

I set the oven to pre-heat while my laptop stirred to life, then I keyed in the log in details for the holiday booking site.

Simon and I were due to go to a rural spot in Wales; the webpage for it boasted little to no phone service, no internet and few neighbours. It would be a perfect way for us to tumble right off the grid for a weekend – and exactly the sort of surprise that

I needed to spring on him to counteract the tensions of the last couple of months. This was a new leaf, I reasoned; a brilliant bright green one that Simon would love.

Meanwhile, Dawn's special holiday was something more glamorous; a week-long trip over to Barcelona during her next half term break at school. It had been two years since we'd last taken her abroad, and I could already hear the howls of delight that would spill out when we told her. There was only one thing left to check on both bookings: I needed to know whether the cottage in Wales was refundable; and whether one ticket could be refunded on the Barcelona trip.

I had started to think in worst-case scenarios in the week since Lily and I had last seen each other. Although we'd spoken on the phone regularly enough, and it had been her idea to dial up the normal at home, too: 'It doesn't hurt to have people who can attest to your character as a reliable, loving and friendly one.'

That's when I'd thought of the holidays; something that would encourage good feeling in everyone. Although I couldn't imagine Simon going alone, if for any reason I wasn't there to go with him; though I hoped he might find energy enough to take Dawn. When Lily had asked what my worst-case scenario was – after I'd mentioned the holidays – I only fell silent on the phone. I wasn't yet ready to admit those particular worries aloud. But she sensed them all the same.

'You're not going to get caught,' she'd said. And I had chosen to try to believe her. But I still clicked the 'refundable' option – at the extra expense of £30 for one trip and £150 for the other – because I was learning that it didn't hurt to prepare. The level of detail in Lily's folder showed me that much.

A folder that now locked in the boot of my car, sandwiched between others relating to authors and panels and public appearances, and a hundred other work-related things that Simon would never think to look through, even if the opportunity for it were to arise. On the day I saw Lily, I spent two hours sat cross-legged in the centre of her office while I worked through the contents of the folder.

I paid close attention to the dates she'd highlighted – they were close, and they were comparatively local against the international destinations Quen had coming up – and I paid close attention, too, to the part where Quen's known relatives and associates were listed. She had a ridiculous amount of detail on those few pages, but I could understand why they were so helpful to have; she wanted to know who was likely to come looking for him.

It would go in our favour, I guessed, that Quen's parents had died in a car accident when he was thirteen – though I'd felt a sandstorm in my belly at imagining that as a convenient thing for us. There were also known hangouts listed, and – a list that both horrified and impressed me – there was a string of hotels he was likely to choose from for each UK city he might visit, alongside the first name of a woman he could call once there, too.

'He's that predictable?' I'd asked.

Lily had laughed and nodded. 'He likes to keep women beholden to him is my understanding. At the back of that you'll find a testimonial from a woman in Oxford, someone he used to hook up with whenever he was there by all accounts. Apparently he enforced a "no other men" policy, even though he was only in the city once every six months. It broke them apart eventually.' She paused to light another cigarette. 'Well, that, and the habitual violence.'

I put mini quiches into the oven to heat for twenty minutes which should allow them time to cool as well – how Simon preferred them. And I tried to bate my worries at being the doting housewife and would-be killer on in and out breaths. I'd told Lily everything I wanted to do – when I wanted to do it – and she promised to take care of practicalities. It felt wrong, not to be doing it, but to be leaning on her after such an argument in the hours before these decisions were made. She'd said all was forgiven but given her extracurricular activities, I wondered how she could forgive and forget so easily. Though I guessed my crimes against her were relatively small compared to the ones she set out to punish.

'One last thing you need to remember,' she'd said as I'd started to collect together the notes from the floor around me. 'Well, two, actually. If at any point you decide you can't do this or don't want to do this, you're in charge of making that call. You pull the plug entirely, or you pull the plug on your involvement, and I'll drop everything, no questions asked. Fair deal?'

I'd nodded. 'And what's the second thing?'

'It's important you remember, Ce, that after this there's really no coming back from it.'

I'd tied the red ribbon loosely around the folder to keep the contents together. 'I know.'

When Simon and Dawn got back from the swimming pool – an hour later than expected, which worked to my favour – the house had been transformed. There was unicorn bunting tacked around the top of the kitchen walls; a unicorn piñata (that promised to be filled with rainbow-coloured sweets) hung between the kitchen and living room, in the small archway that separated the spaces; the dining table was covered in plates of food in as many colours as I could think to cook, and there was a fresh sponge still baking in the oven, too, that would be covered in strawberries and fresh cream when it was done. I had made enough to feed an army, so I knew my small tribe would be taken of care.

Outside, in the sunniest spot of the garden, there was a large paddling pool full of foam balls that I already regretted buying; I could only imagine Dawn's glee at soaking them through and launching them at me and Simon, though, which had been a main reason for buying them. There was factor fifty sun cream and a large umbrella out there, too, because Simon is perhaps the most miserable person in all the land when he feels that he's overheating.

When I heard the front door open I lingered quietly in the kitchen for them. I heard Dawn gasp and I knew she must have caught sight of something, but Simon was slower to react. It wasn't until he ducked under the unicorn piñata and saw the beginnings of bunting that his reaction broke.

'Babe, what the–'

'Surprise!' I announced, arms spread out as though presenting the entire room to them at once. 'I wanted to treat you both.'

'Oh, Mum.' Dawn eyed the food across the table and then looked at me. 'Can I?'

'Go for it! There are small plates at the end there.' I gestured, and Dawn walked around to grab one – taking a handful of grapes on her way. 'Use a plate, monkey.'

'She could do with a shower first,' Simon added, 'we both stink of chemicals.'

'Well,' I wrapped my arms around his waist, 'there's something outside that might help with that.'

The comment triggered Dawn, who immediately dropped her plate on the table and shot through the open doors. 'Oh, score!' And there soon followed an oceanic splash and an eruption of laughter.

'You got us a paddling pool.'

I spoke into Simon's chest. 'I got us a paddling pool.'

He didn't answer, but instead reached down to my sides and started to tickle me – a frantic childish tickle that came complete with my childish laughter while I wiggled and writhed to get away from him, without really wanting to. When the outburst settled some seconds later, he pulled me close to him again and pushed my fringe out of the way to kiss my forehead.

'I'm still getting used to this,' he said, as the hair fell back into place.

Lily had suggested a wig. But I wanted to be a new person entirely when I next saw Quen. So I'd exchanged long hair and a centre parting for a short bob and a fringe. He wouldn't know what was coming, I told myself. *Though that's nothing to do with the hair...* I squeezed my eyes tight and tried to push the thoughts away. *Three things I can smell: chlorine; Simon's aftershave; the rise of a cake in the–*

'Oh, shit.' I pushed away and grabbed oven gloves. 'I was making a sponge.'

I heard Simon laugh from behind me while I ferreted around to pull the cake free from the oven. There was the beginnings of a brown crust around one side but everything else looked to have escaped any incineration. 'We can cover that with cream, or strawberry sauce. Did I buy strawberry...' I started to look through the cupboards for the one thing I might have forgotten to buy, and I wondered whether it would be worth a trip out for it – or I could ask Lily to get it. She was the final surprise of the day, arriving in two hours – after family time, by which point we would all be soaked and, I thought, knackered. It was her idea for us to have that time together first, though, and she said she had a few loose ends to tie together and– There the thoughts were again.

'Babe,' Simon pulled me back into the room, 'what's with...'

I turned around and he gestured to the general state of the room around us. 'You know, the unicorns and all.'

'Dawn loves unicorns.'

He huffed a laugh. 'Definitely not what I mean, and you know it.' He was leaning over the kitchen island eating raspberries straight from their plastic punnet and I wished that I'd bought more. 'Seriously, what's going on?'

I stripped the oven gloves and rested them on the counter between us. 'I know I haven't been great recently, Si, and... I just wanted you to know I'm here, and I love you both and... I want you to always have nice things, and your favourite things and... I want you to have the world.' I turned to catch sight of Dawn wringing her long locks into the paddling pool. Her shorts and T-shirt were soaked through, and her smile was wide. 'I want her to have the whole world.'

He walked around and pulled me to him, his hands grabbing me by the hips. 'You're everything to us, babe, you know that. And she's a firecracker, that one is.' He was looking out to her as well now, watching her sink and squeeze the foam balls, as though testing their potential. 'She'll take the world by force.'

'She'd better.'

'Now,' he pushed me away, 'feed me, woman.'

Dawn came plodding in then, too, and left a trail of footprints from the open doors to the full table. Simon clicked his fingers and pointed to the stairs, 'Clothes, now. You need to throw some dry ones on.'

'These ones will keep me cool,' she answered, with the adult smugness of someone who knows they're right. Dawn looked at me, then, as though seeking support.

'I mean...' I shrugged. 'The kid's got a point.'

Simon laughed, grabbed a plate and started to spoon cheese

coleslaw around one edge of it. 'You two, you're a bloody nightmare.'

Dawn wrapped warm damp arms around my middle. 'Nah, we're just a team.'

'That's right, baby,' I rubbed softly at the crown of her hair, 'it's all teamwork.'

CHAPTER THIRTY-ONE

Quen was staying in a five-star hotel in the centre of Liverpool. For two and a half weeks we had been swapping messages about his time away; how he was looking forward to it desperately, how these work trips were hardly ever work trips at all.

I waited until he laid bait for me – 'It's a shame you aren't closer. Waste of a nice weekend away spending it alone.' – and then I snapped, knowing Quen – despite any changes that he might have tried to make to his scumbag character – was still a man who liked to think he was in control. He had no idea, of course, that this particular situation had been strategically structured around him – and his predictability.

'It's a bit far to travel for a couple of hours,' I replied, knowing his reply would be, 'So stay over. Our secret.'

After that message, I took myself into the disabled toilets at work and cried into a wad of paper towels. Lily had offered to do this part, but she'd already done so much. She handled the booking – hotels and cars alike – all of which was arranged through names that weren't our own. When it came to it, the autonomy I'd wanted in all of this soon gave way to Lily's own voice of experience. She ran everything through me, though, as a throwback, I thought, to the recent accusations I'd slung at her.

Still, the job of texting Quen – the job of baiting him, as much as he thought he was baiting me – was a horrible but necessary one, and I wouldn't have let anyone but me go through with it.

He told me the dates for when he was going to be away – which I already had marked on the calendar in my kitchen at home, having known that it would always come to this. I'd carefully selected them, too, from the list of UK travel dates Lily had filed away as part of the paperwork she'd gathered. Each neat box on the kitchen calendar was marked with an 'L' to indicate Lily and I were away. In two months' time, Simon and I would be away too – and all of this would be behind me.

I hope, I thought as I wedged another pair of black jeans into my overnight bag. Simon was at work and Dawn at school, and I was thankful that they weren't here to see me off. Lily said she'd collect me at midday so we could avoid the clumps of weekend traffic that might appear on the motorway. It wasn't a long drive – because of course we weren't staying in Liverpool – but it was a drive enough. We were heading to Harrogate for the weekend; that was our story. I was there for work to scout out authors at a local festival; Lily was there for companionship, to save me from dining alone every night.

Harrogate also happened to be a reasonable distance from Liverpool; ninety minutes or so, Lily guessed, slightly less if the traffic were right – which it would be, at 11pm or so when Quen was leaving the back-alley restaurant that I'd chosen for us to have a late dinner in, with no intention of turning up.

He questioned the lateness of it – '9.30pm for dinner?' – and I used my home as an excuse – 'Hard to get away.' – which he'd swallowed easily enough.

At 10pm I would text to say I was stuck in traffic but trying to get to him. Lily and I wagered a man like Quen would wait around for an hour or so – have a drink and cruise for alternative arrangements; a woman, any woman – and then he'd leave, and then we'd–

A car horn somewhere beyond the window cut the thought off. I took a look around the bedroom, the fresh floral sheets that I'd put on that morning after Simon had left for his meeting, and I took in the smell of my perfume dancing around his aftershave. After, I repeated the practice for Dawn's room; there were fresh sheets there, too, and the window slightly open to let out the heat of the day. She hated sleeping in warm weather.

Downstairs I hastily scribbled a note that said I loved them both and couldn't wait to get home, and I imagined Simon making a joke to himself about that: 'After the boozing and author schmoozing,' he might say before pinning the note to the fridge. He wouldn't throw it away until I got home; he never did. I'd never asked whether it was superstition or sentiment that made him want to keep them.

I pulled the front door shut behind me, locked up and turned to greet Lily who was leaning back against a silver Vauxhall Astra. She spread her arms wide to make a display of the vehicle. 'Fifth top model car in the UK if you can believe it.'

I laughed. 'That's why you chose it?'

'Jesus,' she turned to open the boot for me, 'why else would I choose it?'

I flung my bag in next to what I assumed was her own overnight bag, though there was another bag wedged next to it.

She must have noticed me looking. 'There are things we'll need.'

I nodded. 'Makes sense to take it. Hardly the stuff you might stop and buy at the service station.' I tried to sound light but it didn't come out right.

'Ce,' she set a hand on my arm to turn me round to her, 'you don't have to–'

'Yes.' I forced a smile. 'I do.'

'Well, all right then.' She slammed the boot and walked back to the driver's side of the car. 'I hope you've got a decent playlist ready because I'm not listening to the *Frozen* soundtrack. That's mine and Dawn's thing.'

And somehow, the thought of Dawn's beautiful innocence – her penchant for dancing around the garden singing Disney show tunes at the top of her young lungs – made it that bit easier to get in the car.

The hotel at Harrogate was exactly what you could want for a girls' weekend away – which is what I had repeatedly told myself this was. The twin room was dressed in golds, reds, and creams, complete with a small terrace that overlooked the centre garden of the hotel.

When I looked through the tall windows, I realised how easy it was to spy on the people in the room across the way from our own, and I made a mental note to pull the curtains together before we left later. *They might notice if we're not here*, I thought as I trod back to the bed I'd claimed with my bag.

I sat to start with, but then flopped backwards and let my arms spread out above me. The car journey had been littered with terrible drivers and awkward small talk; Lily was worried, I could tell. The fact that she didn't have reason to be worried was the thing worrying me, though: *Is this who I am now?* I wondered as I stared into the ether of the ceiling. *Is this how easy this is really going to be?*

'You should get some rest if you're tired,' Lily said from the doorway to the bathroom. 'It's going to be a long night.'

I swallowed hard. 'It takes a long time?' She only smiled, but I couldn't instantly read that as an answer. The silence lingered for a beat longer and then I realised: 'It depends on what you do.'

'Mhmm,' she answered, then, while ferreting through her bag for something. 'Success.' She pulled out what looked like a hand-rolled cigarette but–

'Lily,' I shot up, 'is that a joint?'

'It's a little ritual I have.'

'My God, is it actually?'

She managed a laugh. 'No, Ce, not *really*. But I thought you might need something.'

'A clear head is what I need.'

She crossed the room with a lighter in hand and opened the doors onto the terrace. 'A clear head doesn't always make things easier. Besides which,' she turned back to me, 'it'll be long out of your system by the time we go to meet him later.'

'Can we get food?'

'Now?' She already had the roll-up hanging from her mouth, though it wasn't lit.

'After that.'

'They do room service. We'll order everything.' She sparked up the joint, took a deep inhale, and then handed it for me to take. 'Come on, we can make the most of being here, Ce, even if it is a work trip.'

'It isn't a work trip.' I took her offer, though, and went outside to the small seating area. 'What if someone smells this and tells the hotel?'

'What if someone doesn't and we have a really nice time getting gently stoned in the sunshine?'

'How are you so calm?'

'Years of arduous practice. Are you smoking that or not?'

I took a deep drag of the joint and heard the paper crackle. 'Tell me about Theo.'

'Theo killed himself.'

'No.' I took another drag before I handed it back to her. 'No, he didn't.'

She looked out over the hotel garden and I followed her glance. There were two couples and a family using the space; a mother, father and two girls, one of whom was definitely Dawn's age, the other I guessed was younger. Simon would have collected Dawn from school by now, and I wondered whether they'd spotted their fresh sheets – if they'd read my note together. There was a deep longing for home in the base of my belly, then, as I wondered whether they were both there, and happy, and safe. Though safety was why I was here, too.

'Theo was the only one who seemed to know,' she finally said.

'What do you mean?'

She pulled a deep drag but didn't offer it back to me, and I wondered whether she needed it to tell this story. 'When he saw me for the first time, I remember him looking... relieved? There was definitely something in it. I think he carried it all, what happened that night, I think maybe he'd been waiting... I don't know. The weed is making me sentimental. But there was something in his face that looked relieved, that's all I can say. I told him,' she paused and huffed out a laugh, 'I told him karma was late in arriving, and I gave him the option and–'

'What option?' I wanted to hear her say it.

'Punishment or penance.' She turned to face me, then. 'That's what it always comes down to, Celia. Punishment or penance.'

I watched the family below us for another handful of seconds. I saw the father scoop the youngest into a tight hug and the mother snatch the eldest away from rough brambles that were growing on the border of the landscape.

'I don't want him to have that option,' I admitted, though I couldn't bring myself to look at her.

'Don't worry.' She moved the joint into my eyeline and waited for me to take it. 'He doesn't.'

CHAPTER THIRTY-TWO

When Lily came out of the bathroom I hardly recognised her. Though I don't know why I was surprised; she told me that's what she was aiming for. I was straightening the curls out of my bob; darkening my eyes; wearing glasses with blank lenses. The makeover wasn't essential, but Lily thought it might help.

Meanwhile, Lily had capped her normal hair and replaced it with a long wig; dead straight and brilliant blonde as though the synthetic had been bleached over and over. She must have used a darker foundation, too, because her skin tone looked deeper than its natural shade; her eye make-up was heavier; and her lips were a deep red that made her look as though she just had – or just might – fetch blood from someone.

It was a contingency plan for me to change my appearance – or at the very least tweak it – in case Quen and I unexpectedly bumped into each other before the plan had seeded. But for Lily, it was vital that she looked different. She'd wagered that Quen wouldn't recognise her, but you could never be sure exactly who had seen what on social media these days. So to make sure, she'd done this – this revamped exterior that made her look like the archetypal good time girl in the big city. The type of girl who Quen might drunkenly stumble into on leaving a restaurant, make a pass at, follow anywhere; which is exactly what we were going to make sure he did...

'Will I do?' She splayed herself between both sides of the doorway to strike a pose for me, but crossed the room before I could answer. 'Seriously, do I look different enough?' she asked and I thought there was a quiver of nerves in her tone, though I couldn't understand why. *Do you do this all the time?* I wondered. *Or is this one special?*

I forced a laugh. 'You look like a woman I hardly recognise. Even your... Wait, are your eyes a different–'

'Come on, tell me green doesn't suit me with this hair.' She flicked the wig over her shoulder. And for a second I could believe we were two old friends getting ready for a night in a new city. *We are, that's exactly what we are,* I repeated while I tried to match Lily's smile. But a flicker of something must have given me away because her own smile softened, then, and she took me by the shoulders. 'You're allowed to not be okay with this. You're allowed–'

'I know I am.' I turned back to the mirror to finish changing my face. 'But I'm not going to.'

Lily had thought of everything. When we left the hotel thirty minutes later, I strolled in the direction of the car we'd used to get there earlier in the afternoon – but Lily walked right by it. In the corner of the car park, there was a dark blue Ford Focus that Lily flicked open.

'Second most popular,' she said over the roof of the vehicle before she climbed in, and I followed suit. I was in charge of the bag for the time being, so I wedged it into the passenger footwell and manoeuvred my feet around it. 'It can go in the back,' she said while she adjusted the seat.

'I want it close.'

'I get that.' The car kicked into life. 'Ready?'

I exhaled hard and tried to find three things. 'How did the car get here?'

'Friends in high places.'

Lily pulled out of the space and headed towards the car park exit. We'd checked Google Maps before we left the room and there were no reported delays. I'd texted Quen, too, to make sure he was where he should be; it was just like him to go and fuck up a plan, I thought, and I tried to swallow back those memories that flitted in and out like gnats all evening. I pocketed the phone, though I left its volume on loud, and looked out of the passenger window as we headed towards an A-road.

'Do you need to talk or do you need quiet?' Lily asked.

'I think I need quiet.'

She reached over and softly squeezed my knee. 'Then that's what we'll do.'

The beauty of big cities in the UK is that they're filled to their brims with industrial buildings that no one can afford to use anymore. Particularly cities like Liverpool where the nearby docks had seen one building after another built and then abandoned over the years. The financial landscape of the industry meant that whole offices were going bump all the time. And Lily had picked an out-of-the-way office block, within walking distance of the restaurant where Quen was still waiting, for me to set everything up – taking one implement at a time from the bag I'd brought with us; the one Lily had told me not to open until we'd arrived. I rolled out the blanket that had been wedged at the top of the bag when I opened it, and along the length of fabric I spaced out everything from inside. One lump of steel after another, a stretch of rope, a–

'Is this what I think it is?'

Lily looked up. 'That depends on what you think it is.'

'I've only ever used one for preparing steak.' I weighed the instrument in one hand then the other.

'Then yes, I'd say it's what you think it is.' She walked across to me and wrapped an arm round my shoulders; she gave me a quick squeeze. 'I wanted you to have options.'

I pulled in a shaky breath. 'This is madness.'

'Welcome to my world, beaut.' She handed my ghost phone back to me. She'd been in charge of texting Quen while I got the room ready. 'He thinks you're a bitch for cancelling and wasting his time. That's a direct quote.' I took the phone. 'Madness it might be, but the fucker deserves what's about to happen. How do I look?'

She moved from statement to question with such ease that I flinched. 'Great. Better than great. Are you... Is it time?'

Lily nodded. She held my head between her hands and used a soft voice with me, then. 'Remember, you're not doing this because you're a victim. You're doing this because *he's* a predator. And you can change your mind, change the plan, change anything about any of this, and that's fine.' She waited until I nodded. 'I love you. Everything's going to be fine.'

I smiled. 'Thanks, Lil. I love you.'

'His texting is sloppy so I don't think he'll take much persuading. It's ten minutes here, ten minutes back, which gives you time to–' She was halfway out the room already when she turned back and snapped her fingers. 'I'd forget my head. You need to call Simon.' I felt around in my back pocket for my real phone. 'Alibis, yada-yada. Go by the window so he'll be able to hear something of outside, and just...' She shrugged. 'Be yourself.'

Which is who, exactly? I thought but didn't ask. It wasn't a question Lily was going to be able to answer. I wasn't even sure

I'd be able to answer it any time soon either. But I followed her instructions all the same and perched by one of the open windows to call my husband. It rang out four times and I longed for him not to answer; it felt like making him an unknowing accessory and it hurt my conscience to think of doing that. *Though in the grand scheme of things it's–*

'Babe?'

'Mum!'

I laughed. 'Why is she awake?'

'She's not awake.' I heard a hurried 'Ssh' before he added, 'Okay, she's a bit awake.'

'*Frozen?*'

'No, actually. *Moana.* I bet your night isn't anywhere near as exciting as that now, is it? We've eaten pasta and braided each other's hair as well.'

'Oh, you've *both* had your hair braided, have you?' I laughed along with them.

'I didn't think I had enough but you'll be glad to know that Dawn found a way.'

'And did Dawn manage to take a picture?'

'No, no she bloody didn't.' I heard Dawn gasp in the background. 'It was only "bloody", Dawn, it doesn't even count.'

'So, can I start saying "bloody"?'

'No,' Simon and I said in unison. She couldn't hear me, but it was a knee-jerk reaction, and in those seconds of shared laughter and discipline, I felt a deep well of sadness in the pit of my stomach. *I'm about to ruin everything*, it occurred to me, *I'm about to throw it all away.*

'Anyway, babe, everything okay there?'

'Absolutely. I'm hovering out a window at the venue to find somewhere quiet enough to call you both, that's all. Well, to call you, Dawnie is a bonus. Though shouldn't she...'

'She should,' Simon agreed, 'I'll tuck her in when we're done. Is the hotel nice?'

From there we managed twelve minutes of normal conversation: the hotel was lovely, the area was pleasant, the festival was well-organised. He and Dawn had watched *Moana* AND *Frozen*, they'd eaten pasta straight from the saucepan, they'd raided my bathroom cabinet and found face masks to use on each other.

The black and white contrasts of our evenings felt razor sharp, brittle around the edges, and I swallowed back the urge to cry more than once when I heard Dawn's open and untamed joy in the background of me and Simon talking. I was risking my family, I realised in those moments, but not doing this somehow felt like risking more. *But is that me making it okay?* I wondered, *is that me justifying the unjustifiable?*

I checked my watch and saw there wasn't much time left to make my decision one way or the other. 'I'm going to have to go anyway, babe, I slinked off without even telling Lily I was going.'

Simon laughed. 'I'm sure she'll have commandeered someone by now. Go, see what trouble she's causing. We love you, call us in the morning.'

'Love you!' Dawn's voice came down the phone at a ghastly volume.

'I love you, baby, I love you both.'

I disconnected the call and turned my phone off. I lay down the plastic sheeting that Lily had left me in charge of and then sat cross-legged in the centre of it. No one ever made big decisions with a cluttered head, I reasoned, with panic fluttering like a lost chick in the centre of my ribcage. So I pulled in a deep and greedy breath and– *Three things I can smell: something like oil, or grease; exhaust fumes; Theo's aftershave. Two things I can hear: a thrum-bang-base of a song I don't remember the name of;*

Barnie laughing. One thing I can feel: someone's hand around— No, I force-stopped myself, *I'm doing this wrong.*

From the floor below there came the horror film creak of a heavy door opening, followed by a laughter I recognised as Lily's. There was a man's voice that came through the floor in a mumble, too, a sound I didn't recognise as easily, though I knew it must be him.

I pushed myself up to grab the last of what Lily had left me with – the rag of fabric, the full bottle – and I doused the flannel in fluids on my way to the doorway of the room.

I stood behind, shadowed and well-hidden and hard to spot, even for someone who had their complete faculties about them – which Quen clearly didn't. Lily said she would make sure he came into the room first and when he did, I was to reach up, press down the fabric and hold on with all my might. 'Hold that fabric with the same need that Dawn holds your hand when she's getting on and off an escalator,' had been Lily's exact advice. And when the tall monster walked through the door, that's exactly what I did.

CHAPTER THIRTY-THREE

B y the time Quen came round he was bound with a rough, thick cord; we'd used the same for his hands and feet. Lily had joked halfway through how much easier this was with another person to share the workload and I'd wanted to feel complimented, but I couldn't find the humour in it yet.

Maybe I would, I thought, when we were driving home and I felt better equipped to make a *Thelma and Louise* joke that I already knew Lily would howl with laughter over. But for now, it was hard enough being in the room. I took a considerable step back when Quen started to come round as though distancing myself from the wrath that would come – because of course, there would be a vicious wrath. But Lily stepped forward until she was peering over him.

'Rise and shine,' she said and there was a measure of real enjoyment in her voice, then. She kicked him softly in the ribs and when it didn't prompt a reaction she kicked again, harder. He groaned and shifted awkwardly and I wondered whether he'd wanted to reach and grab the injured part – whether that was the moment he'd realised he was bound. 'Come on, sleepyhead, we've got stuff to get done.'

Quen's eyes moved from a squint through to stretched wide and I imagined his focus clearing, giving way to Lily – minus the wig. *Do you recognise her now?* I thought as I watched the scene play out. Lily was convinced he wouldn't remember her from our university days, the outfit had only been a precaution, but from the look on his face, then, I wasn't sure she'd been right.

'What the fuck? What is this?' He writhed and bucked and tried to move his arms, but they were wedged behind him. 'What the actual fuck?'

'There's our boy,' Lily answered his anger with a snide tone. 'Mitchell came around much quicker than this...'

'What– Mitch didn't– He was– You're the...' Every sentence seemed to die on his lips; words caught between his teeth, and I wished for the panic to dry his mouth out altogether. Better still, I wished for him to have a slow realisation of what was happening. But he bucked harder, then, and I knew that he knew – or at least, he thought he knew – what Lily's presence must mean. 'You're the one who killed him?'

She nodded slowly and then crouched down. 'Don't worry, though; I'm not going to kill you.'

I took my cue and stepped forward from the shadow patch of the room where I'd been lingering. He didn't notice me straight away, his eyes still adjusting to the new space, to the night, but when I was nearly touching distance close to him his head jerked at the sudden intrusion in his peripheral vision. He craned around and stared up at me, and through the new haircut and the changed make-up and the darkness, a slower wave of realisation hit him.

'But she is.'

'Celia–'

Lily stood and booted him again, harder still, and a real burst of discomfort echoed around the hollow space. 'Don't you dare use her name.' She turned to me, then, kissed my cheek and held me to her. The intimacy felt out of place in the context of a killing room but there was a great amount of comfort to take from it, too. 'I'm here if you need me.'

'I know,' I spoke into her mane of hair, tinged with sweat from having been bound beneath the cap for so long. Lily let me go and disappeared into the darkness where I'd hovered before. Quen looked up at me with real fear in his eyes when I trod closer to him – and rather than feel a flicker of guilt, I found that I enjoyed it. Guilt would come, I guessed. But for that moment, I only sat cross-legged on the floor alongside him – a safe distance away. 'You and I are going to talk.'

'Celia, I don't–'

'Sorry,' I interrupted him, 'I'm going to talk. You'll answer when you're spoken to. Nod if you understand that.' He managed that much, though his breathing was jagged by then and there was a sheen of sweat across his forehead, and I wondered how much he must be biting back on the desire for this to stop. But that thought wasn't a deterrent to me carrying on. 'The night of that party at university, you know the one. Nod if you do.'

He gave a shaky nod in response again. 'The other week you referred to that night and you made it sound like I was willing, like it wasn't something that I was subjected to. Is that how you see it?'

'Celia, look–'

'Is that how you see it?' I repeated.

He took an unsettlingly long time to answer but I stared him down the whole while, too. Whether he admitted it or denied it, I decided he could at least have balls big enough to do one or the other to my face. Somewhere in the background I heard the snap of a lighter and the early burn of a cigarette and, like a trance breaking, Quen shook his head, a slow and tentative shift from one side to the other.

'Say it,' I demanded, and he cracked into tears. 'Whatever your answer is, say it.'

'I was a stupid fucking child, Celia, I... I didn't mean for it all to happen how it did.'

I weighed his answer like a small lump of something. 'You meant to gang rape me in another way?'

He flinched at my phrasing.

'Oh, I'm sorry, is there something in that that offends you? Or do you have a preferred phrase for what happened that night?'

He dropped his head and sobbed as close to his chest as he could bend, as though trying to tuck into himself.

'You can cry as much as you want, it won't stop this.' I leaned forward, then, my palms flat on the floor and my mouth close enough to whisper. 'Isn't that what you said?'

From somewhere behind me I heard Lily shift and I wondered whether she'd heard – whether the detailing from then had made her desperate to intervene now. But seconds passed and she didn't move further, so I sat back into my original pose and watched. There was a string of mucus running from Quen's nose to his mouth, his breathing was laboured, and when I scanned down his bent body I spotted the beginnings of a damp patch in his crotch.

'Payback is an ugly thing, isn't it?' I asked, though I wasn't optimistic for an answer. 'The thing is, though, I don't really want payback, Quen.' Again, I heard Lily shift from behind me. 'I've moved on and found some peace and...' I huffed a half-laugh. 'I'm not your victim, or Theo's, or Raff's or... I'm not anything other than a woman, and a mother and... I'm a good friend sometimes, though not as good a friend as some.' I glanced over my shoulder to see whether I could spot Lily, but she was still hidden. *She's keeping her promise*, I thought, *she's letting me do it all.* 'I have another question for you, though. How many other women have there been?'

'What?' He looked genuinely confused; so much so that even his tears eased.

'Since me. Since that night. How many times have you been a stupid fucking child into adulthood?'

'There haven't been– There aren't– Who the hell did you speak to?'

'Rachel, met you at a work event and then couldn't get you to stop calling her for a month straight, which ended in you turning up unannounced at her office. Emily, who changed her mind after getting into a taxi with you but you gave the driver *your* address anyway. Natalie, who remembers *nothing* of her night out with you, but does remember waking up in your bed the morning after. Do you need more prompting?'

'How in the hell do you–'

'You seem to be asking a lot of questions for someone with a gun to their head.' I clicked my fingers. 'Oh, wait.' I stood up, then, and walked to the window ledge where I'd laid out the instruments earlier.

Lily might have wanted for me to have choice, but from the minute I'd set the handgun down I'd known – there had been a noticeable pull towards the cold feel of it, the way it weighed easier in my hand than anything else I'd touched. Besides which, there wasn't enjoyment in this for me. Lily might have liked to take her time, to string things out, but it wasn't what I was there for. *Admission and execution*, I reminded myself as I walked back to Quen, gun in hand and safety catch off, *that's all we're here for.* I looked down and smiled. 'I knew I'd forgotten something.'

The tears started again, then, and the apologies came – like a dam bursting after days, weeks of hold. 'I'm sorry, okay? I'm fucking sorry. I shouldn't have done what I did, not to you, not to any of them. The lads, they were in on it as well, though, Celia, you have to remember that—'

'You think I could forget any of it?' I crouched again. 'I know full well who was involved in that night, and I know full well who encouraged them all to get involved, too. Would you actually have stopped if Theo had told you he loved me, though? Or did it just make it easier that he wouldn't say it?' I moved the gun between my hands to keep it in his sightline. 'Though of course, if he'd loved me then he wouldn't have let it happen so—'

'He did love you,' he stammered out. 'He did. He told me, after.'

'What is it they say about stable doors and horses?'

'It's why he killed himself,' he spat out, tears and spittle following the lie.

'No, it isn't.'

'It is! He told me—'

'Quen, I'd stop if I were you,' Lily added from her perch.

He craned around to see whether he could spot her. When he couldn't, though, he looked back at me. 'Okay, he didn't tell me that. But I'm sure... I'm sure that's why he did what he did... He couldn't live with it.'

But he had, I thought as I stood from my squat alongside him. *All of you have lived with it.*

'It isn't why he did it.' My index finger teased at the trigger of the gun and suddenly the instrument felt heavier.

'Why else would he have, Celia? Think about it.'

But I was tired of thinking about it all. For years, I had been thinking – on and off – about all of them. I wondered what their memories of that night were; whether they even had memories to draw on, or whether all of them, like Quen, had brushed it under the rug as childhood antics. Rather than a night of reckless disregard that might have ruined someone's life. *It hasn't ruined your life, though*, I reminded myself, *and it doesn't need to ruin your life now*. And I wondered, then, whether any of them had had the same tug of guilt, ready to talk them out of it – and if they had, why hadn't they listened?

'Shall I tell you why Theo did it, Quen?' I angled the gun at his head, then. 'It was because he wanted penance.'

CHAPTER THIRTY-FOUR

It took the police ten days to find Quen's body. From there, it took them another five to find their way back to my office.

DS Allen and DC Moss arrived, solemn-faced and stern early one morning, brandishing a slim brown folder and expressions that gave nothing away. They paused and spoke to Rory, only for a second, and he pointed them in my direction.

I actually lifted my arm to a give a gentle wave, as though welcoming a distant friend back into the fold, and I wondered how many times I would need to be questioned by the same detectives before I could think of adding them to my Christmas card list – or whether there never was an appropriate level of familiarity for that. It seemed like something to ask Lily.

They came to a stop in front of my desk, their shoulders nearly touching, and Allen cleared her throat before asking whether she could have a word with me somewhere private.

I wore a concerned look. 'Absolutely, is everything okay?' I shuffled them into the nearest empty meeting room as I spoke. 'Will in here be okay?'

'In here is great, thank you,' she said as she stepped past me through the doorway. Moss followed close behind. 'Everything is fine, Celia, but I'm afraid we're here with some news that may come as a nasty surprise so...' She and Moss took a seat each and she waited until I followed suit before she carried on. 'We're in a bit of a situation here, Celia.' She opened the folder. 'Do you recognise this man?'

'That's Quen Parsons,' I answered in a plain and level tone. 'We went to university together.' I stretched my eyes. 'Oh God, is he okay? Did something...'

Allen pulled her lips down into a sad smile. 'I'm afraid his body was found in an abandoned building up near Liverpool late last week. We're liaising with police there as he was actually local to here. Did you know he was still living in the city?'

'I did,' I nodded with too much enthusiasm, 'I actually ran into him. Christ...' I pushed a hand back through my hair and looked at the floor with what I hoped was a vacant stare. 'Jesus, I'm trying to think when it was. A few weeks ago, I guess? He gave me his card,' I gestured towards my desk, 'I still have it, somewhere. I said I'd call, that we'd catch up.' I forced a slow and shaky breath through the O of my lips. 'I should have called him.'

'It would be helpful if we could ask you a few questions, if you don't have any objections, Celia? I realise you're in some shock right now,' Moss asked, then, and again I nodded, this time with tears pricking the corners of my eyes. I didn't want to overdo it, but I thought a splash of extra feeling couldn't hurt.

During the rest of the weekend in Harrogate, Lily had readied me for all of this. In a plain and unpanicked tone she'd said, 'They'll come for you, and that's fine.' On and off in the hours after she had explained why it was okay: there was no recent link between us apart from a chance encounter at a food court during a lunch hour; Quen and I shared no paper trail; and best of all, I had an alibi. 'But still, it doesn't hurt to be prepared. So when they ask, you tell them everything.'

'*Everything?*' I'd repeated, and when Lily had looked up at me with a worried expression I fell over myself with a laughter that didn't feel quite right – but still, it felt too natural not to give in to. She'd slapped my leg and then laughed along, too.

'Christ, I thought you were about to cock everything up, then!'

I'd taken my jeans off and thrown them to her; the last of the bloodstains. 'I'm not going to tell anyone what I did, Lil.'

'No, but here's what you *are* going to tell them...'

Moss cleared his throat and pulled me back into the room. 'You mentioned that you bumped into Quen recently? That must have been strange, after so long?'

That's an interesting opener, I thought, but I only shrugged. 'It wasn't, really. I mean, it was in the sense that we both work in the city but haven't seen each other sooner. But I was trying a new food court, waiting on a friend to arrive, and I guess it just,' another shrug, 'it just happened. Quen said it felt like a weird coincidence, though, after Mitchell and all.'

'He mentioned Mitchell's passing?' Allen leapt on the mention.

'Mhm. We didn't talk about it for very long, to be honest. Quen seemed... I don't know, not nervous... He was unsettled when he mentioned it, though, I suppose. But then they were quite close in their first year of university, I think?'

'We've got quite a few pictures of them, testimonials from a few others who have said they spent a lot of time together in their first year, but not so much in the year that followed. I don't suppose you know why a friendship break might have...'

I was already shaking my head. 'Honestly, I'm not best placed for answering that.'

'We've also spoken to a Raff Hall. Is that name familiar to you?'

'I... I don't know that it is, I'm sorry. Do you have a picture?'

They did, of course, and when I glanced over his grubby teenage face, I tilted my head from one side to the other as though thinking him over. 'Honestly, I'm not sure whether I remember him or not. I'm sorry that's not much help.'

'Raff tells us that the friendship just drifted apart.' Moss took back the picture and filed it away. 'We've spoken to a Barnaby...'

'Colt,' Allen filled in the hesitation but stared at me as she spoke. I wondered whether she was trying to read my reaction. 'He said something similar, about the friendship breaking apart.'

'I mean...' I shrugged. 'These things happen, don't they? Especially when you're at university. I remember Barnie a little, though I remember him being quite flaky, too, so I can see how drifting apart would have happened there.'

'Flaky?' Allen parroted.

I waved the word away. 'A law unto himself kind of character. That's how I remember him, at least. Other people might have better things to say about the man.' I smiled, then, and forced out another slow breath. 'God, sorry, this is all just a bit mental, isn't it? Like, the three cases being connected and being all close together–'

'Three?' she interrupted me.

'Well,' I looked from her to Moss and back again, 'you came to ask me about a second name, didn't you? God,' another hand through the hair; all the shy panicked gestures I could manage without seeming obvious, heavy-handed, 'I feel terrible but I can't remember the man's name.'

She nodded. 'That's being treated as a second investigation for the time being.'

When she didn't offer any more information I decided not to push. Lily had told me to be careful with how much interest I showed, and I thought knowing their thoughts on whether the cases were connected was helpful enough to be getting along with.

'I really wish there was more I could tell you about... Well, any of it.'

'What you've told us has been really helpful already, Celia, thank you,' she said and I thought she sounded sincere with it. 'This is a horrible thing but I hope you'll understand that we're dotting and crossing things as we go on...' *Here we go.* 'I assume, if we needed you to account for your whereabouts two weekends ago...'

She didn't want to ask outright, which I thought was very sweet of her. 'Oh, I was in Harrogate with a friend. A university friend, actually, so I guess not everyone drifts away.' I flashed a tight smile. 'I can give you her details if it would help at all?' I brought my hands palms-up as I spoke, as though showing them physical evidence that I had nothing to hide, nothing stashed up my sleeve. In fact, there was nothing buried at all. My clothes were burned through; the cars were valeted and returned to their dealerships; the gun was at the bottom of the River Mersey. *I have nothing to hide*, I repeated to myself – because I really didn't. 'Her name's Lily, I'm sure she won't mind accounting for our whereabouts that weekend. Anything to help.' I smiled again, then, and stood. 'I'll just go and note down her details.'

'That's great, Celia, thanks for that.'

'And if we have any other questions,' Allen added as she stood, 'we'll be in touch.'

'Please do. It's terrifying what's happening. Anything to help put a stop to it,' I answered, and I really meant it – though I suspected we were perhaps talking about different things by then...

After the police left I waited two and a half hours before updating my social media status: 'Being a grown-up means treating yourself to a Just Because ice cream on the walk home from work.' It was somehow both an intricate and entirely simple system. Lily had set her own social media platform to ping a notification whenever I updated mine, which I seldom did. We agreed to the code for me to use after the police had visited – she was *so* sure they would – because anything showing an immediate phone call to her might look suspicious at a later date, if our records were ever checked. I closed Facebook and huffed a half-laugh into the then empty office. *Because these are the things I have to think about now...*

Since Quen, I'd avoided spending too much time on my own. Though I was always surprised to find that the thoughts, the guilt, didn't flood in how I expected them to. Every now and then they would appear like the singed outside of a bread roll left to bake for too long – but I found there was always a way of chipping off the browned bits and being left with something quite filling at the end of it all, too.

I leaned back in my chair, placed my hands either side of my ribcage and breathed in a hefty mouthful of air. I forced it out through a tight O and repeated it once, twice, three times until I felt the churn of my stomach ease. I hadn't counted three things since we left Liverpool. Though I had had to practice breathing quite often.

After – after the gunshot and the blood splatter and the grim realisation – I had sat balled on the floor in tears with Lily behind me, her legs around my body as though she were my Lamaze partner – as though this were some kind of rebirth. She had let me cry until I'd run out of tears and then she had placed a hand either side of my ribs – 'Here and here, move your hands with me, Ce.' – and she had told me to breathe, long and slow and evenly. 'It will be fine,' she'd said on every in-breath, 'I promise,' on every out.

When I left work that day Lily was parked outside the office, leaning back on a car that I didn't recognise as hers. She tapped the roof. 'Work trip, outgoing. I'm leaving tonight.' She pulled me into a loose hug, then. 'But I've got time for an ice cream, if you're game?'

'I think I did good, Lil.'

She kissed the side of my temple. 'I'll bet you did great.'

'What happens next?'

'Next,' she crossed round to her side of the car, 'we get ice cream.' She climbed in and waited for me to join her. When my door was closed she added, 'Next you forget about it; next you move on. If the police come back, you only know as much as you told them in that talk today; if they find evidence then we'll handle it.'

I was surprised at my lack of nerves, then, at the thought that there might be evidence leftover. I didn't know whether it was my confidence in Lily – or the invincibility that comes with committing a major crime. I was first-year-university-student-cocky with an energy that could have carried me for days, though, and I was ready to burn through it.

'I don't think that's what I meant,' I answered.

'Okay, beaut,' she pulled the car away from the kerb, 'what do you mean? Next what?'

'Next, what about the others...'

NOW

TEN MONTHS LATER...

CHAPTER THIRTY-FIVE

It was blue and grey and green and even black, where the shadows fell. But there was a core of yellow in the centre of the image where sunshine was breaking through cloud formations. The sea looked tranquil clear and the stretch of landscape matched it. There were clifftops in the background, white teal and worn, that eventually gave way to miles on miles of fields. They were a brilliant green too, polka dotted with cattle and other animals too out of focus to name. There were houses, too, some tall in stature and others squat in a way that made them hard to see on the first look. Simon kept coming back to that yellow centre, though, and he wondered whether the sunlight had tinged the landscape or whether there were crops, flowers, even, that accounted for the colour change there.

He propped the card up against the vase on the dining room table and then carried on with dinner preparations.

Dawn had been whisked away by another mother for a pool party and Simon had been happy for the break – or rather, he'd been glad of a party that he didn't actually have to stay for. The last few school events had been heavy on parent participation, and he'd spent the majority of them thinking about blueprints and building materials.

While the house had been quiet that morning he'd worked through his backlog that had been looming large for weeks – and he'd found time to make cinnamon rolls, too. They were Dawn's latest fad, and to start with he and Celia had opted for shop-bought-and-bang-in-the-oven versions. But he'd got it into his head that he might be able to work up a home-grown batch instead and, from the smell leaking out of the oven, it looked as though he'd managed it.

He lowered the temperature and trod into the living room to finish fort-building. There were pillows and blankets all over the place, and he couldn't wait to see Dawn's reaction when she got home. With the set-up finished, he booted up the television set and got *Encanto* ready – despite having 'Let It Go' stuck in his head for the second hour running. It was just his luck that now Dawn had *finally* moved away from *Frozen*, he would realise he did in fact know *all* the words to her favourite song in it. *Still*, he thought as he clicked through the options to the right film, *I'll learn these words quickly enough, too.*

He was midway back to the kitchen when the doorbell went with an enthusiasm he recognised. He rushed to let his daughter in and found Dolly standing behind, her hands resting on Dawn's shoulders and her smile too wide. Celia had joked that in the last ten months – with his gym routine *and* their sex life back on track after a severe blip in both a year or so ago – Simon had become the ultimate Dad Pin-Up, and he'd laughed it off every time. But there were moments…

'Dolly, nice of you to bring my order right to my door.' He forced a smile. 'Dawn, I hope you thanked Dolly?'

'I did but,' she tipped her head back to look at the woman, 'thank you, Dolly.'

'You're most welcome, young lady.' She ruffled her hair. 'She's been a superstar all morning, no trouble at all.'

'Well, I appreciate you ferrying her there and back. I got a boat load done–'

'So I smell,' Dolly interrupted him, and he thought she leaned forward with the comment, too. 'Something smells good in there.'

Dawn gasped. 'Dad, did you?'

'I did.' He grabbed his daughter and pulled her into a loose hug. 'Go on, wash your hands and put the kettle on for us.' She followed instruction without a further word, though she did shout back a, 'Bye, Dolly!' from somewhere behind Simon. He laughed. 'I'd better go before she starts gnawing at the oven. Thanks again, Doll.'

'Any time, Si,' she answered, and she leaned heavy on the abbreviation of his name.

Simon shut the door before she'd even turned to walk away. But he worried that if he didn't signal an end to their doorstep conversation, he might actually have to share a cinnamon roll with the woman – and he couldn't see that going down well with Dawn, either! He trod the length of the hallway to find his daughter clutching the postcard that he'd left on the table for her to find.

'I'll put the kettle on then, shall I?' he said, noticing Dawn hadn't quite got that far.

'So, this is the Isle of Wight?'

Nice to have my voice heard, Simon thought as he knocked the cold tap off. 'Yep, looks pretty amazing, doesn't it?'

'Can we go?'

'Now? Surprise Mum?' he joked. 'I don't see why not. Your mum seems to be having a nice time, though. Did you even get to the writing?' He opened the oven and waved away the heat before it had the chance to fog his glasses. 'Dawn, do you want to grab us some plates and we'll have one each while they're still warm?' There was a long pause where no answer came. 'Dawn.' He craned to look over his shoulder.

'Dad, I'm reading...' She held her face close to the script as though inspecting it for something. 'Missing you both terribly. You'd love it here. So many cake shops and bookshops. Sea is beautiful. Hotel is dead posh. Lots of treats to bring home with us already. Hope you're taking care of each other. Love you and wish you were here. Celia and Lily. Xx'

THE END

ACKNOWLEDGEMENTS

I had a lot of back and forth doubts while writing this particular book – for a whole host of reasons. Without naming names, I'd like to thank everyone who gave me their support and advice through *Penance*. There were times when it took a lot of encouragement to arrive at the end of Celia's story, but I'm glad that we got there. To those who were kind enough to share their own experiences with me, thank you.

Thanks, too, to Clare for another outstanding edit; your attention to detail stuns me every time, and I'm so glad we've got to work together on another book. Thank you to the Bloodhound Books team for giving Celia a home, too. Finally, thank you to my ARC group who kindly give their time to reading these novels and sharing their thoughts. Putting a book out there is a glorious and terrifying experience, and it certainly wouldn't be worth it without the people who are willing to read every story. So thank you, over and again.

A NOTE FROM THE PUBLISHER

Thank you for reading this book. If you enjoyed it please do consider leaving a review on Amazon to help others find it too.

We hate typos. All of our books have been rigorously edited and proofread, but sometimes mistakes do slip through. If you have spotted a typo, please do let us know and we can get it amended within hours.

info@bloodhoundbooks.com